burst

Praise for BURST

"Otis delivers a psychologically acute vision of a mother and daughter and their haunting waltz in which allegiance, dreams of escape, the desire for dignity, and the urge for self-destruction play their part in a dance that spreads over three decades. A powerful debut."
—Janet Fitch, author of *White Oleander* and *The Revolution of Marina M.*

"A profound, propulsive exploration of what it means to be a mother, a daughter, an artist, and an addict. A transfixing, singular evocation of the precarious, terrifying predicament that constitutes being a woman alone in the world. *Burst* made me think deeply about my own choices and compulsions and changed, forever, the way I see myself and the world."
—Joanna Rakoff, author of *My Salinger Year* and *A Fortunate Age*

"Otis is so gifted at giving us two full and complicated women in this captivating novel, allowing each her brokenness and her dignity. Plus, the gorgeous writing about dance! I was making a list in my head of readers I want to give it to."
—Aimee Bender, author of *The Particular Sadness of Lemon Cake* and *The Butterfly Lampshade*

"When it comes to stories of mothers and daughters, Otis's *Burst* is up there with Mona Simpson's *Anywhere but Here* and Elizabeth Strout's *Amy and Isabelle.* Otis writes with complexity and heart. We are all richer and wiser after reading her work."
—Natalie Baszile, author of *Queen Sugar* and *We Are Each Other's Harvest*

"Beautifully written, propulsive, and utterly transcendent, this is a mother-daughter story for the ages."
—J. Ryan Stradal, author of *Kitchens of the Great Midwest* and *The Lager Queen of Minnesota*

"*Burst* is a wallop of a novel — it is about risk and pleasure, the way a body or mind can feel like a boundless possibility and a small prison, the way a mother and daughter set loose in the world can make everything shine, even if the shiny things also have teeth."
  — Ramona Ausubel, author of *Sons and Daughters of Ease and Plenty* and *Awayland*

"The mysterious bond that occurs between troubled mothers and their daughters has been written about endlessly, but almost never with such perfectly modulated electricity, such humor and deep wisdom, such enveloping — but utterly unsentimental — tenderness. *Burst* is a taut, economical novel that nonetheless contains multitudes. Its interrogations of what we owe ourselves and one another, how we love our parents and struggle to escape their shadows, and how we reconcile our dreams with our disappointments, is wonderful indeed."
  — Matthew Specktor, author of *Always Crashing in the Same Car* and *American Dream Machine*

"Otis writes about the ineffable — the high of being a dancer, the terrible closeness of mothers and daughters — with clarity, soul, and grace. *Burst* is a radiant first novel, its characters impossible to forget in their individual vividness and their complicated love for one another."
  — Sarah Shun-lien Bynum, author of *Likes* and *Madeleine is Sleeping*

Also by Mary Otis

Yes, Yes, Cherries

burst

a novel

MARY OTIS

Zibby Books
New York

Excerpts of this novel were published in earlier forms in *Los Angeles Review of Books* and *Zyzzyva*.

Library of Congress Control Number: 2022939277

ISBN: 978-1-958506-01-1
eBook ISBN: 979-8-9862418-4-5

Cover design by Mumtaz Mustafa
Book design by Ursula Damm
www.zibbybooks.com

Printed in the United States of America

For Vincent

PART ONE

chapter one
1979

Her mother had two speeds: drunk or driven. Here she is on an August afternoon at the helm of their VW van, laughing and waving her hands, alternating one and then the other on the steering wheel. Momentarily, no hands on the wheel. Then Charlotte's left hand flies out the window, slices the air carelessly, her fingers stretched wide as if she'd flung a fist of pearls at passing cars.

Charlotte drives without a seat belt—doesn't make Viva use one, either. This was before safety awareness, before worry was a sport, before you could be cited for mowing your grass the wrong way. Beers in hand, mothers and fathers sloshed around town in big-boat cars and cruise-ship vans, vans that held flip-flops, firewood, stray arrows. This was when children walked by themselves—uptown, downtown—alone while singing, together in packs, silent, not silent, shrieking at the sky like birds.

They are on Cape Cod, on Route 6, trying to nudge the flat nose of their van into the middle lane—the passing lane for cars heading in both directions—the "reversible" lane, the "suicide lane," the "every man for himself" lane. Charlotte said the highway people got the idea from ants, because ants are polite, don't panic, and basically everyone should take a cue from ants. Everyone calls it the "crash lane." Everyone drives it anyway.

Earlier they'd stopped for a drink. Charlotte drank most of her first glass of white wine, and Viva drank the last few sips when she ordered another. When Viva learned the planets in science class, Mrs. Kenmore said that when the earth is closest to the sun that point is called perihelion, and that was how she thought of herself and her mother. She was the closest anyone could get to Charlotte, maybe until the end of time.

"People used to drink wine for breakfast. Did you know that?" said Charlotte. She was worldly and once toured with a band called Yesterday's Horoscope.

"What people?" asked Viva. She looked at her mother's face, which had softened since her first glass. Charlotte had that look in her eye, as if many things she'd tried to recall, very good things, had all flown back to her.

"Renaissance people." She tapped her index finger on their table. "Oh."

That past year in the Fifth Grade Melody Makers, Viva had learned a madrigal—a fussy, overwrought song that circled round and round. A Renaissance person wrote it, and it did make perfect sense to her that they might have been drunk when they did.

Charlotte ordered another glass of wine from their waiter, Kenny, who had a bar towel crammed into his back pocket. When he walked it bounced like a tail. Charlotte whispered to Viva, "Men become delicious after fifty." They both laughed without making any noise. They were alike that way—a society of two.

Back on the road, Charlotte jabbed at the accelerator with her bare foot as they sped up to pass a Mustang. They were going fast, but the Mustang went faster. The air became thick and warm, the oncoming traffic looked tight and crinkled. On certain gray days, their van was hard to see. It had been custom-painted "cloud color" at Charlotte's behest. The paint was a strange bluish gray, the color of white socks that go through the dark wash by accident.

Then there was a third car in the crash lane coming toward them. It might as well have sprung from the pavement because Viva was watching carefully, and it had not been there just a moment before. Red station wagon. Primer on the hood. The man driving looked as though he was deeply considering something, the way a person stops in the grocery store mid-aisle, stops with their entire body, and tries to decide whether they want chops or spaghetti. The van began to shake.

Charlotte said, "Why didn't anyone tell me?" as if something had just occurred to her, and she found it both hilarious and tragic.

Viva had no idea what she was talking about—it wasn't about the passing lane—but Charlotte had that faraway look she'd come to recognize.

Her mother bent over the steering wheel, squeezing it as if that would make their van go faster. The smell of burgers, grease, and cotton candy poured into their open windows, which meant they were only yards from the La Pierre campground where they'd stayed for the past month. They would have to turn. Which meant they would have to crash. Which meant they would have to be dead. And then they would have to *start all over again* in another life, because Charlotte said souls travel in packs, and Viva did believe in reincarnation, but she knew it was possible they might not come back again as mother and daughter but perhaps as farmer and pig.

She was worrying about these things as she always worried about everything, and she had ample time, more than ample because all at once time was very slow. It was like they'd driven through an invisible door where time was so slow it would take a week for a man to put on his shoes. The top of her head buzzed, and it was not unlike hearing an entire city's worth of flies and bees on a summer's day, and it was not unlike a shock treatment or what she thought one might be like. The camp was near a state mental hospital, and sometimes Viva thought she could hear the treatments happening at night—sharp, electric buzzes like stars spinning from the sky. Under no circumstances did she ever want one. And now this would be a moot point, this fretting about elective electrocution, what with potential deadness in the offing. The bad shaking got worse, and in her mind things started to come loose, random things—scraps of conversations, the names of water formations in caves. They'd been on a science test earlier in the year. *Stalagmite, stalactite, and you can remember which one grows up and which hangs down, because you just think of tights and how they roll down, see like stalac-TITES!* And then there was Mrs. Kenmore, who popped into her mind saying: *Viva, I could tell your mother the school burned down, and she'd show up with a box of Frosted Flakes.*

Charlotte shouted, "Fucking hell!" She was honking, and the man in the red station wagon was honking, and neither of them would take their car back into the proper lane.

Then Viva's head went quiet, and she could feel the bones of her skull, as if someone had their hands around her brain, holding it still while a kind of information poured into it. It wasn't fancy, only different, like breathing from your elbow instead of your nose. It was a knowing that they would not crash, but she didn't know it from her brain. Her brain was the tollbooth they'd passed through a mile back. It was necessary only to get to a larger territory that didn't involve thinking and remembering. They were alive. They were alone. They were alone but together.

chapter two

"I'm thinking of a number between one and ten, what is it?" said Charlotte. They were sitting at the picnic table between their trailer and the next camping space.

"Seven," Viva said quickly, because in truth nothing had come to her.

"Not bad," Charlotte said. Seven. Five. Close enough." She looked at Viva intently, lit up a clove cigarette, and inhaled deeply. "Have there been other times you knew what was going to happen before it happened?"

There hadn't been, but Viva knew she was psychic. She could feel it like a weight in her head, like a tourmaline stone, dark and shiny, nestled in the velvet folds of her brain. She'd been psychic for a week now since Charlotte suggested she might be when Viva correctly guessed the number of beans in a glass jar at the supermarket. They'd won twenty-five dollars and a case of paper towels.

When they received the news, Charlotte pulled Viva to her and said, "Did you have to think about the number, or did it come to you in a flash? Because I'm going to give it to you straight—knowing what you don't know is tough work. Not everyone can be psychic. It's special."

For a single instant, Viva felt as if her mother saw her as a better girl, a smarter girl, one capable of doing great things. "A flash."

A young girl ran toward them. She stopped by a pine tree and stared. She wore a maroon women's top that fit her like a nightgown. A piece of blue ribbon was tied around her waist. About six, her lank blond hair stuck to her skull, and her pallor was oddly bloodless. She pulled out a compact mirror and stared at herself.

"Tell me her name," Charlotte said.

Every name in the world that ever existed flew from Viva's mind, but she thought she could feel the shape of one in her mouth. "Something like crate?"

The child laughed and rapidly flashed her compact mirror as if trying to communicate in frantic Morse code.

"Little girl, come tell us who you are," Charlotte called to her. She ran toward them but stopped a few feet away.

"I'm Kate," she said.

Charlotte turned to Viva. "Maybe you are psychic." She picked a loose piece of tobacco off her lips, threw the clove cigarette beneath the heel of her clog, and ground it out. Most mornings she quit smoking around eight and began again by ten.

Without invitation, the girl sat down across from them. Her shirt was filthy around the hem, and she smelled like campfire smoke and urine. A seagull landed on the table not two inches from her arm, but she didn't flinch. "Seagulls are trash cans, did you know that? And you can't eat them," Kate said. She pointed at Viva's mother. "Now you tell me something about birds."

Charlotte held her chin in her hand and thought. "Here's something about birds," she said. "Birds in the wild hide their hurt. Bet you didn't know that."

"Tharen!" a woman called, and for the first time, Viva saw not far from the table a large wool blanket hung over a large tree branch. It was held down on each corner by different items—an anchor, a boot, a can of paint. Next to it was parked the red station wagon. Quebec license plate. The new neighbors. The car was so rusted on the passenger side that what red paint was left looked like drops of blood.

"Tharen!"

"I'm coming," the girl shouted.

"But your name is Kate. You said it was." Viva looked at the girl's fingernails, which were rimmed with dirt.

"It's my vacation name," Kate said. She looked over her shoulder at a figure who stood by the blanket tent, a woman wearing a lavender leotard and a silver cuff bracelet around her upper arm that glinted in the sun. She was barefoot, and Viva could see her long legs through her muslin skirt. Her black hair was plaited into a single braid that fell to her hips. Undone, it might fall to her knees. "Greetings, fellow travelers, I'm Simone," she said. Charlotte rolled her eyes at Viva before introducing her daughter and herself. Simone beckoned to Kate, and they disappeared inside their tent.

The next day, on the hunt for gossip and bad behavior to report to her mother, Viva walked along the camp road, where she saw Marcus, the camp manager, making his morning rounds. A ubiquitous presence at the La Pierre, he was constantly checking on things as he traveled the paths between trailers, stabbing at litter with his trash picker, always in a hurry, walking in his inimitable way, leading with his right shoulder, his torso pulling left, as if his inner compass was permanently askew. A boating accident as a boy was the rumor.

Marcus waved at Viva and asked, "How's your mother?" She was used to men noticing Charlotte and, taking her mother's advice to never share more information than necessary, she said nothing. "Tell her I need to talk to her," he called. "It's urgent."

Viva picked up her pace, passing tents and trailers of all types—Nuggets, which barely fit a single person, pop-top trailers, and the single extravagant Holiday Rambler owned by the McQuigs, a family who were forever barbecuing. Outside their trailer, their meat brander hung menacingly from a hook. She continued past mothers lathered in Crisco, frying in their lawn chairs, and kids playing tag, jacked on Fudgsicles and Tang. The air was filled with the usual sounds—the ice cream truck, TVs fading in and out, snippets of conversation. Viva finished the loop and, returning to her trailer, found Simone washing her panties beneath the spigot between their campsites.

Simone was wearing the same clothes she'd worn the day before. She looked up at Viva and continued to scrub her underwear with a bar of brown soap. Kate stood next to her, playing with a loose front tooth. She was the type of girl, Viva thought, who must always show off something—a tooth, a wart, a scab on her leg. She'd seen her type before.

"Hello, precious pearl," Simone said. Her voice was low and sounded scraped. It wasn't like the voices of mothers or teachers or even women on television. Who said something like that to kids? No one she knew.

A man poked his head out of the makeshift tent. "Cairo," he said, as if Viva should have already known his name, as if he was famous. He squeezed his beard the way someone tests a piece of fruit for ripeness. "Are you the little mind reader my daughter told me about?"

Before Viva could answer, Cairo demanded, "Do you see a face in that tree?" He gestured at the large pine from which their blanket tent hung. She didn't see anything but sap. "Because you should if you're psychic," he said. "Shamans do."

She looked at the tree again. Viva thought she saw a president's head for a second, but she couldn't tell which one, and then it vanished.

Cairo said, "You're the spitting image of your mother," which wasn't true. Viva had an olive complexion and brown eyes, while her mother was pale and green-eyed. He seemed to mean it some other way.

Kate cranked up the volume on their transistor radio, which sat next to a pail of peanuts by their tent. "Sympathy for the Devil" sprang into the air and Cairo began to smack a half-full gallon of milk in time to the music. Simone stopped her washing and looked skyward. She closed her eyes and, still kneeling, swayed with her arms stretched overhead. Kate flapped her hands like they were wet and broke into an awkward shimmy.

Simone opened her eyes. "Viva, move!"

Viva shook her head. Her body went rigid, and she could feel her face flush.

Simone jumped up. "Come on! Come on! Do what I do!" She hiked up her skirt and jumped from two feet to one. Then she extended her left leg and circled it. Viva did the same. Simone thrust her arms sideways and backed up before running and leaping over a rock. Viva copied her movements, but when she jumped, she traveled twice as far.

"Again!" shouted Kate.

She repeated Simone's sequence, and this time, when she leaped, Viva felt as if her body, thin and runty, gained access to a larger power—a flash pass to transcendence. Her own strength was harnessed to something invisible and intoxicating, and immediately she wanted more. For an instant, it seemed she'd burst free from the confines of her body and gravity couldn't hold her.

"Praise be!" shouted Cairo, and he turned up the music.

Simone grabbed Viva's forearms, and they began to spin. They were laughing and as they went round and round the world flashed by—Cairo doing a wild jig, Kate clapping and shrieking. Faster they went as jittery pine trees flipped past mercilessly, magnificently.

Simone abruptly stopped and Viva almost fell. Catching her balance, she saw her mother standing next to Kate, arms clamped against her chest. Charlotte's eyes traveled around the campsite, taking in the ratty sleeping bags hanging from tree branches, peanut shells scattered everywhere, a large white ankh scrawled on a tree.

"Entrez," Cairo said, half smiling as he mimed doffing his hat to her, though the gesture didn't completely hide his contempt.

Charlotte didn't move. "Viva, let's go."

Simone wiped perspiration from her brow with the hem of her skirt and sighed.

"Now," said Charlotte.

Cairo cracked a peanut with his teeth and spit the shell on the ground. "Let the child have some fun."

Charlotte squinted at him. "You're one to give advice—you almost killed us yesterday."

"The lane goes both ways, madam."

Kate began to wail, and Simone pulled her close.

"You're upsetting my daughter," said Cairo. "You should go."

"You're a shitty driver, so don't act so high and mighty with me," Charlotte shouted.

"You!—you were swerving all over the place. You shouldn't even be on the road."

"You're going to tell me what to do? What do you know? Leave my kid alone." Charlotte's voice cracked, but she took a deep breath and straightened her skirt. She grabbed Viva's hand and they walked away slowly to show that nothing he said meant anything to them. Viva was shaking, and before they stepped into their trailer, she looked back. Cairo, hands clenched at his sides, was still glaring at Charlotte.

Charlotte sprayed a cloud of Fracas in the air, paused, and walked through it. Charlotte had a date with Kenny the waiter. If she was a little late getting back that evening, Viva wasn't to worry—it might be the type of date people in France make. She made a ham sandwich for Viva and left it on the counter for later. Charlotte was wearing a white gauzy top embroidered with little birds. No makeup except for frosted-peach lipstick. She stood before the small mirror hanging on the side of the refrigerator and stared at herself. She frowned and absently touched her jaw. Charlotte had told Viva that when she was a child, she had a "broken mouth," but Viva didn't see any scars. How could a thing be broken but invisible?

"All right, my big girl, the night is yours," Charlotte said. She grabbed her purple suede purse, and as she did, Viva felt a pang of fear—she and her mother were seldom apart. But Charlotte said she was twice as mature as other kids her age, and Viva didn't want to disappoint her by asking her to stay. Before driving away, Charlotte waited on the other side of the trailer door while Viva locked it. She gave three short ebullient raps, and Viva gave one—their private signal.

Charlotte had barely hit the camp road when Viva jumped into bed with her sandwich, something Charlotte didn't allow. When she'd finished eating, she got Charlotte's playing cards and spread six facedown on her blanket. She would practice being psychic. But it was much more difficult than guessing the beans in the jar. Viva had dozed off when she heard a child crying and then a pine tree scratching the side of the trailer. She got up and turned on the radio to drown out the noises. She wasn't a baby.

Charlotte returned near dawn, rapping softly for Viva to unlock the door. She pressed something into Viva's hand. A beaded necklace. "Found it on the beach. Good as new."

She sighed happily. "What a night, my dear girl, what a night."

Charlotte woke up a few hours later and wordlessly made a pot of coffee. Viva could tell that she was hungover, so today would be a not-drinking day. On these days, when Charlotte was irritable, a particular phrase would run through Viva's mind on a mental ticker tape: *She's off the giggle juice, sir.* It gave her a kind of fierce pleasure, as if she was relaying an update to someone who completely understood her side of things.

A not-drinking day involved mending clothes, doing laundry, and cleaning the trailer—the penance and absolution of chores. On a not-drinking day, Charlotte was fiercely industrious, sentimental without provocation, but the most she would ever admit to Viva was feeling "wobbly." Charlotte liked to say she was queen of the hard stop, and the tone she used indicated that she was actual royalty.

Viva watched her mother wash the previous day's dishes. She left her crystal goblet for last and dried it carefully before setting it on the counter. She had inherited an entire set of Rogaška from her mother, which they kept in the van, and which, if necessary, Charlotte often reminded Viva, they could sell. She fished a Kretek out of her jeans pocket and lit it.

Charlotte cranked open the levered window in their rented trailer, which smelled of Bain de Soleil, cigarettes, and Charlotte's perfume. "How Deep Is Your Love," a song Charlotte scoffed at, but which Viva secretly liked, drifted in. Viva heard gravel crunch and peered through the window at an old blue Subaru as it slowly rolled past their trailer. The back seat was packed with open-mouthed kids whose faces floated behind windows as if the car was an aquarium on wheels. Someone's father clutched the steering wheel, pausing to squint and slowly, dopily read the numbers staked in front of the campsites. Viva scrutinized the man's face. She had recently begun to tell herself that her father might one day appear at the La Pierre. She knew it wasn't likely since she'd never met him. Yet whenever Viva heard a car slowing in front of their campsite, she rushed to check.

Charlotte made up Viva's bed, which served as a kitchen table in the day. The bed was perfect in its geometry. The table folded down, and the side cushions could be pushed together to serve as a mattress. The trailer was inexpensive to rent, and at only eleven feet in length, it was the opposite of the old sprawling farmhouse where they'd stayed for the past year. That situation had been rent-free, since the owner of the house, Ona Prince, an old classmate of Charlotte's, needed someone to take care of her chickens while she taught art history in Europe. But then the semester ended, and they had to leave. That was how it was—they lived according to other people's schedules.

Viva studied her mother in the morning light. If she closed her eyes a little, the sun streaming through the window angled across her head like a cap. Charlotte wouldn't describe herself as beautiful, although she was. She preferred to be called handsome. She would allow that she had moxie. She had a habit of lifting her eyebrows in an imperious manner, followed by a crooked half smile, a habit that reliably revealed one dimple, and Viva obsessively practiced her mother's face when her back was turned. It seemed to her, if she did this enough, Charlotte's features might one day become her own.

Someone banged loudly on the trailer door. Charlotte opened it a crack.

"You've blocked my car, and my family is late for work," said Cairo. He, Simone, and Kate spent most afternoons in the parking lot of a nearby general store, where they sold horseshoe-crab shells and beach glass displayed on their blanket—the same one that served as their home at night. Pathetic, Charlotte called it. They never appeared to have any customers. Only the most idiotic tourists would go for such a thing. "I saw you slink in at four in the morning," he added. "Unbelievable."

"You saw me *slink*? You spying on me, Cairo? Maybe you need more excitement in your life."

"Move it now or I'm calling a tow truck." Wordlessly, Charlotte snatched the keys off the kitchen table. Viva followed her out the door and saw their van at a wild angle, inches from the picnic table and crosswise to Cairo's car. Simone and Kate were squatting in the road, staring at the spectacle. Simone calmly gnawed on the end of a large carrot, its green top frothing from her fist.

Cairo turned to Viva. His face was narrow, and his eyebrows were high and thin, almost womanly. "Where is your father?"

"He's coming." Charlotte turned and caught Viva's eye. Her look said, *Good one*.

Charlotte got in the van, made a rough three-point turn, and flew into their assigned space.

"Find yourself a new nighttime hobby, Cairo, and mind your own business." Before he could answer, Charlotte pushed Viva into the trailer. She walked straight to the counter and contemplated her crystal glass, gleaming in the sunlight. Swiftly she reached beneath the sink where she kept her wine. Charlotte poured a glass and drank most of it in a single shot. Not a not-drinking day.

An hour later, Charlotte roared up to Quinn's General Store. She and Viva passed by Cairo and his family, and saw them rearranging their stinky crab shells. As if that would help. Kate was asleep on a corner of the blanket, clutching her blue ribbon in her hand.

"It's awful how they use that child," Charlotte said loudly when they walked past.

"What do you mean?"

"They want people to feel bad for them."

Simone and Cairo studiously ignored them. They were pale and still, like people in a religious painting. Viva felt like she'd done something wrong. A horsefly buzzed around Cairo's head, and he killed it with his hands. He raised his palm as if to send Charlotte a healing beam.

"Oh, for Chrissakes," Charlotte muttered as she stepped into the store. Viva trailed behind her. They were on an important psychic-related mission, the return of a map Charlotte had purchased. The map was supposed to feature a cemetery without headstones packed full of unidentified Quakers. Charlotte had planned for them to go to the cemetery that afternoon so Viva could psychically identify them.

"This map is entirely defective," said Charlotte to the man behind the register. She had a way of speaking after a few glasses of wine that was elevated, almost British. Charlotte slapped the map, which she had already crumpled up twice, onto the counter and flattened it. She had changed her nail polish color earlier that morning from Honeycomb to Coral Reef but only got as far as the first three fingers on her left hand.

The man squinted at her. "How's that?"

"It's missing the Lost Quakers Cemetery, which is why I purchased it in the first place, and it's not even drawn to scale." She crossed her arms over her chest. Viva had seen Charlotte return all kinds of things over the years—a coat, a lamp, a partially drank bottle of wine.

"This is a Cape Cod map," the man said.

"Are we not on Cape Cod?" Charlotte turned to a couple of nearby surfers clutching cans of beer and rolled her eyes. They stopped chatting and listened to Charlotte with amusement. Playing to her audience, Charlotte threw her hands up in mock exasperation.

"Well, the cemetery isn't on Cape Cod, lady. It's in Nantucket."

"I'd like to speak to the manager."

"About what? Moving the cemetery?"

"I want a different map of Cape Cod, because this one"—and she struck it with the back of her hand—"is a bad map, and it doesn't show us where to go." She braced herself against the counter and turned to the growing line of people behind her. She tipped her head at them as if they had assembled not to buy things, but to show their support. And this was when Viva knew the man behind the counter would give her what she wanted. He would give her what she wanted because he wanted her to leave. Viva felt a familiar twist of embarrassment in her chest spread quickly to her arms until they felt heavy and useless. Charlotte dramatically shook her head as if she'd argued a difficult court case. One of the surfers saluted her with a Budweiser, and the other said, "Tell him, sister! Sexy don't take no guff!" Charlotte clasped Viva's hand, turned to the other shoppers, and triumphantly raised her fist.

chapter three

"We were here first!" said Charlotte.

Viva awoke to hear her mother and Cairo fighting over picnic table rights. The more expensive camping sites featured a private table, but those staying at the Econo-Sites had to share. Cairo insisted that because there were *three* in his family and Viva and her mother were *only two*, they deserved more time. Plus, he and Simone needed the table from five to six for their daily meditation session. "Heaven forbid you skip a night of the high-and-holy show, Cairo!" shouted Charlotte. "Just because you eat sanctimony for breakfast doesn't mean you can tell me what to do!" She stomped away to join the line for the pay phone across the road.

Charlotte planned to invite Kenny to dinner and had discussed numerous possible menus with Viva in the previous days. Cairo crossed in front of their trailer and caught Viva's eye. She yanked the blinds shut. She ate her cereal and waited for her mother. A few minutes later, Charlotte burst in the door. She wiped her eye with the edge of her poncho as if she might cry, but she didn't.

"What's wrong?" asked Viva.

"Men."

"Are we still getting lobsters?"

"Change of plans," Charlotte said. "Let's blow this joint." She put on her sun hat and grabbed her canvas bag, the one that said *Damn Everything but the Circus* on it. She quickly threw some snacks and two bottles of wine inside it. "Grab the beach towel off the line, Viva."

They were nearing the public showers by the border of the campground when they saw Marcus pushing his cleaning cart. He stopped and ran to them. "Charlotte, I . . ." For a moment he seemed to forget what he wanted to say. He tucked in his shirt and coughed. "I'm sorry, but . . . your rent." He said the word as if it was entirely too distasteful for the creature before him.

Charlotte tucked a piece of hair behind her ear and smiled up at him. "Did anyone ever tell you you look like Tom Selleck?"

Marcus flushed deeply but didn't respond.

"Could I have another week, Marky?"

Marcus mopped his brow with his cleaning rag. "I can do it one more time, but I'll need cash. No checks."

"Are you sure?" Charlotte asked, but before Marcus could answer she added, "If it's cash you want, cash it will be." Charlotte prided herself on never overplaying her hand. She grabbed Viva's arm, and they hurried to the opening of the beach trail. Charlotte stopped and took a swift drink from one of her bottles. "Still got it," she said. Charlotte returned the bottle to her bag and tugged at Viva's cowlick. She was in the right phase of drunk, and Viva knew from experience it was the best time to ask for something.

"Can I take a dance class?"

"Where?"

"I saw a place on the highway."

"What place?"

"Taffy's Dance Girls."

"Taffy's Dance Girls is a strip club."

"What's a strip club?"

"Let's just say you don't need a tutu at Taffy's."

"Well, then a different place."

"Maybe," said Charlotte. "Once we get our ducks in a row."

The previous week, Charlotte said they might stay on at the camp until it closed for the season in late fall. Before then, they needed to replenish their funds, and Charlotte planned to sell some of the Rogaška. Just the crystal vase to start. Then they needed to find Viva a school. There was no local public option, only a private one. But there was the Jonas Sparr Center for Truth, an experimental school that eschewed compulsory lessons, time-tables, or rules. Viva had studied it numerous times when they drove past the low-slung wooden building bordering the salt marsh. The shake-shingle roof was covered in patchy moss in which all manner of detritus was caught—golf balls, pieces of crashed kites. It didn't look like any school Viva had ever seen, and she'd seen a few. Ten, to be exact. She was unsure if she'd repeat fifth grade, given that they'd left midway through the school year, or simply skip it as she had with second grade.

They'd almost reached the beach when Charlotte squeezed Viva's shoulder and remarked on her height—she'd grown two inches that summer. Charlotte murmured, "You got that from your father." Viva tucked away the information to later savor along with the fact that he was a good swimmer and allergic to shellfish, things Charlotte had mentioned in passing a year ago.

Suddenly, they heard a high-pitched, exaggerated laugh and turned to see Kate trailing after them. She was dancing slowly and snapping her blue ribbon in the air. They kept walking and Viva hoped that Kate would fall behind, but she began to sing loudly, a sort of nonsense song.

"I don't want her to come," Viva said.

Charlotte stopped and put her hands on her hips. "Go back to camp, Kate. Can you do that?" Viva put her hands on her hips, too. "Viva and I are having a private mother-daughter meeting."

Kate stood completely still. She was pale and thin and seemed to waver in the wind. She stared at Charlotte and played with her loose tooth.

"Go find your parents," Charlotte called. She waved her hand, and Kate took a quick step backward like a dog that's about to be hit. Violently, she began to cry. Charlotte frowned and bit her lip. "Okay, Kate, you can come with us but only for a little while."

Viva was shocked. Her mother would never let Viva pull those theatrics. "What? No!" she said, but Kate had already run to them.

Charlotte found a spot on the beach near a massive black rock and set out the snacks—a Rice Krispies square, half a cucumber, orange fruit leather, and an actual orange. Charlotte hugged Viva and said, "This is going to be the best year yet, you'll see. A fresh start." Kate nodded in agreement as if she knew what Charlotte was talking about. She stuffed a strip of fruit leather between her lips and chewed with her mouth open. Viva could barely look at her. Charlotte took a drink from her bottle.

Charlotte jumped up and stretched out her arms like a great wild bird. Then she linked arms with both girls. As if they were sisters. Viva was furious. Charlotte began to run in a circle, and the ocean breeze sliced one way, then another, causing their hair to fly in all directions. They went faster and faster until abruptly Charlotte stopped and put her fist to her mouth. "Oh, no," she said. She turned and ran, disappearing behind a nearby dune. Viva knew not to follow her.

In the distance Viva saw a flash. She tried to remember the rules of lightning, which she'd been taught in a school assembly after a local woman was electrocuted. She'd been walking on the beach, wearing a swimsuit that zipped up the front. Walking one minute, dead the next. "Dumb bunny," Charlotte had said. Viva recalled that if your hair stood on end you were supposed to take an action, but what was the action?

Without warning, Kate took off after Charlotte. Viva chased her and Kate stopped short at Charlotte's feet. There lay Charlotte, her right arm flung over her head as it always was when she slept, as if she were trying to flag someone for help. "She's dead! She's dead!" shrieked Kate.

"She's not dead, you dumb ass. She's resting." To use her mother's own words.

Kate leaned over Charlotte and peered at her. With her index finger she touched Charlotte's nose and then her mouth.

"Stop it! Leave her alone, Kate." Kate snatched Charlotte's hat off her head and ran back toward the water, zigzagging until Viva tackled her. Viva shook sand off the hat and carefully placed it on the beach towel, which she pulled back a few feet. The surf was coming in. Kate jumped on the towel and stuck her face close to Viva. She crossed her eyes and wiggled her loose tooth, which bled a bit. "Kate, go back to camp."

"No."

"I said *go*."

Kate flipped around and stuck her bottom in Viva's face.

"Stop it."

Kate plunked down on the towel and sucked her thumb. "Sing me a song." Viva could have shaken her. But then an idea came to her. "If I let you stay, you do what I say."

Kate stared at her and slowly nodded.

"Act like a monkey." Kate hunched over and dangled her arms. She pooched her lips and scratched her armpit, giving Viva a beseeching look.

"Eat that dead fly," she said.

"What?"

"You heard me."

Kate gingerly picked up the fly and stared at it. With a look of defiance, she quickly swallowed it. *Stand on one foot until you fall. Pull a hair from your head. Slap yourself.* As Kate carried out her orders, Viva felt an ever-increasing rush of power. "Drink that salt water," she said, pointing at a tide pool. "Now."

Kate shook her head. "Or leave," said Viva. Kate walked to the pool and cupped her hands, and there she stood for a couple of minutes. "It smells."

"Too bad." Waves were rolling in quickly, and Viva pulled the towel back again. She put her mother's hat on her head. "Drink it, Kate!"

Kate started crying for real this time, but she bent over and scooped up some ocean water. Suddenly a wave crashed in and left her on the sand. It was almost like a cartoon. Before she could get up, another wave broke over her. She fell again. Struggled to stand. There was blood on her face. Then she managed to get up. "My tooth! My tooth!" she shrieked, and ran after the receding wave.

"Kate!" Viva shouted.

"Stop!" Viva looked up and saw Cairo frantically stumbling down the dune. "Oh my God!" He ran and scooped up Kate. "Where is your mother?" he asked Viva.

Viva dug her foot into cold, wet sand.

"Is your mother back at camp?"

Viva shook her head.

"Is she *here*?" he shouted. Scared, Viva pointed in the general direction of where Charlotte lay.

Cairo ran to the dune, disappeared around the side, then quickly returned. He wrapped Kate in the towel and ordered Viva to take his hand. "Come on, it's going to storm."

"I'm not going." Viva tried to pull away from him.

"I'm not leaving you here with that drunk."

"But the ocean might take her."

Cairo grabbed Viva by the arm. "We'll get her later."

"I want my mama," Kate shrieked, and started wailing.

Then Viva was crying, but there was nothing she could do. Though she struggled to break free from Cairo, she couldn't, and already they were halfway up the beach. Viva looked back once but Charlotte was hidden from view.

It was getting dark by the time they reached the campsite, but there was a full moon, which shone on oak trees that appeared to crowd in, conspiratorial, full of gossip. Simone screamed when she saw her daughter, wet and with blood on her shirt.

Cairo handed Kate to her mother and turned to Viva. "When is your father coming? Where do you folks live?" He squatted in front of her. "Where is your home?" he asked, as if Viva hadn't understood the question. Viva just stared at him. You wouldn't get her mouth open if you tried for a hundred years. She ran to their trailer, where she slammed the door and locked it.

Inside, Viva sat down stiffly at the table. She never did the honors of making it into a bed herself. Her mother did that. She put her head on the tabletop as they'd been told to do in school when things got out of hand. Thunder shook the trailer, and finally, it began to pour. She closed her eyes and tried to psychically connect with her mother. Nothing. The opposite of being psychic is wanting to forget what you already know.

"Oh, for heaven's sake, I'm fine!" It was her mother's voice. Her tone was familiar—high-handed, jovial, irritated. Like a song cutting through static on the radio, Viva could hear something else: shame. But you had to have a trained ear to pick it up.

Viva looked out the window and saw Marcus leading Charlotte toward the trailer. When they reached Cairo's station wagon, she flung herself on the hood. Motionless, she looked like she'd fallen from the sky.

"Goddamn it! Get off my car!" Cairo shouted.

Charlotte struggled to get up. Marcus lifted her from the hood and slung her arm over his shoulder. For a moment they looked like a couple attempting some kind of complicated square dance promenade. They headed toward the trailer, Charlotte's feet catching on unseen objects.

Campers began to crowd around their site, eager to watch the spectacle. "This isn't a free show!" shouted Charlotte.

Cairo shook his finger at Charlotte. "You took my daughter, you took your own daughter, and you pass out on the beach. You're damn lucky someone didn't get hurt." He turned to Marcus. "What are you going to do about this?"

"My daughter!" Charlotte suddenly stopped. "What did you do with my daughter?"

Viva opened the trailer door.

"There you are!" Charlotte stood there swaying, and the mixture of joy and relief on her face was a thing to behold. "Viva . . . Viva . . ." She seemed to want to say something very badly. Whatever it was, the words sat silent and frantic in her mouth. "My daughter's here," she said. She pulled a cigarette from her pocket and lit the wrong end. "She's right here."

Marcus tried to steer Charlotte toward the trailer door. She suddenly turned and shouted, "Everyone thinks it's so easy. You try it. You try it. And get your hands off me, Marky. I'm perfectly capable of walking on my own." Marcus looked stricken. Charlotte backed up and knocked into a garbage can overflowing with paper plates, cans, and bottles. She whirled on the gathering crowd. "What are you staring at? For your information, garbage still answers to the name of trash!"

"What the hell?" said Cairo. "And pick up that mess. Marcus, if you don't take care of this, I will."

"What are you going to do, Cairo? Pray me away?" Charlotte laughed, and elbowed Marcus as if he, too, was in on the joke. Frantically, she started to shadowbox, and Marcus caught her by the arm. "Stop, just stop." He took a deep breath and Viva could see how hard this was for him. "Charlotte, you need to leave tomorrow. I have to keep my campers safe."

"Am I a danger, Marcus? Because I won't sleep with you? Thanks, you fickle fucking friend." She turned back to the crowd and lifted her arm in a grand fashion. "Watch what they do, not what they say, folks. Watch what they do." Abruptly, she leaned on the picnic table, and Viva thought she might topple over. "Everyone just *leave* me alone!" Then Charlotte sat at the table, folded her hands, and stared into space. Viva knew that when her mother reached this point, like a wound-down doll, she was spent.

Early the next morning, Charlotte quickly and silently packed up. They simply left the trailer at the camp the way a crab leaves its shell. The highway was empty, and they had the suicide lane to themselves. It was raining, and Charlotte opened every window in their van. As she drove, a cold wind rushed at them—her handmade storm. She looked in the rearview mirror and said, "Don't worry, Viva, you're safe with me."

chapter four

Sometimes, Charlotte's jaw still hurt. Though the accident was long ago, her body had not forgotten. Today, she felt an inexplicable shooting pain like a tiny bomb detonating in her maxilla. Clutching a baggie of dimes in one hand, Charlotte rooted through her purse innards to locate her address book. The phone booth was streaked with yellow—mustard? Worse?

She saw Viva in the park across the street, lining up with other kids according to height. There was a free day camp, and miraculously, today there was a dance class. Tap. Not the type of class Viva wanted to take, but it would do. The teacher, a man wearing spandex pants and a tuxedo T-shirt, pressed play on his cassette player and showed the kids a basic step. Charlotte watched Viva roll up her too-long bell-bottoms. She had meant to hem them. The kids who had tap shoes practiced on an old piece of plywood while Viva practiced on the grass. Even without the shoes, she could see Viva had something the others did not. It was there in her sense of rhythm and the ease with which she picked up the choreography. Viva possessed a natural cohesion of movement, a sense of personal placement that Charlotte envied, one so unlike her own energy, which she felt wavered around the edges, vibrated too wide or simply vanished when she most needed it. Drinking didn't help. Until it helped. Charlotte would give anything to feel the sense of transport she saw Viva experience when she danced. She felt a stab of guilt. What kind of mother envied her own daughter's joy?

Charlotte would figure out how to get Viva real dance lessons. Charlotte herself had pleaded for riding lessons when she was Viva's age. It was 1955 and her mother vehemently refused. Her mother said horses were hinky. Her mother said stables stank. But what her mother meant was horses break hymens.

Charlotte saved up her allowance and paid for one introductory lesson, which she snuck out of the house to take. She recalled the riding instructor, Mrs. Cordelia Waller, whose painted-on eyebrows smudged to her hairline, leading an old skewbald horse out of the barn for her. Standing in the center of the corral, Mrs. Waller blasted warnings:

Horses are five hundred times stronger than humans.
A fall from a horse can be fatal.
If you ride a horse, you will fall off. When you fall off, let go.

Mrs. Cordelia Waller said more about falling off a horse than staying on, and it seemed to Charlotte that she secretly loved to fall, as if that might be the entire point of riding.

Charlotte did get her left foot in the stirrup; she did grab the horn of the saddle. She even sat for a moment. The problem was that Charlotte's right foot never found the other stirrup. She lost the reins and reached out senselessly, grasping handfuls of air. For a second, her fingers caught the horse's mane, but she lost that, too.

Charlotte told the horse to stop, she told it to wait—but *wait was too late*. They'd learned that in school. A person who waits doesn't get the worm, can't find their shoes, and turns out terrible. But how does a person stop a thing already in motion?

The horse began to gallop, and its speed seemed to quicken her vision, articulating rock and tree, and stable gate, their outlines buzzing as she flew past.

And then she fell. The fact that she knew she was going to fall did nothing to lessen the shock of the hard ground against her back and the absence of breath that felt like the bottom of a cough in its ache and completeness. Where was her air, the current that makes the invisible machinery work? Something was wrong with her jaw, it was off its hinge, and her chin and lips, where were they? She couldn't feel them.

Her jaw was wired shut the next day, and Charlotte's great ability to keep things to herself was born. She never told Viva where they were going, she never talked about money, and she refused to reveal the identity of Viva's father.

Charlotte pulled out her address book and scanned the names she'd collected in the last ten years. Some were smeared or illegible—she'd accidentally dropped the book in the ocean the previous week. She dialed up an old friend from Manhattan who now lived somewhere on the Cape. She thought. Disconnected. In the near distance, cars inched along the Bourne Bridge. Yesterday, they'd traveled only two hours south from the La Pierre campground before Charlotte had pulled over by a park. She wasn't sure which way they should go once they crossed to the mainland. They had nowhere to go. She and Viva had slept in the van last night and they both could use a shower. Charlotte waved at her daughter and watched.

Charlotte would call her older sister, Ardel. Newly married, newly Christian Scientist, she lived on the West Coast, but her husband's family lived somewhere near Rhode Island. Didn't they? Charlotte and her sister had never been close, and before she began to dial, she felt a familiar unease. She remembered Ardel, a high school senior when Charlotte was in sixth grade, arriving home from cello practice, sweeping into the kitchen. Ardel would sit in her slip and drink coffee with Charlotte's mother, recapping the highlights of her day. Charlotte could not compete with their gossip, their womanly bodies, nor could she join their conversations about the recordings of Maria Callas and Joan Sutherland, whom they constantly played. The music flooded the air above their heads as they shared a cigarette, and Charlotte would despair of ever catching up.

Quickly, before she could change her mind, she slipped a dime into the slot. The operator said, "Fifty-five cents for the next three minutes." In her haste to grab more coins, Charlotte dropped her bag of dimes and they scattered on the warm concrete. She scooped up a handful, redialed. The phone rang and rang.

Charlotte had been a child who talked a lot, to everyone and everything—strangers, dogs, cars, bugs. Her father told her, *The empty wagon rattles the most.* And yet, there was no one to talk to at home, certainly not her mother or sister, or her father, a developmental engineer with GE who spent his days among massive turbines and who, when home, seemed vaguely disappointed by the confounding and messy design of female humans. Quiet and hardworking, most nights he stayed up late, drinking Scotch. It barely seemed to affect him. He never became belligerent or maudlin and would rinse out his glass before going to bed. Then he'd sleep five hours and leave for work before dawn.

Sun beat down on the phone booth. It was past noon. Charlotte felt a dull throbbing in her jaw and cradled it in her palm.

Due to the trauma, due to the fact she'd had her jaw wired shut for two months, Charlotte's parents had sent her to the only child psychiatrist in Poughkeepsie, Dr. Drzybylski. The doctor asked inane questions like how she felt about having to stay home from school, what it was like to not be able to talk on the phone. Her mouth encaged, Charlotte wrote brief answers on a piece of paper like, *mad, bad, sad*. But mostly she was mad. And Charlotte was never going to that doctor again.

When she came home after her appointment, she found her mother on a call with their neighbor, Mrs. Dennehey. She was making Charlotte a special blender drink—canned peaches and graham crackers. Peaches for vitamin C, graham crackers to quell sexual urges. Last year, the teenage girl down the street got pregnant, and the closer Charlotte got to puberty the more anxious her mother became.

Charlotte sat at the kitchen table and picked up the reading material her mother had left for her—a young ladies' primer called *The Modern Girl* published by the Modess sanitary napkin company. Its cover displayed an angel hovering above a stove, rays of light emanating from her bottom, or perhaps it was smoke blowing upward. A kind of quasi-Christian, home-ec compendium, it featured the chapter headings "House," "Kitchen," "Church," "Body."

Charlotte had immediately flipped to "Body" only to find the word *menstruation* spelled out phonetically with no explanation as to what the thing entailed. Instead, it offered a single helpful hint: *Remember: Modess rhymes with "Oh. Yes."* Charlotte dreaded joining the ranks of her mother, sister, and basically all womankind.

Her mother cranked the dial on the blender and shouted to Mrs. Dennehey, "Why do girls like horses so much? I'll tell you why, because Hasbro and Elizabeth Taylor told them to. This wouldn't have happened if Charlotte didn't insist on disobeying me. Willful, that child is willful."

Without touching her pulverized-peach slop, Charlotte ran upstairs, slammed her bedroom door, and except for using the bathroom, stayed there until the wires came off fifty-three days later. At mealtimes, her mother knocked and left a tray outside the door, but after the first week, Charlotte pretended she lived in a hotel. Isolation be damned. She'd show them willful.

Day after day, Charlotte lay in bed almost suffocating from the smells of Lemon Pledge, cigarette smoke, and fried chicken, while she listened to her mother's blender gun from chop to purée, endless competing operas, the daily drag of the Hoover across the hardwood floor, and outside the sound of Mrs. Dennehey's dog whose vocal cords had been cut, standing at their gate, day after day, barking with no bark, and she would lie completely rigid for so long and with such perfect resolve, she could feel herself float up and out of her body, no longer a girl full of words with no way to say them, but free.

A man banged on the phone booth.

"Fuck off!" Charlotte shouted. She pulled a jam jar of Southern Comfort from her purse and took a sip. Just one. She put it on the shelf beneath the phone. Sometimes when Charlotte drank, it felt like she walked through a door, and on the other side of that door, she was free of her memories, body, and past, and before her lay a clearing where the present moment beckoned in beautiful potentiality. But today that door was closed to her. She picked up the jar and took a gulp.

Charlotte considered trying to find a cheap motel, but their funds had almost run out. She'd been able to save a couple hundred dollars from her job last spring as a makeup artist at Sears, but she was down to four twenties hidden beneath the van's floor mat. Charlotte dialed a woman named Amaryllis she'd met at a flea market, and of course, Amaryllis would be happy to put them up for a few days, and what great fun it would be to have a youngster in the house, and why, just that afternoon she'd made a coconut cake! But alas, her house was being fumigated. She tried the youth hostel. No vacancy. Kenny the waiter? God, no. Who was the nice man they'd met at the clam shack? He'd offered her a job at his bookstore if they stayed through the fall. She didn't have a number. She was out of dimes and already at the Ts.

And there, written in tiny letters that snaked along the inside spine of her address book, she saw a phone number and the name *Bill Titus*. A painter she knew from a college art class. Bill had always had a crush on her. Charlotte called collect.

chapter five

They'd been at the Titus home for three days, and Viva hadn't seen her mother drink a drop. She watched Charlotte pace before the dining room window of the Titus house, which appeared caged, due to the twelve-foot-high fence that surrounded the property. The wrought-iron bars served as a reminder that someone important lived there, someone whom others might go to great lengths to see. Bill Titus bragged that the gate's remote control, special-ordered from Switzerland, was château-grade. The Titus family possessed an enormous sunken living room, which, covered in purple shag carpet, looked like a lake of grape juice. A swinging bed hung from the ceiling on boat chains.

"We're so happy you've come to visit us, Viva," Bill said, looking at Charlotte.

Charlotte turned from the window. "Bill, do you have any vino?"

"Wine?" Bill asked, and there was something distasteful in his tone.

"What?" said Bill's wife, Sheila.

Sheila was a beautiful woman whose bangs fell to the side of her head in perfect cascading wings. She'd barely spoken during dinner and seemed firmly ensconced in a personal dream world.

"Chenin blanc, rosé, whatever you have on hand," said Charlotte in a tone that would indicate she hardly cared if they had any at all.

Bill wiped his mouth with his napkin. "Sorry, Charlotte, no wine. No libations in this house."

"Not a problem," said Charlotte. She reached for her cigarettes. Here they were—Charlotte and Viva—with Bill, Sheila, and their children, Poe and Tommy, gathered around the dining room table. Poe, with thick eyebrows and blond hair that looked like dandelion fluff, was eleven, like Viva. Tommy, fourteen, said little but smirked, as if he knew something bad about a person but with great restraint would not reveal what it was. Behind him on the dining room wall hung a "family heirloom," a cigarette smoke–stained painting called *Pastore Sè Riposarse*. Gazing imperiously from the painting, the pastor looked like he'd never skipped a snack.

They were eating dinner at 5:00 sharp, the Tituses' preferred time, which now would become their own. Viva and Charlotte had barely slept the previous night, and toward early morning, Viva asked if they could sleep in the van. But no, it might appear ungracious. When they'd crawled into bed, Viva carefully folded back her bedspread the way Charlotte demonstrated. There was no telling whether the Titus family slept under their bedspreads or used them for decorative purposes only. As a guest, it wasn't worth making the wrong move.

Charlotte lit her cigarette, and Bill and Sheila followed suit. Red, orange, and striped packs of cigarettes lined the edge of the table like so many tiny racing cars. Charlotte, who'd recently ditched her clove cigarettes for a carton of Camels, smoked in brisk wet pops. Bill took rough drags of his Winston, and Sheila inhaled and exhaled two dainty puffs before depositing her lit Benson & Hedges on the edge of her dinner plate. She left for the kitchen.

Smoke hung thick around the savage-looking dining room chandelier that featured jagged pieces of metal soldered together in concentric circles. If it were to fall from the ceiling, it would surely kill whoever sat beneath it. "That's quite a piece," said Charlotte.

"It's brutalist," said Bill.

"Brutalist?" asked Charlotte.

"It refers to a design style. It's from the French word for *raw*."

"That's wonderful," said Charlotte, and she made the slightest motion of dipping her head, like a woman about to be crowned. Then she slowly lifted her eyes, and a ripple passed between Bill and Charlotte, something that excluded everyone else at the table.

Bill ran a hand through his hair, which was thick and uniform, like dog fur. Charlotte said Bill had long ago abandoned his artistic aspirations and for a decade now he'd owned a hardware store thirty miles outside of Boston. He drove a canary-yellow Camaro Berlinetta and had his own TV commercial that ran on the local station.

There was much to learn about the Tituses:

The Titus family did not believe in self-delusion. Bill Titus had gone through EST training twice, and he was a firm believer in the idea that you do something or you don't. Bill Titus did not believe in *trying*.

The Titus family did not believe in small talk or organized religion.

The Titus family did not believe in vitamins, gift wrap, or cold cuts.

The Titus family did not believe in soda, with the exception of Tab.

Charlotte and Viva took quick note of these things, but the problem with being a guest is that a person must be useful, listen to stories that hold no interest, and in Charlotte's case, not drink. Not in the house, anyway. Before long, a bottomless thermos of red wine appeared in the glove compartment of the van.

After the first week with the Tituses, Charlotte enrolled Viva in sixth grade at Hoover Middle School—just for a semester, she told Sheila and Bill. Just until they got on their feet. Bill didn't seem to mind; in fact, he said he had some work for Charlotte. Sheila received the news with her usual equanimity, like a woman always slightly anesthetized.

A few of the teachers seemed to think Viva was Tommy and Poe's younger sister, perhaps one who had been away at boarding school, and Viva didn't correct them. When they walked to school in the morning, Tommy led the way, bouncing on the balls of his feet, his white painter's pants mottled with dirt. Poe stomped along behind him. Viva silently brought up the rear, crossing the street when they crossed, stopping when they stopped. On occasion and without provocation, Poe gave her the finger behind her back.

While Viva was at school, Charlotte worked mornings at the hardware store, and in the afternoons, she worked on *Pastore Sè Riposarse*. Charlotte had studied art restoration for only a single semester in college, but she said if you could spit, you could do it.

The first Friday of the fall semester, school let out early due to a teachers' conference. When Viva returned to the Titus house, she found her mother in the basement working at an easel by the washer and dryer. Next to her Bill stood on a folding chair, fiddling with a work light, which he trained downward on the painting. Charlotte had told Viva that restoration work should be completed in daylight, but since *The Husky Pastor*, as she called the painting, was no *Last Supper*, she'd said it was a moot point. On top of the washing machine sat two opened beers—in the short time they'd been there, she'd managed to convince Bill that beer wasn't real alcohol.

"Is this the best angle, Char?" Viva knew she disliked the nickname, but as a guest she'd put up with it.

"Whatever you think, Bill," Charlotte said, rubbing her neck.

"Oh, there's the sweet spot," said Bill, shining the light directly on Charlotte's face. Charlotte smiled at him and lifted her chin.

"Over here," Viva called, and Bill swung the light in her direction. She did a single pirouette. Not well.

"She's good, right, Bill?"

"What?"

"I think she has raw talent, the kind that blossoms with a little instruction."

"Sure," said Bill. He turned the light from Viva and trained it on the awful painting.

Viva did a second pirouette in the shadows, and this one was stronger, but she knocked into a bed frame stored in the corner.

"Viva, I know you can do better than that—now come show Bill again."

"Oh, that's okay, I saw how good she was the first time. Viva, honey, why don't you go play *Pong* with Poe."

Fat chance. Earlier that day, Poe said that in profile Viva looked like a zipper, referring to her flat chest and prominent nose. "I want to stay and watch."

"You'll be bored out of your mind," Charlotte said and gave Viva a look that told her she should leave. Bill stepped off the chair and stood behind Charlotte. He began to massage her neck and she sighed with pleasure. "This is a big job, Bill, and it's going to take some time."

"You take all the time you need, Char. We're honored to have a real artist in the house."

Viva had never heard Charlotte or anyone else describe her this way, but her mother's eyes lit up. "Oh, you're gilding the lily, Bill, but thank you."

Viva climbed the basement stairs and went into the kitchen. She popped open a Tab and practiced a shuffle ball change she'd learned in the free class until she had to stop and catch her breath.

Already, Viva liked to push herself, and her strength was a secret no one could touch. Not her mother. Not the Tituses. The brief physical rebellion was intoxicating.

Sheila wafted past her wearing a mauve chiffon muumuu, clutching a book from the Sunshine Query, a cult in upstate Maine that Charlotte said was in the business of changing lives one $49.99 book at a time. Charlotte also said Sheila was depressed. Sheila didn't acknowledge Viva's presence and disappeared into her private bathroom, which featured a pink velvet swivel chair with a deep indentation that Charlotte called "the cervix." If Viva was completely honest, she was impressed by the splendor of the bathroom — the flocked wallpaper with its pattern of fuchsia pelicans in repose; even the air seemed opulent, drenched in the fragrance of potted gardenias and Charlie perfume. "An exercise in gauche excess," Charlotte called it, and out of loyalty to her mother, Viva completely agreed. Charlotte said, "You and I are wired the same way, Viva," and it thrilled her to think she shared her mother's circuity, which she imagined as complex and sparkling, far more remarkable than that of people like Sheila Titus.

Viva heard the theme from *Sanford and Son* blaring from Tommy's bedroom. She tried to time her dance moves to the music, but it didn't work. Swathed in a gray wool blanket, Tommy watched the show every day, huddled like a gargoyle. He kept his reading material close by — stacks of a magazine called *Porno Smile*, which, since it was published in Japan, Bill approved as foreign reading material.

Suddenly, Tommy appeared in the kitchen doorway, clutching a box of Fiddle Faddle. He was always slinking around, and sometimes she could smell him before she saw him — Aqua Velva, and beneath that, dirt, and beneath that, something that lingered, like ammonia.

Tommy leaned against the refrigerator and began to sing made-up lyrics to the *Sanford and Son* theme song:

There's a lady
There's a lady we all know
She's got sugar, she's got sugar all the time
She's got sugar running down her legs . . .

"Screw off, Tommy." Charlotte's line.

"Make me a cheese sandwich."

"No."

"Make me a cheese sandwich."

Tommy stepped closer to Viva and thrust his neck forward. His smell was overpowering. "Do it."

Viva saw three single black hairs on his jaw, which he never trimmed, hoping they would encourage a beard. "No."

Before she could stop him, Tommy leaned in and licked her neck. Viva kicked his shin. Tommy opened his mouth and his eyes rolled back in his head. He winced and reached for his leg. The cellar door flew open, and Charlotte appeared, carrying a basket brimming with the Titus family laundry—Tommy's T-shirts, and a pair of Bill's blue boxers atop the pile. In addition to her restoration work, Sheila had asked her to take on the task since she'd be spending so much time in the basement.

"What the hell is going on?"

Tommy smirked at her and didn't move. "Nothing, Mrs. Charlotte."

"Go to your room. Now."

"Like you can tell me what to do."

Charlotte slammed the basket on the table. "You want me to get your father?" She jerked her thumb toward Bill, who was now in the backyard with Poe. Even though he couldn't have heard her, he suddenly looked up and caught her eye. The longer they stayed, the stronger his Charlotte radar grew.

Tommy slipped out of the room and Charlotte spun around. "What happened?"

Viva flushed. "Nothing."

"If that little fucker gives you any trouble, you let me know and I'll straighten him out. You got that?"

Charlotte was an expert at handling men. Men loved Charlotte or at the very least feared her, and in part, Viva had concluded, this was because she never loved them. Not Kenny the waiter. Not Marcus, always finding reasons to fix things near their trailer. Certainly not Cairo.

Charlotte leaned in and whispered, "Viva, I have a hot piece of news for you. Bill said he'll pay for lessons at the local dance school, Penrose Academy for the Performing Arts. So you be very nice to him."

"When do I start?"

"I don't know, but we'll sign you up soon."

Viva hugged her mother. Charlotte said, "I'm going to give it to you straight—your dancing needs work, but I think you've got something."

They heard a shriek and looked out the window. Bill was giving Poe a piggyback ride in the backyard. Poe savagely clutched her father's neck, and when Bill pretended to choke, she kicked the heels of her snakeskin boots against his back with glee.

Viva sometimes missed the physical presence of her own father as if he were a phantom limb. She would become very still and try to sink into the yearning and could almost picture her father coming to see her. But immediately and maddeningly, the feeling dissolved. Where would he be coming from? Possibilities flooded her mind—a man on a boat, a bus, an operating table, a man on a toilet, taking tickets, plucking a bird. It was ridiculous and embarrassing, and yet the longing itself refused to abate, a dark interior patch that she could do nothing but bear. Viva told herself she wasn't like girls she saw who clung to their fathers, whining for money or records or roller skates, and her noble ache made her feel superior, pure.

Charlotte pulled Viva outside and made a production of enjoying Bill and Poe's game. "Go, Bill, go. Yeehaw!" she shouted. Viva stood there silently.

Bill and Poe flew past them, and Poe pumped her fist triumphantly. She gave Viva a simpering smile and flung her rabbit-fur hat to the ground. As if she expected Viva to pick it up. Viva didn't move. If the hat was ruined, Bill would buy her a new one. They circled past again, and this time Charlotte sharply elbowed Viva, who clapped twice. The nick of self-betrayal was instant.

chapter six

It was late at night, the first week in November, when Charlotte and Viva slipped out the back door of the Titus home. Charlotte put the van in neutral, rolling it backward out of the driveway. Time for another nighttime run.

Early snow had begun, and as they drove through quiet streets it seemed like they were the only ones on earth. Charlotte was smoking hash out of a meerschaum pipe she'd filched from Bill. The pipe was carved into a sultan's head, which became darker as she smoked.

"Pilot to copilot?" said Charlotte.

"We read you loud and clear." Viva looked out the window, and there was the night—the quick black overtake. "Where are we going?"

"You'll see."

They'd left the tony neighborhood where the Tituses lived and sped past the Rexall with its riotous *R*, past the town hall, the Carter underwear factory, and the state prison. When Viva looked out the window the night gobbled up the last two houses on the town's border, a blue Victorian and a green two-story.

Viva put her hands over the heating vent, which barely worked anymore. "Can we go to *The Fantasticks* tomorrow?" she asked. It was playing at the local community theater, and the entire Titus family planned to attend, even Sheila. The hardware store was a full-page sponsor, and Bill said he could get Charlotte and Viva in for free.

"It's not really my thing," said Charlotte. She blew a smoke ring and squinted at the sky. "Besides, we're not joiners and we never will be."

"Are you depressed?" Viva asked.

"I don't get depressed," said Charlotte.

Viva mentally reviewed the mythological animals they had been studying in school—the griffin, a creature with the body of a lion and the head of an eagle, and the chimera, which was also part lion as well as goat and snake. Both would be on a test next week. She thought Charlotte was like these animals—part mother, part unknowable creature.

"I'll go without you."

"Fine with me," said Charlotte with a smile that indicated she knew Viva wouldn't go if she didn't. And really, Viva couldn't bear the idea of being alone with the Tituses. Their jokes and family shorthand were incomprehensible to her. Why did everyone think it was so funny when Tommy would randomly blurt out "ka-ching, ka-ching!" It was impossible to crack the family humor code, and she wasn't willing to ask for help. Without warning Charlotte swerved into the almost empty parking lot of a twenty-four-hour grocery store. Viva stared up at the Price Chopper logo, which featured Lady Liberty with an ax stuck in her head.

"Did you know some people drill holes in their skull to achieve nirvana?" asked Charlotte.

"What is nirvana?"

"It's purification and liberation, it's being free from fret. It's the Price Chopper."

The automatic doors of the supermarket popped open with a delighted gasp, and the store air felt fresh and welcoming, redolent with the smell of baking bread and peppermint floor polish. Viva saw a wild display of what looked like glinting grass hanging from the ceiling—row after row of sparkly green streamers, which lifted and danced on some unseen air current. In this moment the Price Chopper seemed to her a kind of mad church of goodwill and benevolence.

It was four in the morning, and a single checker sat on a stool near aisle 6 reading *The Boston Phoenix*. Atop her head sat a dish of gray hair, upswept and swirled by mysterious forces. Behind her an old man cleaned the vast body of the grocery store floor, buffing scuffs and spills from its endless parallel limbs.

Charlotte grabbed Viva's hand and swerved right at aisle 5, jerking to a halt before a display of lavender Yardley soap. "Thirty-three cents a bar, what are they thinking?" She shook her head as if Yardley had personally let her down and she was doing them a service by diminishing the display by one, two, then four bars. Into her book bag. The Tituses had soap, but that wasn't the point.

"Greensleeves" wafted around them, piped in from an invisible source. Charlotte lit up a Camel. "'Nirvana' means blown out," she said absently, shaking her match.

Viva clasped her arms around Charlotte's waist and trailed behind her, shuffling her feet in an exaggerated manner like a zombie. Charlotte didn't react, but she didn't stop her, either. Viva knew she was getting too old to do these things, and time was running out. Before long, she would have to join the ranks of the junior high school girls she saw perched on the wall near the school incinerator, where they sat silent and unsmiling, heads cloaked by hooded sweatshirts, faces spackled with Revlon foundation, only the occasional nose or cigarette protruding. But not yet, not yet, and this was turning out to be the best night ever.

She spotted a jar of pickles. Classic Vlasic. "Look, Mom, *classic!*" Viva never used the word *Mom*, but they were in an alternate world where everything was brighter, better.

"Stop it," said Charlotte, but she tossed the jar of pickles into the bag and zipped around the corner, where she came to a complete halt.

The liquor aisle. Charlotte stared at the hard liquor on shelves to her left, the beer and wine in a cooler to her right. She crossed her arms and stepped back, as though she was contemplating a complicated piece of art. Viva had seen her do this before, as if there was someone for whom she needed to perform.

Viva caught sight of herself in a strip of mirror within the cooler—skinny, thumbs hooked in belt loops. She looked to herself like a sort of terrible old, fusty sheriff in a cowboy movie. She pursed her lips and stuck out her breasts, which made no difference at all. She did a quick pirouette for fortification. Charlotte had told her she'd grow into herself, but meanwhile, what was the poor self to do? How long must it wait? Her body was incomprehensible to her.

"That's good, honey." Charlotte picked up a bottle of Smirnoff, took a drag of her cigarette, and peered at the label like she was trying to make out a blurred phone number, the type one sees in a dream.

Viva studied Charlotte's face—the straight no-nonsense eyebrows, almost boyish, her broad mouth and pale lips that turned down slightly when she smiled, and her green eyes, which were shining like she had a fever. In this moment she was completely absorbed, and Viva knew better than to interrupt.

Charlotte ran her fingers through her hair with her free hand and began to sing along with "Greensleeves," which was still playing and perhaps on a loop. Then she was talking very quickly, talking about the Tudors, how the Tudors really knew how to write an unrequited love song, how every love song since 1580 was based on "Greensleeves."

"And the thing people forget is that in those days sleeves weren't always attached to the dresses. They used pins! Can you imagine? Pins!" Charlotte laughed and her energy began to crank in a way that Viva had witnessed before, a spiraling current of glee. She slipped the bottle into the bag.

Her mother grabbed her hand, and they were off. Charlotte's chartreuse caftan whirled around her legs as her bare feet slapped the grocery store floor. Viva could barely keep up with her. Charlotte took a sudden hard right and swooped down upon the meat counter, where she slipped a ham—so quickly that Viva wasn't sure she saw her do it—into her book bag. Neither Charlotte nor she liked ham. Bill Titus liked ham.

"Why do we have to get Bill a ham?" Viva asked.

"Because his wife won't let him eat it is why." Charlotte took a drag from her cigarette and blew a smoke ring.

"Ma'am, you can't smoke in here." The man wore a uniform with a white apron over it. He looked more official than a checker, but not bloody enough to be a butcher. "No smoking," he said again, but he wasn't looking at Charlotte's cigarette, he was looking at Charlotte's bag. The ham was clearly visible, defenseless as a baby's head.

"Did you buy those items?"

Charlotte took a deep breath, tilted her head, and exhaled. "What is your position in this establishment?"

"I'm the night manager."

"Then you know that at night sometimes people are simply too tired to push a cart."

Viva saw the man look at her pajama top covered in pink parrots and her blue corduroy pants. They'd left the Titus house so quickly she hadn't even put on her underpants.

"You *planned* to buy these things?" The man directed the question to Viva, and there was something softer in his voice now. Viva didn't answer—a trick she'd learned from her mother—*never defend, explain, or justify*. Charlotte set her bag on the floor. She was the picture of calm, but Viva could feel something within her like a wire shorting out. The man pulled a walkie-talkie from his pocket.

"We stole," Viva said.

Charlotte looked off into the distance as if she heard someone calling her name. She took a tube of ChapStick from where she kept it in her bra and began to apply it. "This is a beautiful store, the displays are exuberant yet phosphine," said Charlotte. She put great faith in the idea that using an unusual word threw people off their game.

No one said anything, and Viva had a terrible urge to laugh. The air in the store suddenly seemed silly and jittery, manufactured, too bright. "Greensleeves" cranked on and on, inescapable.

"You need to buy those things or get out of here. And I'm giving you a break to leave it at that."

The man had a large mole on his right temple and Viva fixated on it.

"Have you ever been hungry, sir?" Charlotte asked the question softly and carefully, as if she was asking the man something quite personal. She bowed her head and put her hand on his forearm. The way she asked the question, she might have been talking about people who worked at night because they had nowhere better to be, people who slept all day because they had no friends. She might have been talking about stray cats, fatherless girls, and people whose love isn't returned for four hundred years.

The man was saying something, but Viva had a hard time hearing him because she was sure he was going to turn them in. Her nose began to bleed, and she wiped it with the back of her hand. Then she turned and ran.

She ran through the store, past brooms tightly wedged in grim vigilance against the wall, past pyramids of tomatoes and embarrassing penile vegetables, past diddly cotton swabs, which everyone knew were bad for your ears and could puncture your brain, past Freshen-up gum, which squirted when you bit into it, and a boy at school called "cum gum," past a no-neck cardboard scarecrow waving a fat wheat paw, a conversation bubble emerging from his lips: *Howdy, lady! Howdy!*

This was not Nirvana.

The automatic door stuck, and she almost crashed into it. Viva stomped on the black rubber mat, trying in vain to find the special spot that would make the door swing wide and release her into the night. And then she was outside, alone with a shiny black pony, the type children ride for a quarter, paralyzed mid-leap with gaiety. On his back, he bore a sign that read: *For Kids Only. No Rough Ridin'.*

Viva ran to the van and waited there for her mother. A single floodlight shone down upon the Price Chopper, illuminating a stand of straggly pine trees that lined the chain-link fence at the store's perimeter. Her feet were cold and her pajama top was too thin. She crossed her arms over her chest.

And then there was Charlotte, walking slowly toward her, like a woman treading the bottom of the ocean, all her wild flying energy tucked back inside.

Charlotte didn't immediately start the engine. A potato chip truck rattled past, and "Sisters of Mercy" leaked from the window. They both stared at the truck as if there was something to see. Charlotte gave Viva a tissue for her bloody nose, then handed her a cellophane-wrapped doughnut. The lights in the parking lot clicked off. Two crows winged up and over the Price Chopper. Charlotte stared through the windshield like she could see the entirety of their lives unfurled before them. She seemed very tired. Her bag, which now held only a single item, slumped between them on the seat. "That bottle is paid for." Charlotte turned on the radio and they heard the song continue. She took a hit from her pipe, and sank back in her seat, closing her eyes.

Viva took a bite of her doughnut and watched a small pale sun begin to rise in the distance. "We better go home."

"That's not our home and Bill is not our boss. No man is our boss." She took another hit from her pipe and solemnly nodded as Leonard Cohen sang about leaving everything you cannot control before it comes for your soul. "It does come 'round to your soul,' Viva." Charlotte blew a delicate stream of smoke from her lips and added, "Bill Titus, Father of the Year."

"Bill isn't my father, is he?"

Charlotte coughed out smoke and laughed. "What?! No, Viva. No."

"Well, who was my father?"

Charlotte sighed. "Your father was very sure of himself, but he had a knack for believing people who lied to him."

Viva blew on her bare hands. "Like who?"

"Losers and cheats. One time he bought a TV set from some men selling one by the side of the road, and when he opened the box there was no TV, just an old outboard motor. Can you believe that, Viva?" She put the pipe in the ashtray and grasped her hand. "He was *that* trusting." It seemed to be something she admired and disrespected in equal parts. A hacking cough gripped her. "Viva, promise me you'll never smoke. Not cigarettes or J. Not even hashish. Please."

"Was he buying the TV for me?"

"Oh, he never met you, honey."

Viva felt a wild shock of joy not unlike the amusement ride the Gravitron, where you're held in by centrifugal force, and the bottom drops out, but you're happy, because something greater than yourself has taken over, and there's not a damn thing you can do about it. This was new information, good information, because if a person had never met you, how could they not like you?

chapter seven

It was as if she had no body prior to this day. Viva raced to the Titus house to tell Charlotte she'd been accepted into the advanced beginner class at Penrose Dance Studio. She knew Bill would be happy to hear the news. Increasingly possessive of her mother, he complained that she and Charlotte spent too much time together. After Charlotte had finished her repairs on the ghastly painting, he needed her to work extra hours at the hardware store. Then it was a two-week store inventory that required late-night hours. Sheila had become progressively reclusive, eating nothing but bowls of blue Jell-O in her private bathroom. Poe still ignored Viva, and Tommy continued to hassle her. But Viva had dance now, classes twice a week, and even though it had been only a month, she'd been bumped up to the next level, which was taught by a locally famous teacher, Danita Lavoisin. Danita, who had danced two seasons on *The Dean Martin Show*, was almost six feet tall. Her platinum-blond hair was cut in a savage wedge, and she wore no makeup except for lavender lipstick. Tied to her leotard were multicolored scarves, and as she made her way across the dance studio, she appeared like a bright traveling carnival—body rolling, scarves flying.

Danita began class by asking the students to stand motionless for nine minutes. Nine, because in numerology it signifies initiation. The girls nodded like they knew what numerology was. As they stood in stillness, Danita spoke about "the gathering," which entailed willing one's force and focus. She said a dance was the after expression of something internally summoned. In fact, she said, *a dance was over before it began*. No one knew what the hell she was talking about, but it didn't matter, because as Danita's eyes traveled around the studio, she seemed to have a numinous ability to calibrate their talent before they even took a single step. Already, everyone wanted to please her.

When the nine minutes were up, Danita sat cross-legged on the floor and stretched forward to show the dancers how to draw energy from the ground. "When you lift from this position and throw your head and arms back, it should be as if you have a spear in your chest," she said.

"Like you're dead?" Viva asked.

"No," said Danita. "Not dead. Pierced. You know the difference?"

"Yes," she said, lying.

They continued the warm-up and Danita laid down the rules. They would be on time for class and practice every night. They would make sacrifices and they would like it.

For the remainder of the class, the dancers were to do one single thing—press the sole of the foot into the floor, extend the leg, and slowly, slowly, lift the foot. Point. Hold. Repeat. Again and again and again. This would teach them precision and stamina and control. If their ankles were hot, good. If they were on fire, better. Danita was building them from the ground up. Serious work.

"We're talking about artistic commitment, ladies," said Danita. "And if you don't have it in you, go join twirl club."

It was a freakishly warm day for early March, and as Viva rounded the corner from Farleigh Drive to Wedgwood Lane, she saw the Titus house in all its glory. Except that something was not right.

There was the Titus front door, which Bill had recently painted an odd, urgent blue. There was the brass pug door knocker, which commemorated a long-dead pet named Tally. The replica dog had the appearance of being lodged in the door—its imaginary rear end forever stuck in the foyer, its poor head eternally gazing onto the street. And there was the narrow stained glass window that bordered the front door, its red panes ablaze as it always was at this time of day. And there was Charlotte.

Charlotte lying on a lounge chair on the front lawn, wearing shorts and a halter top sewn from multicolored bandannas. Lathered in Bain de Soleil. Stomach down, rump up. It was only seventy degrees, but she looked melted.

Bill, clutching two cans of Budweiser, flew out the front door and ran down the steps. He shouted to Charlotte, "I could teach you golf in a single lesson."

Viva knew Charlotte hated golf.

Charlotte rolled over and opened one eye. "A single lesson? You must be good," she said, watching Bill as he walked toward her. She reached out her hand. Her movements were languid and there was something different about her energy. She seemed to be shining. Charlotte looked up at him, tilting her chin. A woman who wished to be kissed. It came to Viva with startling clarity. Her mother was no longer a guest. Something in her chest tightened and she couldn't catch her breath. Viva felt the same panic she'd experienced the day her mother disappeared on the beach. She needed help from someone who would know what to do.

Ridiculously, she thought of Danita Lavoisin, but she had no idea how to contact her.

Bill Titus looked at Viva and waved. "How was your class?" he shouted with exaggerated interest. "I said, how was class?"

"Good."

"Well, as long as you're happy."

As long as you're happy. A thing that could be said of a dog licking its bottom. Viva gave him the finger behind his back.

Bill brandished the gate remote and with a clank the bars began to groan and part. "Like welcoming arms," he'd gushed on the day of their arrival.

"Viva, why are you standing there?"

Charlotte glanced at her but remained in her lounger, one hand idly stirring the air as if it was water and she was lying on the bank of her own personal river. She'd gained some weight, and it made her look regal, like an empress. Bill kissed her head, pulled her to her feet, and swatted her bottom.

Viva ran past them and into the house. Tommy was in the kitchen, leaning against the counter, shaking an open box of Trix into his mouth. He stopped and stared at her. "Is your father dead, or what?"

"Dead," Viva said. "Dead from the war."

"That's too bad," he said, stepping closer to her. "Don't you get lonely?"

Viva pushed past him and grabbed a Budweiser from the refrigerator.

"You want to be my girlfriend?"

"No."

"I can buy you all the beer you want. I know a guy."

"Leave me alone," said Viva. She opened the pop-top and swigged from the can. It tasted terrible. Her eye fell on a milk carton on the kitchen counter. A photo of a missing girl was featured, a girl about her own age who seemed to look directly at her.

"Hey, give me some," Tommy said, and tried to grab the Bud.

Viva pushed him away. "Get your own!"

"Viva, don't get so mad. You want to come play a game in my room?"

Viva heard her mother call her and she drank half the beer before fleeing out the kitchen door. Cutting across the backyard, she turned down an alley that ran behind the Titus house and neighboring homes. Garbage cans lined the passageway and atop one sat a doll in a red voile dress edged with lace. A perfectly good doll. She never played with dolls or wanted one, but she stopped and looked at her. Her blue eyes stared back with glee, and in that moment, Viva felt the doll understood her. In fact, she felt that everything understood her—the tall pine trees that bordered the alley and seemed to lean in conspiratorially, a piece of pink cellophane that blew in the wind, and even a crow that pecked at an open bin, staring at her side-eyed. The world was open and speaking to her somehow, and there was no other side to anything—no worries, no Tituses.

So this was what it was all about. She'd seen her mother in this state, and when she closed her eyes, she suddenly felt she became her. Viva exaggerated Charlotte's crooked smile and walked a few paces, mimicking Charlotte's stride, slightly pigeon-toed, a swing in her hips. She took a drink from the beer, turned to the doll, and said, "Who do you think you are, Bill?" Bill. The person who so swiftly had replaced her. Viva's mood plummeted. She picked up her pace, but it was almost dusk by the time she reached the main road. She wasn't sure if she should go left or right. Viva stood beneath an ash tree, and when she looked up, its leaves spun and jumped like sparkling green fish. Then the fish morphed into a face—the face of the girl on the milk carton. The ad had said she was bright and curious and that it was *urgent* she be found. People all over the country were probably looking for her. In her lostness she'd become special and famous. And that's when it came to her—she would go missing. Viva would keep walking until she reached the bus station and she'd figure out where to go then. But the problem was she had no money. She finished the beer and decided to return to the Titus house. She'd clip the emergency fifty her mother kept hidden in her boot and hit the road.

When Viva reached the Titus house, her mother and Bill had vanished, and his car was gone. The front door was locked, but through the foyer window she saw Sheila float down the hallway in her caftan. She banged on the door. Sheila didn't acknowledge it—one of the few benefits of being a specter in your own home. But Viva knew she could see her, and she knocked on the red window that bordered the front door. And knocked again. Hard.

And then her arm was on the other side of the glass.

She looked at her wrist and was shocked to see layers of skin within the cut, as if until this moment, her body hadn't had an inside.

The Berlinetta swung into the driveway, engine rumbling, radio blaring. Her mother was driving, Bill next to her. Tommy and Poe were in the back seat, and Poe's bare foot protruded from the window, a gold snake bracelet spiraling up her ankle. At first, no one seemed to register anything was wrong. Charlotte cut the engine and bounced out of the Berlinetta, laughing about the car's sticky second. Bill slapped the hood and said she was a damn fine driver all the same.

Viva held up her arm and blood gushed down her sleeve. Poe stared at her with a look on her face like a person who had crashed into a snowbank, a stunned and incomprehensible look of shock and delight.

Bill was shouting. Charlotte was shouting. Tommy ran up the steps two at a time.

Sheila never opened the door.

Everyone back into the Berlinetta. Blood on the white leather seats.

Bill said, "Viva, what's your name? Tell us your name," as if Viva had put her head, not her arm, through the window.

Charlotte sat with Viva in the hospital room while the doctor sewed up her right wrist, twenty stitches in all. They'd left Bill and his kids in the waiting room. Uncharacteristically quiet, Charlotte held Viva's hand and squeezed it every few seconds. Beneath the fluorescent lights, she looked completely different from when Viva found her with Bill in the front yard—her hair hung limply on either side of her face, and she had bags under her eyes.

The doctor cut a piece of gauze and wrapped it around Viva's arm. The smell of coffee on his breath was nauseating and she had a headache. "How did this happen?" he asked.

Charlotte locked eyes with her daughter. "I was trying to get in," said Viva.

"Where?" he asked.

"I knocked too hard on the window."

"Of your house?" he said.

Charlotte bit her lip and nodded ever so slightly at Viva.

"Yes, our house."

The doctor paused and considered something. "Well, it seems to me you don't know your own strength, young lady. Next time try the doorbell." He left them with instructions for wound care and a bag of bandages.

Charlotte leaned in to Viva and lowered her voice. "Tommy said you were drinking."

"One beer."

"Viva, you can't drink beer."

"You drink it all the time."

Charlotte took a deep breath. "Things are going to change. You'll see. We're going to get the hell out of here and make a fresh start."

Viva looked at her blankly.

"Pilot to copilot, is that a yes?" Charlotte bit her thumbnail and waited, as if Viva's answer was the most important thing in the world. As if it would make a difference. She began to hum a lullaby she used to sing to her daughter, "Ding Sally Shinepath," a melody Viva now found babyish and annoying.

"I'm not your copilot."

"Viva, please, I'm trying."

"Yes."

"Then we have a plan. You know, I broke my jaw when I was about your age, and I was scared that when I got the wires off, I'd never stop talking. Isn't that silly?"

"Where are we going?"

"So don't be scared. A wound is a secret only you and your body know. You'll have a scar, but a scar just means the hurt is over."

"Where are we going?"

"Remember I said you had an aunt? Well, she's got a very nice house in a beach town. You like the ocean."

"What about my dance classes?"

"We'll get you into a class. I bet the teachers are better there."

Viva rolled her eyes.

A nurse stuck her head in the doorway and asked Charlotte if she wanted her husband to join them. Charlotte stared at her as if she'd asked a complex question, then shook her head.

"What about Bill?"

Charlotte knelt in front of Viva and tucked a stray hair behind her ear. "You are my one and only. Ever since you were born. You know that, right?"

Viva looked at the floor. "I will never be like you."

Charlotte picked up the bag of bandages. "Put on your jacket," she said, and her right eye began to twitch—as close as she ever came to crying.

chapter eight
1985

Charlotte said that Viva was too high-strung, a phrase that Viva detested. But it was true. Too often, she felt her nerves twist and sizzle, her senses crank to high alert, and with little discretion she would take note of anything and everything—things like the word *cricket*, the metallic smell of ketchup, a particularly nauseating color of blue, lyrics, slogans, TV ads, and words on the side of a bus. Sometimes, a kind of inner tornado seemed to spin and toss these things within her, cranking faster and faster, until she felt like the world was about to overtake her. But modern dance, especially the Graham and Cunningham techniques she was learning this semester, gave her a place to put all that. And dance had nothing to do with her mother.

"Crush this," said Bethany Clay as she snaked her long fingers under Viva's spine. The class was practicing pleadings, a contraction done on the floor. Bethany continually urged them to go to their core, expel their most primitive energies, and find the "inner gasp." To Viva, it all seemed like code for sex. And here they were on a Wednesday morning, divided into two rows, contracting and contracting, breathing in the dance studio air—a fragrance that smelled like Secret roll-on, musk oil, and the sweat of a dozen girls ages fourteen to seventeen.

A hot-for-February sun pierced the studio window and blinded the entire front row. But this was good for the girls. You had to know how to dance even if you couldn't see where you were going.

The Marble School was one of the finest performing arts high schools in the state of California. Viva had a partial scholarship. She and her mother had been visiting Charlotte's older sister, Ardel, for almost five years. Charlotte was careful to never use the phrase *living with* Ardel because this wasn't to be a permanent thing.

"Ardel is just like my mother," Charlotte had said to Viva when they arrived.

"What does that mean?"

"It means we're going to make the best of it."

Aunt Ardel, who lived in Encinitas, was an average Christian Scientist but a Shaklee saleswoman extraordinaire. Charlotte said to Viva, "If she asks whether we're Christian Scientists, say yes. Just don't get sick or hurt yourself."

Ardel was passionate about crafts and had a near fetish for tiny pom-poms that jiggled from the curtains in the kitchen, from the bathroom towels, and from the hem of the maxi dress she wore to her Shaklee fiestas. An entire basement cabinet was filled with vitamins, cleaning solutions, and makeup, and Ardel was a master at "sponsoring" new sales recruits. Prominently displayed in the living room was her gold Shaklee saleswoman-of-the-year trophy, which stood atop a three-foot marble stand.

Sometimes Viva, returning home from school, would find a group of women huddled around a display of Shaklee vitamins while Ardel intoned the Prayer of Faith, a kind of spiritual and financial twofer. As she'd pass by, Ardel would say, "There she is now," or "What a lot of work it is to raise a teenager," as if Viva was her own daughter. She never contradicted her. Viva knew Ardel wanted to have children with her husband, Brock, but was unable to, and as a guest she had an obligation to play the part.

But maybe Ardel wasn't so bad. Last week when they were doing the dishes, Viva asked Ardel if she'd ever met her father. "The *artiste*? No, never met the man." When Viva asked what happened to him, she said, "Who knows, but I guess that's the artist's prerogative. You know how they are." Viva wasn't sure if she was more pleased to learn that her father was an artist or that Ardel indicated Viva herself was an artist. But if both were true, then maybe she got her artistic commitment from him—a piece of information Viva would savor for months.

Bethany stood and demonstrated for the dancers a classic Graham move, heel of the hand to the forehead. The first day of class she shouted at Viva, "Take. More. Space. MORE!" This was the best invitation of Viva's life so far—sanctioned physical greediness. More. More space, more almost-sex, more no-eating, more less-sleep. Some days all she ate was an apple, and she did her homework at one in the morning after practicing cave turns and bison jumps for hours.

And then there was Phinneas Phelan aka Fender. Fender had an IQ of 148 and took special math classes at San Diego State. Fender was a part-time pot dealer and played drums in a band called Pavlover. He had large hands with which he frequently encircled Viva's entire waist. His head, heart, and lifelines were collapsed into a single slash across his palm, a unique feature, he told Viva, shared by kings and Robert De Niro. He drove a '76 midnight-blue Dodge Charger, a vehicle he'd never have been able to afford without his side business. The smell of his car, like rubber and dewberry air freshener, was on Viva, in her clothes and hair, and maybe even inside her. Although they had not had sex, they had had everything else. Tonight, they had an appointment.

"Movement never lies," Bethany shouted at the new girl, Sandy Mapes, who'd arrived three weeks into the semester. Sandy had tried to play the ballet card and roamed the halls in turnout, telling anyone who'd listen that for the best results one should sew her shoes with dental floss. That lasted about a week with Bethany Clay.

Bethany paced between the girls. "A dance position is not a dead static thing. It is a picture you have in your mind."

Out of the corner of her eye, Viva saw the head of the dance department and senior instructor, Mr. Muich, sitting in a corner, smoking a cigarette. An original member of Pilobolus, he wore the same gray tank top and dance pants every day. His broad face, all planes and angles, gave him the bearing of a disgruntled royal. He often gazed out the window, seemingly mystified as to how he had ended up there. Sometimes, without warning, he would violently clap his hands and, cigarette still dangling from his mouth, chase a dancer across the floor as if she was a chicken.

"What does développé mean?" Bethany asked with a curious little smile that always preceded a scolding. Everyone knew to not answer this question because whatever one said would be wrong.

But Sherry DeSoto took the bait. "It's when a dancer stands on one leg, brings the other through coup-de-pied, retiré, and attitude positions before extending it to the front, side, or back."

Bethany Clay shut her eyes and fluttered her eyelashes, a habitual expression indicating disgust. "It means development, like a photo going from black-and-white to color. I want to see the colors changing, I want to see your energy. To do a turn, don't just turn, gather the space behind your leg, gather the space." *Scoop, scoop.* The way she moved her arm looked obscene, but no one dared

laugh. They respected and feared Bethany Clay and pushed themselves so hard for her that after class, exhausted and jubilant, their
bodies lurched from the studio and staggered down the hallway,
crashing into each other.

Breathless, Viva stood before her open locker and adjusted her
underwear—silk panties the color and texture of an oil slick that
she'd bought on sale at Bullock's. She thought about seeing Fender
later and a pang of nerves hit her gut. Charlotte had once described
a lover as "pointy." She'd said he was so big he'd almost impaled her
lung. Was that possible? Viva was wishing and wanting, fearful and
fearless, her entire being angled toward that night.

Viva stayed late to practice in the dance studio. It was four
o'clock when she rushed down the hall, leaping across scuffed-up
floor tiles. The school was almost empty, and the teachers were long
gone, having piled into their cars, most of them lighting up before
the key hit the ignition. The Winter Wonderland Choir and Dance
Extravaganza had been weeks ago, jazz band didn't resume practice
until after spring break, it had rained for ten days, and with every
window closed, the entire school smelled like tuna casserole and
green beans. But the second-floor corridor of the Marble School
was a different matter. At a certain point in the late afternoon when
the sun fell at a particular angle, the hall became submerged in light,
as if broken off from the rest of the school, like a golden corridor
from an abandoned passenger ship.

Viva ran down the staircase, and as she did, she saw through the
long rectangular window that faced the parking lot, Fender. Waiting
for her. Leaning against his car, arms crossed, head slightly bowed, he
almost looked like he was praying. Viva thought she would never be
the same after this day, and as she ran toward him, she suddenly
seemed to slip free of herself. It was as though she could look back at
herself from a distant time in the future, past adulthood, middle age,

old age, even death. She felt completely at home in the world in a way she'd never felt, and this moment of pure belonging felt like it might last forever. Then Viva hit the bottom step and it was done. She hadn't summoned the moment, and she couldn't make it return.

Viva and Fender walked through the back door of Ardel's house past Brock's size 13 black patent leather loafers, past his Arturo Fuente cigars stashed near the pantry, past the black velvet jacket of his uniform, which, because it always smelled like cigarettes, was never allowed in their closet. Brock, a taciturn former Marine, was the maître d' at Gagliardo's, a local Italian restaurant, and he would be upstairs getting ready for work. He didn't like Fender (the one thing he and Charlotte seemed to agree on), and Viva tried to make sure they didn't cross paths. Fender grabbed two of Brock's cigars and stuck them in his pocket. He turned to the pantry, where canned goods, paper goods, and spices were arranged alphabetically per Ardel's decree. He grabbed a box of baggies.

"Can I take these?"

"What for?" said Viva, but before he could answer she added, "Oh." They didn't talk much about his part-time job, and she sometimes worried he'd get into trouble, but Fender said half the school was dealing. "Sure."

Fender began to drum his hands on the top of the washing machine, then the dryer, then both. Always practicing. Friday night his band was opening for Better Than Murder at the Lions Club Mardi Gras party. Viva reached up and kissed Fender on his neck. Pressing into him, she could feel his hard-on. "I'll be quick," said Viva. She left to shower and change her clothes.

Upstairs, she saw that the door to the room she shared with her mother was closed. Charlotte often took a nap this time of day before she went to her second job as a telemarketer. As she passed by Ardel's bedroom, Viva saw her polishing the head of her Shaklee trophy, which she held in her lap like a baby. Behind her, Brock was buttoning up his work shirt. He looked like a disgruntled turtle, his thick neck jutting from the black ruffles.

"Viva," said Ardel, "you need a curfew. If your mother won't set one, then it's up to Brock and me. Ten thirty."

"Ten thirty!? I'm not in sixth grade."

"Well, you and Fender don't want to grow up too fast."

Viva almost laughed in her face.

"Ten thirty. No back sass." Brock often spoke as if he was reading a telegram. A cheapskate, he was miserly about everything—toilet paper, soap, even his words. He snorted and with a flourish knotted his velvet bow tie. "The punk is bad news."

Charlotte suddenly appeared in the doorway. "Don't tell my daughter what to do, Brock. And Ardel, it's not your job to set my daughter's curfew."

Charlotte looked at Viva. "Can you make it home by eleven thirty?"

Viva smiled.

"Unbelievable," Brock muttered.

"My house, my rules," Ardel protested.

Charlotte bit her lip, and the color rose in her face. Viva thought she was about to fight Ardel, but she didn't. Late on her contribution to household expenses, she couldn't afford to. "Get your own kid, Ardel," she said. She turned on her heel and returned to her room, slamming the door.

chapter nine

Charlotte sank into a large wicker chair parked in the corner of Ardel's guest room. It featured a six-rayed sun woven into its back and was designed by the preeminent wicker maker of Encinitas, a fact Ardel never failed to mention when she passed by the guest room, poking in her head, trying to entice Charlotte into Mo Short's Pinnacle group—Shaklee upper echelon.

Charlotte had always been able to get a job, she always would, and for the past year, she'd been employed at a local real estate office. She would save enough for Viva to go to college, and she would do this without becoming a Shaklee salesperson, no matter how many times Ardel tried to "sponsor" her.

Charlotte inhaled the fragrance of plumeria, which wafted through the guest room, the house, and the entire neighborhood. Her daughter collected the fallen blossoms and floated them in bowls atop every surface in the house that Ardel would allow. People in Encinitas were crazy for plumeria trees, but if Charlotte heard one more person attempt to describe their fruity, green, heavenly qualities and floral ambiguity, she would scream.

For a few months now, Charlotte had been feeling to the side of herself. Not beside herself, as in distraught, furious, or frenzied. Oh, how she longed for some frenzy. She hadn't been on a date in a year, and there weren't any real candidates at the real estate office. All the men were marrieds or milquetoasts. Her loneliness seemed to compound with every passing month, and it pained her to see Viva and Fender so in love. Or in lust. Charlotte would settle for lust. She thought about making a cocktail. Surprisingly, Ardel kept a fair amount of liquor, albeit sweet liquor, on hand for the Shaklee parties. Baileys Irish Cream, Drambuie, crème de menthe. But no, she hadn't drunk since New Year's, almost nine weeks. That is if you didn't count an embarrassing episode the previous week. After a particularly hard day at work, and following a fight with Viva, she'd had one drink that turned into seven drinks. She remembered dancing in the kitchen in her underwear, music blaring. Viva shouting at her. Everything after that was a blur. Thank God Ardel and Brock were at an overnight Shaklee conference. The next day Charlotte promised Viva she would quit drinking. And she did. After all, she was queen of the hard stop. She'd done it before, and she'd do it again.

Charlotte wrote a note that read *Don't Touch* and pinned it to the lapel of her blue silk real estate blazer. Ardel, in a weekly fever of good works, swept through the house every Saturday morning, grabbing anything that might go to Sassy's Cleaners. She took a drag of her Capri Ultra Lights Menthol. It tasted like a stale candy cane but was the closest thing to not smoking at all. She reached for the seashell ashtray that sat atop the desk in the corner of the room and there she saw a file containing Viva's college applications. For early admission, no less. She'd been working on them for weeks. Charlotte felt a moment of pride before a crushing wave of envy rolled over her. If only she'd had the guts to pursue painting. If only she hadn't become pregnant. But if she was completely honest with herself, she wasn't sure that was what had held her back. Not if she'd been a real artist.

Charlotte hovered for a moment over the file and looked at Viva's neat, precise handwriting. So different from her chicken scratch. Charlotte's own mother said she had the handwriting of a serial killer. She considered that she should wait for Viva to show her the applications. *If* she showed them to her. But wasn't Charlotte the one who was going to foot the bill? Certainly, she deserved to at least take a peek.

Charlotte opened the file and flipped through a couple of forms containing basic information when she saw a document titled "Self Statement." Her eye fell on the phrase *I had a peripatetic childhood . . .* Charlotte stopped to consider the meaning of *peripatetic.* Spicy? No, she knew what it meant—adventurous! Charlotte smiled. Yes, indeed, she and Viva certainly had plenty of adventures and her daughter had experienced people from all walks of life. Not many kids could say that. She scanned the following paragraph that listed some of the places they'd lived and jumped to the next one.

My mother is a complex and troubled person, and—Charlotte stopped. She felt as if she couldn't breathe and quickly turned the document facedown. She heard laughter in the street. Charlotte stood to the side of the open window and looked down upon Fender and Viva.

Two figures standing by the curb, intertwined and unmoving, as if they'd magically grown into each other like trees. Fender was wearing his Cure T-shirt with the cutoff sleeves, the only one she ever saw him wear. And Viva wore a black T-shirt ripped on such a fierce diagonal, it threatened to reveal a nipple. Black leg warmers. She wore her dance clothes all the time now so she could squeeze in extra practice. Fender's arm was at an awkward angle. Was it down her daughter's pants in broad daylight? She leaned forward and peered at them. Told herself to look away. Didn't.

"Where are your hands, Fender?!" Charlotte shouted.

Viva dropped her house keys on the sidewalk, and they broke apart. Fender, impenetrable, slowly swiveled his head, removed his hand from Viva's pants, and shoved his hand in his pocket.

"Can you act like civilized human beings for Christ's sake?"

"What?" Viva looked up at her as if she didn't understand.

"You know what I said, Viva. Or am I being too peripatetic!"

Fender glanced up at Charlotte and quickly looked away.

Belatedly, Charlotte realized she was still in her slip. Shaking with fury, she pulled the curtain across her torso.

The three of them held their positions. Charlotte at the window, Viva unmoving, Fender affecting the stance of a man waiting for a taxi.

Once, many years ago, Charlotte and a boy from art class were kissing on the subway when an old woman screamed at them, "Boodlers!" Charlotte hadn't heard the word before, but the woman's fury and loneliness had shaken them apart.

Viva whispered something to Fender, and he exploded with laughter. She saw her daughter wobble and wave a pretend cigarette in the air. They turned and walked down the street.

Charlotte felt her entire body flush and suddenly her jaw throbbed. She remembered the isolation of the days in her childhood bedroom, recuperating. Sometimes she would hear other kids playing in the street, and Charlotte would spy on them. Sometimes she would sketch them. No one ever saw her, and at one point, she believed she had the actual ability to become invisible. Charlotte turned from the window, grabbed another cigarette, and lit it. She paced for a few moments before snatching the "Self Statement" off the desk and picked up where she'd left off.

Sometimes, I feel sorry for my mother as she struggles with her personal problems and addiction, but I am grateful that she has given me something to push against. I believe this has made me a more resilient person, one who is better equipped to handle life's challenges.

Charlotte felt dizzy. Was that all she'd been good for? Someone to push against? She looked out the window and saw Viva and Fender nearing the end of the street—a flash of Viva's purple knapsack, her hair whipping in the wind—and then they turned the corner. Charlotte had no idea where they were going or when they'd be back. She was now that lady on the subway, the don't-touch lady. The lady to be laughed at and mocked.

Well, she'd show them. Viva wasn't the only one with plans for the night.

chapter ten

After they left Ardel's house, Viva and Fender drove south on the 101 past Cardiff State Beach, the surf unfurling parallel to them.

"Where's your father this week?" asked Viva.

"Bermuda, Calcutta, who knows," said Fender.

Their appointment was to be conducted in the bedroom of none other than one Captain Dirk Phalen of Pan American World Airways. Fender's bedroom was used for storage, and he usually slept on the sofa.

In the planning stages, Fender's father's bedroom seemed like a sophisticated option, what with its wet-look leopard-print wallpaper and masks worn by real Borneo tribesmen tacked to the wall. Viva had met Captain Phalen for the first time the previous week and she'd become flustered when he asked her if, being a dancer, she ate a special diet. But then, all fathers made her nervous.

She sometimes wondered what her own father was like or what he looked like. On occasion, she'd find herself attached to an imaginary physical image only to realize it was someone she'd seen in a movie or on the news. It was an embarrassing, futile business, this imagining. The last time she'd asked Charlotte for facts her mother said, "Don't poke at it," but the recent information Ardel had told her—that her father might be an artist—gave her some small satisfaction.

"It's my mother's birthday," said Fender.

Viva was surprised by the comment. Though she and Fender both lacked a parent, it wasn't something they often discussed. Instead, it was an almost physical bond between them, the deep, silent recognition of loss—a missing father, a dead mother, ever-present.

"How old would she be?" asked Viva.

"Forty, I think." Fender's mother was killed when their car was T-boned on this very highway by a bunch of drunk kids from San Diego State. Fender, who was ten at the time, walked away untouched.

"You know, I sometimes smell her in the house—the perfume she wore. Like somehow it got stuck in the walls or maybe the ceiling. It leaks out sometimes and I don't think I can take it."

Despite Fender's good looks and a certain kind of fearlessness, Viva felt within him a deep wariness, as if the great good fortune that had spared him from death would someday turn on him.

"How is your mother?" he asked.

"She's on the Almaden drip again."

Charlotte had sworn off liquor since New Year's Day, but the previous week Viva awoke to music blaring in the kitchen. It was almost 3:00 a.m. and she found her mother in her bra and panties, dancing with Ardel's beagle, cradling him as she swayed back and forth. When she saw Viva, she abruptly stopped. The next morning, by the time Viva woke up, Charlotte had already left for work. The jug of Almaden Golden Chablis on the kitchen table was replaced with a plate of blueberry muffins. As if nothing had ever happened—one of Charlotte's few predictable behaviors.

"I can't wait to get away from her," said Viva.

Fender reached across the seat and grabbed her hand. He gently kissed the back of her wrist. Her scar had faded some but was still quite visible. Viva tried to hide it whenever possible, especially after one of the girls in dance class asked if she'd tried to kill herself. She recalled Charlotte saying a scar means the hurt is over. But was it? It didn't seem so when it came to her mother.

"I'm sick of her lies." After the Winter Recital, Charlotte cornered Viva's dance teacher, and while clutching her jaw with her hand, told the story of her childhood horseback riding accident in an urgent, hushed tone. As if the pain she'd experienced as a girl worked through a kind of invisible circuitry to power Viva's performance. Viva was tired of her mother dining out on the story, embellishing the details—in one version she was a burgeoning master of dressage, in another she barely clung to life.

"She's a piece of work, for sure," said Fender.

Viva nodded but felt an instant pang of betrayal. She thought of Charlotte at her real estate job. Her mother said she wrote copy for listings, but Viva knew she passed out flyers at open houses, had seen her waving them at passersby at an open house near school. But she stuck with the job to help pay for Viva's education. And by God, she'd gotten her dance lessons wherever they lived. Viva's anger swung to guilt as she considered that her mother came to all her performances, even if she was sometimes half in the bag.

"Are you all right?" asked Fender.

"Definitely. Let's just not talk about my mother anymore."

"Of course."

They drove to Fender's house in record time.

Fender sped up the driveway of the old Spanish with its stucco exterior the color and consistency of soggy Wheaties, the overgrown yard, and the decorative elves prancing on the roof—some of them arranged to look like they were climbing into the second-floor window, their fat jolly bums in shiny red pants visible from a block away. They'd been up since last Christmas.

Viva and Fender entered through the kitchen, and as if he could suddenly see his home through her eyes, Fender snatched the garbage can from beneath the kitchen sink and swatted at a cluster of balled-up Doritos wrappers sitting on the kitchen table. They missed the bin and hit the floor, where he kicked them beneath a counter. On the stovetop was a half-opened box of frozen Ore-Ida french fries, which, now thawed, looked like a box of dead slugs.

"Sorry," said Fender. He grabbed a couple of beers and pulled Viva into the living room, which was empty except for his drum kit and a red leather ottoman embossed with gold zodiac signs. "My father bought this in Malaysia." Fender pushed her onto the hassock, lifted her hair and kissed the back of her neck. Then he bent down and licked the strip of skin between her jeans and shirt, marked by a mole in the southeast quadrant. Her body was no longer a single entity but frenzied territories competing for his attention. "Go upstairs," said Fender. "I'll be there in a minute."

Viva could hear waves crashing in the distance, and she could smell mildew, ever-present in all the older beach houses. One of Captain Phaelan's pilot caps sat atop a mammoth cherrywood dresser that faced the bed as if the man himself contemplated them. Viva sprang up and threw his hat into a drawer. On his desk was a blue marble chess set, stopped mid-game, and colonized around the board were stacks of loose change, tie stays, partially eaten rolls of Tums, unopened mail, and a jumbo box of Asian condoms, from which they would not partake since they'd already bought a box of Trojans at the 7-Eleven the previous Tuesday.

Viva sat on the bed and waited for Fender. The sheets smelled like they'd hadn't been changed in a while, and the yellowing pillows lacked cases. Viva heard the old furnace clunk on, a behemoth hidden in the cellar like some batty relative, its temperature gauge long broken. Maybe they should have just gone to the beach like everyone else.

Viva debated whether she should take off her panties and get under the sheets. Waiting in her underwear made her feel like she was at the doctor's office. She thought of something Bethany Clay frequently said in class, something she'd never quite understood until this moment— *We are here to confront the body.*

Fender appeared at the bedroom door lugging his Sharp MR-990 boom box. Viva's preselected cassette tape, Roxy Music's *Avalon*, was already loaded.

Fender flicked off the overhead light. In his free hand, he carried the only candle in the house—a citronella bug candle covered in white plastic netting. He was whistling, something he never did. He put the candle on his father's bureau and took off his boxer shorts. Fender was sticking straight out, and though Viva had already touched him in this state, he now seemed altogether bigger.

The sound of a car alarm spiraled up through the neighborhood and into the bedroom. Viva jumped up, arms across her chest. She heard herself laughing, although she didn't find it funny.

"Don't you want to?" said Fender.

Viva felt a trickle of perspiration run down her arm.

Fender stood motionless. They were each deeply alone in this.

Viva knelt in front of him and took him in her mouth. She'd never done this before and wished she knew some special trick. A girl in dance class said she used Pop Rocks. But that same girl said to douche after sex with Mountain Dew. So. Tentatively, she continued, and Fender went completely still. With one arm, he seized his father's brass hat rack, which, like an unwitting hostage, now lurked in Viva's peripheral vision.

Fender grabbed a condom off the bureau and thrust it at Viva. The thing felt slippery and alive like a goldfish she once had that jumped out of its bowl. She'd simply thrown it back in and—miracle of miracles—it lived. She had the composure to do that, and she would have the composure to do this. She tried to strike from her mind the image of the wooden penis in health class, the one they called Barnaby, the one they had to practice putting a condom on, the poor old disembodied, testicle-less thing, nicked and full of splinters. But Barnaby, with his eternally immobile erection, was a breeze compared to the real thing.

Before she could even unroll it, Viva dropped the rubber on the carpet, which, littered with cracker crumbs, surely had not been vacuumed in months. "Should I wash it? I'll wash it!"

"No, wait!"

Fender grabbed another condom, ripped it open, and quickly put it on.

Viva pulled him to her and they fell on the bed. They were grappling, they were missing, and no one was laughing. The baseboard heaters in the bedroom began to click and ping, and soon they would be sweltering.

Then Fender made a sound she'd never heard before. He was done before they'd started.

But they would try again. And this time, when he finally entered her, Viva felt her entire being shake. It didn't really hurt.

Fender paused. "Push back a little."

"Oh." She had thought that him simply being inside her was the sex. There was more?

They were sweating and the room felt airless. But it didn't matter because, now moving with him, they were beyond air. They were beyond reason. They were hooked up to a mutual electricity machine, hurtling through space, and whatever it was that held the world together was fast receding.

chapter eleven

An hour after Viva and Fender left, Charlotte snuck down the back stairs and slipped behind her sister, who sat at the dining room table, working on a macramé owl, her fingers nimbly looping and twisting, pulling tight a knot around the bird's neck with the satisfaction of an executioner. Charlotte carried her red cork platforms in her hands, and the Fracas she'd sprayed behind her right knee kicked up as she strode down the hill near Ardel's house. The single shot of crème de menthe, the one she'd thrown back in the kitchen, coated her throat like a terrible medicine. Not worth it. But to make it worth it, she needed a chaser. Because sometimes the hard stop was too hard.

Charlotte wore her Peter Max minidress, the green paisley one that in certain lights looked like fish scales. She'd bought the dress ten years ago and it still fit. There was that. No slip, no bra. Cricket-colored eyeshadow. Narcissus #6 lipstick. Charlotte was going to the Kraken, a bar named for the mythical many-armed sea creature that could seize a ship and drag it to the bottom of the ocean. She flashed on Viva's application and felt she was capable of similar violence.

The bar was about a fifteen-minute walk, and when Charlotte arrived, she planned to order ginger ale. Maybe one glass of wine. One. She told herself it was company she was looking for, not drinks. And maybe she'd find someone who could carry a conversation. Someone with an actual sense of humor. Something sorely lacking at the real estate office. Those people! She was sick of the burnt-Sanka smell that permeated the place and disgusted by the days-old glazed doughnuts that she was supposed to foist on potential clients. Viva could try passing out flyers for hours at an open house. Talk about smiling! Sometimes people handed her their empty soda cans, and once, a disposable diaper. People could be pigs. Viva wouldn't last for a minute at her job. She didn't possess Charlotte's grit and moxie and fuck-'em-all fortitude that powered her through the long, dull hours of her workday.

A breeze off the ocean made it colder than she'd estimated, but her fury at Viva and Fender made her numb to it and gave her strength of will and purpose. Charlotte stopped to put on her shoes and began to walk south on the main drag. Cars rushed by and more than a few heads turned. Charlotte didn't acknowledge them, but to say she was displeased would be inaccurate. In the distance and across from the bar, she could see the lights of a small roadside carnival. Ardel had told Viva and Charlotte to steer clear of the Zing Zang because last year a carny forgot to check a safety bar on the Zipper, and a man plunged to his death. Charlotte loved rides, the wilder the better, although she hadn't been to a carnival in a long time. Viva was afraid of heights and always had been.

When Charlotte reached the bar, she saw the parking lot was completely empty. She walked around to the front of the building. No lights, no people. A piece of cardboard hung in the front window. Scrawled on it in purple Magic Marker were the words *Closed for the Holiday.* What holiday? It was well past Valentine's Day, not yet St. Patrick's. Plus, didn't bars need to stay open on holidays? Was this a joke?

She stood on the side of the freeway across from the Zing Zang and considered her next move. She could take a taxi into town, but the nearest phone booth was another mile down the road. Charlotte watched the Tumbler careen into the night sky as Gloria Gaynor blared from overhead speakers. Near the ride she saw concession stands, one of them a beer booth ringed in flashing lights that featured a mural of a snowcapped mountain peak, a girl in a dirndl skirt sitting atop it, hoisting a frothing mug. Beer wasn't her favorite drink, but it was something.

She waited for a break in the traffic and ran across the freeway. In front of the ticket window, a large plastic clown head spiked on a metal pole bobbled about, crazy eyeballs rolling in opposite directions, its open red mouth large enough to swallow a child whole. Charlotte walked straight past it. Surely the carnival wouldn't be open for much longer, why pay full price?

She hurried past the drown-the-clown game, the balloon darts, and the milk-bottle toss, looking for the beer booth. She stopped before the Tilt-A-Whirl, the only ride she'd ever been able to get Viva to try.

Charlotte watched a mother and teenage daughter disembark from the ride, clinging to each other, laughing, putting on quite a show, she thought.

Viva hadn't had the common courtesy to leave a note when she left that afternoon with Fender. So rude. And just last week, when Charlotte saw them in the drugstore, they ducked out the back. Later, when Charlotte confronted Viva about it, she insisted they never saw her, all the while maintaining an indulgent, patronizing smile as if Charlotte was a simpleton. Then she had the gall to accuse Charlotte of being jealous of Fender. As if. But deep down,

Charlotte had to admit she ached for the allegiance they once had, the way Viva so easily took her cue from her.

The mother and daughter passed by arm in arm. Was the mother trying to be the girl's best buddy or something? Charlotte knew the type, and she didn't like it.

———

Viva was late. Very late. After they left Fender's house, he had to do a pickup at an apartment in Carlsbad. When he pulled behind the building, he cut the lights, grabbed a wad of cash from his glove box, and ran inside. Viva waited in the car. On the way back, they parked at Beacon's Beach and sampled the product—some good-quality Colombian. Fender passed her a joint. Viva took a hit and squinted at the Cure logo on Fender's T-shirt, a flower with sharp teeth and a menacing red eye. At that moment, it seemed like a secret but obvious message—Fender was her cure, and she was his cure. She laid her head in Fender's lap, and Viva felt as if a membrane had been stripped from the world, revealing the real and electric one sparking just beneath it. Fender stroked her hair, and maybe they stayed at the beach twenty minutes or maybe it was much longer, but by the time Viva noticed the hour it was almost one. They sped to Ardel's, Fender's Charger blasting through the night, cold air pouring into their open windows smelling of orange blossoms and ocean. When Viva turned her head, the moon seemed tethered to the car, a joyful conspirator in this magnificent night. Everything lay ahead of them, everything was possible.

Miraculously, Ardel's house was dark. Her aunt and uncle would be asleep, and when Charlotte was on the wagon, she went to bed around eight. "I don't want you to go," said Viva.

"Then I won't," said Fender. It seemed a magical empowerment had descended upon them—all obstacles were surmountable. He

locked his glove box and hid the bag of pot beneath his car seat. He
laced his fingers through Viva's, and they ran up the flagstone walk.

Viva unlocked the front door and pulled Fender in behind her.
For a moment she imagined what it would be like if they were married, what it would be like if this were not Ardel and Brock's house
but their own. There would be lavender roses everywhere, velvet
draperies, a music room for Fender, a dance studio for herself.
They'd have a four-poster bed, a mural on the ceiling, and satin
sheets. She and Fender would walk around the house nude and eat
every meal in bed if they felt like it. Someday.

Fender pulled her to him, pushed her against the foyer wall,
and they kissed for a long time. It seemed entirely possible they
might have sex again, right there in Ardel's foyer. Viva unbuckled
Fender's belt.

"What are you doing?!" Ardel's voice.

Viva and Fender were suddenly caught in the glare of the overhead light. Not ten feet to their right sat Ardel, ensconced in the
brocade wing chair. She looked like a mad Kabuki actor, her face
lathered in white face cream, mouth slack with exhaustion. How
long had she watched them? "You're late." Next to Ardel, like a
preposterous sentry, sat her Shaklee trophy on its marble stand, the
little woman now buffed to a high gloss. Fender giggled and Viva
caught him by the arm. But then she, too, couldn't help but laugh.

"What's so funny? I allow a generous curfew extension, and this
is how I'm rewarded. You have relations in my hallway!"

"Get in here," said Brock. Viva hadn't seen him until this
moment, standing in the rear of the living room, legs wide apart,
arms crossed over his chest. "I said get in here."

Fender quickly buckled his pants, and he and Viva joined them.
They stood in silence while Ardel and Brock stared at them as if
they were specimens from another planet. Viva felt like the walls
were closing in on her—the ticking faux-colonial clock on the wall,

the bunch of fake gladioli on the coffee table, and Ardel's latest creation, the two-foot macramé owl, which now hung above the TV, no longer inanimate objects, but alive, witnesses all. "You're not my mother," Viva said to Ardel. "Charlotte!" she shouted.

"She's gone," said Ardel.

"Gone? Where?" asked Viva.

"Took off hours ago and didn't have the decency to tell me where she was going or when she'd be back. I'm sick with worry." But Ardel was more angry than worried, and beneath that was something else in her tone. Triumph. Tonight, *she* was the mother. "What do you two have to say for yourselves?"

Viva looked at Fender. The overhead light shone down upon him like an unremitting sun as he stood there wearing a tight, grim smile, but Viva could only see his face as it had been earlier in the bedroom, his secret face, which she'd glimpsed in shadow. Fender coughed and shot her a look—*keep it together*.

"What's that on your neck?" Ardel sprang from her chair, and Viva covered the blossoming hickey with her palm. Ardel pulled her hand away and shook her head in disgust. She inhaled dramatically. "And you reek."

Brock stepped closer to Viva as if he would make his own assessment, but then he stopped. "Just like your mother," he said.

"You don't own her," Fender said.

"No, we don't own her, Fender, but we pay the mortgage, keep the house running, and put up with rude and disrespectful behavior!" Ardel's voice broke, and she dabbed at a bit of face cream that had congealed near her eye.

Brock stepped forward. "You have no say in this, young man."

"I have more say than you."

Something in Brock swiftly shifted, and like a dog that's about to attack, he went completely still. He leaned toward Fender and dropped his voice. "I know about you, you two-bit punk."

"You don't know anything," said Fender.

The two men stood motionless — Fender three inches taller than Brock, Brock almost twice as wide. Then Brock shoved Fender. Fender didn't react and almost looked like he might laugh. Brock pushed him again. Hard. This time Fender shoved back and Brock, arms flailing, lost his footing. He toppled backward, knocking into Ardel's trophy, which crashed to the floor. Decapitated.

"Look what you did, bastard!"

"What I did? What you did, you old fuck."

Ardel stood frozen.

"What did you call me?" Brock rushed Fender and slammed him to the floor. Then he was on top of him, pinning his arms. Fender spit in his face.

"Stop it!" screamed Viva.

But Brock was just getting started. He started to choke Fender. Viva bolted to the kitchen and called 911. "My uncle's trying to kill my boyfriend!" She ran back into the living room just as Fender managed to break free from Brock.

"You asshole!" Fender screamed. "What's wrong with you, psycho!"

The police arrived quickly. Ardel rushed out to meet them. When they came back in Ardel pointed at Fender. "There he is!"

"He was defending himself," Viva shouted, but no one listened to her.

"Kid's a dealer. High as a kite," Brock said triumphantly.

Fender looked at Viva, and the air in the room seemed to congeal. Viva felt a strange sensation, as if she was on an elevator going upward. If only Charlotte was there. Charlotte would handle this. A policeman pulled Fender outside. Viva tried to follow, but Ardel held her back. A cop was shining a light in Fender's eyes. Then Fender was against the side of his car, legs splayed, while another cop checked inside. Then Fender was in handcuffs. Then he was gone.

Viva sat in a lawn chair in the middle of the driveway, and there she waited for Charlotte. Like a mother waiting for a daughter on a date. Disgusting. Viva imagined what might unfold with her mother. Maybe a taxi would drop her off a block away, and she'd try to sneak in the back door. Maybe Charlotte would appear riding a child's bicycle as she once had when they lived with Ona Prince. Maybe she'd have found a dog. Viva's anger fueled a sizzling alertness to the lone plane cutting through the sky, sprinklers clicking off, the babble of the neighbor's TV. She was cold but wouldn't budge to get a sweater. What was going to happen to Fender? She'd called the police station, but he'd already been booked. How had this night, the best of her life, fallen apart so quickly?

If Charlotte hadn't disappeared, probably on a bender, her aunt and uncle wouldn't have waited up. If Charlotte had ever provided a real home for them, if she and her mother hadn't been "guests" since Viva was born, they wouldn't have been here in the first place. Viva felt like she couldn't breathe. She stretched her right foot and marked a basic dance sequence on the concrete. She repeated it again and again until the familiar sense of order and certainty clicked in. Relief. But only for a moment. Viva thought of Charlotte's expression when she'd presented her with a new dance bag the previous day. It wasn't the black leather one Viva had coveted in the Capezio store window—it was the polka-dot vinyl one from the clearance bin, but Charlotte had saved for it. Viva pushed the memory from her mind, clinging to her rage until something inside her swung shut, and it seemed impossible to her that it would ever open again.

Winner, winner, winner! Charlotte whirled toward the recorded voice issuing from the shoot-'em-up booth—a dozen stars on placards affixed to a saloon facade. A man in purple jeans clutched

the toy gun set on a pivot, his face screwed up in fierce concentration. He shot and missed again and again. Charlotte knew the
games were gaffed, but she was a pretty good shot. Maybe she
could win a prize for Viva. She studied the plastic dolls suspended
from the ceiling. One wore a leotard, her leg extended in a perfect
arabesque. She'd win the dancer doll for her daughter. But just as
quickly, she was sure Viva wouldn't want it. She wasn't a little girl
anymore. Viva hadn't even liked dolls as a child. But Charlotte
paid for a round and stepped up to the shooting range. She missed
every shot. Not even close.

Was there nothing she could do right? Was she only a cautionary
example, the type of mother who came in handy for college applications? Charlotte stepped aside from the shooting range and stood
there, hands clenched at her sides, not sure where to go next. The
manic bouncy pops emitting from the shooting gallery seemed to
fly past her head, and she felt as if she was drowning in the crazy
noise of the rides, clanking, crashing, whirring.

And then she saw it, there at the end of a row of games—the
beer booth. A shirtless man in vinyl lederhosen was tapping a new
keg. He paused to wipe his hands on the fake felt snow stapled to
the sides of the booth.

"Genesee or Schlitz?" The man chewed on a paper clip that
disappeared into his mouth, reappeared, and hung from the corner
of his lip like a fishhook.

"Do you have any other drinks, like Asti Spumante?" said
Charlotte.

"Genesee or Schlitz."

"You pick," she said and gave him her most beguiling half smile.
She reached into her dress pocket and frowned. "Oh, you best cancel that, looks like I lost my ticket."

"Here, pretty," he said, handing her a beer in a large cup. "On
the house."

Charlotte turned from him and took a swift gulp.

The beer was warm and tasted terrible.

Charlotte looked upward and her gaze fell upon the Ferris wheel in the far corner of the parking lot. Why hadn't she noticed it before? Ringed in blue lights and quietly spinning, it seemed majestic and certain in its endless trajectory. Charlotte took another gulp and threw the rest of the beer into a nearby trash can.

The Ferris wheel was almost empty. Beside it a young man sat backward on a red vinyl kitchen chair watching the wheel turn with abject interest, as if it represented the hours and days of his life rolling away. He wore a button-down shirt with his work pants, and his hair was cut short, military-style. He pulled a lever, and the wheel began to slow. As he freed the last few riders from their cages, she heard him say, "Look lively now," and something in his tone seemed generous, almost concerned.

When the last passenger was taken care of, he turned toward Charlotte.

"How's it going?" she said.

"It's going."

The Ferris wheel operator didn't look like a carny. Maybe he was a college kid. "You old enough to run this thing?" said Charlotte.

"You old enough to get on it?"

Charlotte stared at him. So this was how it was going to go.

"Naughty schoolboy."

"What?"

Charlotte instantly realized she'd miscalculated something about him, and if she was good at anything, she was good at the quick pivot.

"Let me guess, UC San Diego?"

The man lit a cigarette and exhaled in a put-upon way.

"Well, you look like a gentleman and a scholar to me."

"Look, lady, we're closing in five minutes."

Charlotte clipped the cigarette from his hand and took a drag. "I want to take a ride."

"No single riders."

"Why?"

"Because we had a jumper last year is why."

"I need this ride," said Charlotte. "I'll make it worth your while."

"How's that?"

Charlotte walked up to him and kissed him full on the lips. The kiss went on for a few minutes, though neither one lifted their arms to embrace. When they pulled apart, the man blinked. He didn't even ask for a ticket.

The Ferris wheel began to creak and click, and then roughly Charlotte's yellow gondola shot backward and up. Very quickly she was very high.

Zeppelin's "Rock and Roll" blared from the carnival speakers, and the ocean wind swayed her bucket from side to side. Up above it all Charlotte went—the red-checkered flag on the calliope, people swarming, a boy screaming, his parents running, and even from there she could see it was too late. Goldfish dropped, goldfish dead. The Ferris wheel lights rippled out to sea as waves rolled in, a miraculous and mysterious convergence. Then Charlotte heard a loud ding. A loopy ding, signaling something. Had she won a prize? Hell, she *was* the prize. From the ground, the man watched her go round and round. The sky flew by in pieces.

Then down Charlotte went past the ghastly clown, wagging his head in interminable consternation. "Faster!" she shouted as she passed the ride operator and faster she flew. The gondola shook from side to side. Something inside her accelerated, a kind of reckless transcendence, and Charlotte felt like she herself was powering the ride. Surely this must be how Viva felt when she danced. For a moment Charlotte felt all-knowing, all-seeing, and below her she saw cars on the freeway, cars in the car park, cars bearing humans on earthly errands, and one car, perhaps a blue Dodge Charger, bearing her daughter away. Was she losing her? Had she lost her? The Ferris wheel sped upward once again, and in a flash, Charlotte thought it wasn't too late to change her entire life. Anything was possible. Wasn't it?

chapter twelve
1968

Charlotte unzipped her skirt, stepped out of it, and stood there in her blouse and panties, waiting for Wilson. The light in his bedroom seemed to have shape and force, and things almost appeared to vibrate—Wilson's bureau with the chipped corner, his desk, and on it a vase of yellow tulips, stems yearning for water. Last Saturday, Wilson had bought her the flowers for her twenty-fourth birthday, and she'd deliberately left them there. Outside his window, the long, green arm of a linden tree caught in the breeze and scratched at the glass. Charlotte waited. She had wanted Wilson for a long time and waited for him a long time—a kind of painful, slow-motion, voluntary conscription.

Charlotte heard Wilson walk up the stairs, open the apartment door, and throw his keys into the ceramic monkey dish on the credenza. She quickly undid the buttons of her blouse, shook it off, then stepped out of her underwear and placed her forearms against the cool bedroom wall—a pose she'd seen in one of Wilson's photography books.

She waited. Charlotte had a terrible itch just above her right buttock, but she couldn't scratch it lest he walk into the room at that very minute. She summoned her strength, pressed her forehead into her hands, and waited some more. The itch traveled down her right thigh. She began to perspire around her hairline. Charlotte didn't move a muscle. She galvanized. After all, she'd waited this long.

Wilson Bernays had moved into the rental cottage next to her parents' house in Poughkeepsie when she was sixteen and he was twenty-five. He'd lived there for a few years until he moved to Manhattan. The first time she saw him, Charlotte was seized by everything about Wilson—the way he got into his car and sometimes paused before turning the key in the ignition as if he had a great deal on his mind, the way he mowed the lawn, in a labyrinthine pattern versus rows, how he sometimes sat in his open garage, sketching with a beer in his hand. He was too old for Charlotte. Then.

But now Wilson was a man of thirty-three, and the nine-year age difference no longer seemed an obstacle. How she had longed for him as a teenager, looking for any excuse to go to his door to borrow garden sheers, a pail, a dictionary. Charlotte looked at these brief visits as a sort of repeated inoculation against the virus of her desire. Once she showed up at his door and he answered with a bowl of ice cream in his hand. He'd offered her some, but, overwhelmed by sudden crushing nerves, Charlotte declined, saying she didn't eat sweets. "Except for caramels," she'd managed to get out.

"Good to know," said Wilson. This phrase alone undid at least five inoculations, because what could he be hinting at? That someday, somewhere, he might bring her caramels?

During those years Wilson had a girlfriend, one Leila Greenleaf, a woman from the city who visited him every weekend, one Leila Greenleaf who kissed him in his driveway when she left each

Sunday afternoon, one Leila Greenleaf who shaded her face with her delicate palm in a way that infuriated Charlotte—not as if she was protecting herself from the sun but as if she was protecting the entire world from her great beauty. A don't-look-at-me-please-look-at-me gesture if Charlotte ever saw one. Peering from her bedroom window, Charlotte had studied Wilson and Leila many times, her own face slathered with blue clay facial mask, a mask that claimed to both moisturize and prevent acne when it did neither and left only a deathly tinge to her skin for days afterward.

Charlotte's neck began to stiffen as she held her position against the wall. She lifted her head and turned it to the side. She could hear Wilson puttering in the kitchen. Above his desk and tacked to the wall were the proofs of a recent portrait series he'd shot. Wilson talked about the coherence of gesture, and in each photo the subject's hands were lit separately from their body. He told Charlotte that everyone had a secret they express all day long—in the way they hold a pencil, walk down the street, or shake salt on their food—and he said it was the photographer's job to locate that secret. Charlotte worried that by now he must have guessed her own secret—that she didn't feel worthy of him. Maybe this stupid stunt would only underscore it.

After a while, it began to feel to Charlotte as though the people in the photographs were watching her, particularly an old man who sat on the edge of his bed, clutching a bowling trophy, staring straight into the camera. She returned her head to her arms.

Charlotte heard Wilson's chair scrape, then she heard him sigh. Was he reading his mail? A book? How long must she wait?

Earlier, when Charlotte arrived at Wilson's apartment, she'd quickly washed off her lipstick and face powder, which she wore at her afternoon job at an art supply store. And this was part of it—she wanted him to see her exactly as she was. Hers wasn't a girlish face, had never been, but with her hair parted down the center, she thought she looked resolute, resolute but passionate, like a Civil War woman. She'd pinned up her hair so that he could see her back, which she considered one of her best features. She had no freckles or spots, and her skin was very pale. A boy whom she'd dated at school, her first lover, called her "lush." It had pleased her even though she broke up with him the next day. The boy had stood outside her dorm room shouting that she acted like she didn't need anyone or anything. That wasn't exactly true, but in her mind, she was saving herself for Wilson.

Charlotte could hear some children playing and a ball smacking against the blacktop outside Wilson's apartment, mocking her it seemed, over and over and over. The rhythm was almost more than she could bear, and suddenly her fragrance, Fracas, which she had sprayed at the base of her neck and on the backs of her knees that morning, seemed cloying. A last push of sunlight suddenly flooded the room. Charlotte was a nude woman pressed against a wall, basting in her own perfume.

And what was Wilson doing? Had he fallen asleep in the kitchen, arms crossed over his chest as she'd once seen him do in his backyard? It had seemed incredibly sexy to her at the time, the self-containment, but now it irritated her.

She thought back to the day two weeks ago when she bumped into him in Manhattan. It had threatened to rain all afternoon, and there was a stubborn, unyielding feeling to the air as if the sky would never let go. Until it did, just as Charlotte crossed Fourth Avenue near Union Square. She was wearing new celery-colored leather flats, just purchased at a sale. Charlotte never did have the patience to wait to wear new shoes, and the minute she left the store, she junked her scuffed Mary Janes in a nearby trash can. And now her new Pappagallos would be ruined. When she reached the curb, Charlotte ripped them off her feet and ran down the block barefoot.

When she burst through the door of Schulte's bookstore, the sphinx at the counter barely seemed to register her entrance, let alone her bare feet. The staff was known for its haughty manner—it was the kind of store where you didn't ask for help.

Charlotte was about to take the one free chair near the botany section when she saw Wilson scanning the Buddhism shelves nearby. He was shorter than she remembered, but her estimate of his height was skewed from a girlhood of watching him from her second-story window. Same intent concentration, though, same broad shoulders. Black raincoat. Long sideburns. Strong profile—a nose Charlotte considered regal.

Wilson suddenly turned and looked at her. Deep-set eyes, unnerving gaze. The circles beneath his eyes were more pronounced now, something Charlotte had always found sexy. "Charlotte?"

"What have you been up to?" asked Charlotte, trying to sound casual. She began to shake and thrust her hands into her pockets.

Wilson asked about her parents. Charlotte asked him about his photography, and he said he had an upcoming show at the Elijah Decatur Gallery. He also mentioned he taught part-time at Pratt. Charlotte told him she was studying art history at Cooper Union. Within two minutes it seemed the conversation had completely run its course.

"I heard this store is going out of business," Wilson said.

"What a shame," she said, even though she favored the Eighth Street Bookshop.

"It is," he agreed, and they both fell silent.

Charlotte could feel that blue-faced girl at the window, peering down, digging her nails into her palm.

"Do you want to get a cup of coffee?" asked Wilson.

"Now?" asked Charlotte.

"I could carry you."

"Why would you do that?" Charlotte hadn't meant to sound accusatory.

"It's a joke," said Wilson, looking at her bare toes rimmed with dirt.

"I have shoes," she said like a charmless dolt. Her mother always said, *The essence of charm is ease*, but what if you're out of ease? Charlotte's right eye started to twitch, which happened whenever she was excited or about to cry.

Wilson grabbed her by the wrist and Charlotte felt as if she'd been pleasantly electrocuted. "Come on, let's get out of here."

The next weekend, Wilson took her to his apartment for the first time—a railroad flat off Seventy-first and Columbus. Charlotte was stunned by the lack of privacy. His roommate lived in the bedroom one had to walk through to get to Wilson's bedroom. They passed Ben and his girlfriend, Minka, in bed, seemingly asleep, but there was a feeling of sex in the air, a kind of sharp sparkling, almost audible, like the sound a television makes when you turn it off.

They sat on the edge of Wilson's bed directly across from a large mirror with a carved wooden frame. It seemed unreal to Charlotte to see the image of herself sitting on Wilson's lap—something she'd long imagined. And yet that feeling was immediately followed by a kind of preemptive aguish. Though waiting for him all these years had been torture, the idea that now she could lose him was worse.

Wilson leaned in to kiss her when they heard Minka's laughter. Charlotte pulled away.

"Are they leaving soon?"

Wilson looked puzzled before he looked amused. "Oh, Lottie," he said, using her childhood nickname. He brushed the hair from her eyes and Charlotte blushed. "Nobody calls me that anymore," she said. And she was no prude, if that's what Wilson was getting at. But the moment was lost.

Charlotte hadn't been able to stop thinking about him since. And here she was, standing nude against Wilson's bedroom wall.

Charlotte's left foot was falling asleep, and she rotated her ankle. The phone rang and she heard Wilson say hello then fall silent. Perhaps it was another girl. Charlotte strained to hear with no success. He spoke softly and occasionally cleared his throat. She had no idea what to do. Maybe a different position was called for. Her head began to pound.

For fortification, she recalled a moment earlier that day when a businessman in a green suit ran up to her and gave her his card. He'd scrawled his home address on the back and invited her to a party that night. Thrusting a fifty-dollar bill into her hand, he said, "Buy a dress." Charlotte tossed the card but kept the bill. She had options. But she didn't want options.

She looked out Wilson's bedroom window and she saw trees waving back and forth, back and forth. *We have all the time in the world,* they seemed to say. Then the sun vanished from the room, and a breeze blew in the open window, giving her goose bumps. Charlotte could cross the room and shut the window, but no. She heard a child crying in the street and could smell meat cooking in a nearby apartment. Someone began to play "Red River Valley" on a trumpet. They played the first few measures, then stopped. Started again and stopped. Each time the musician paused as if he might continue but then returned to the beginning. At this moment, she would gladly kill him.

Charlotte heard Wilson laugh and say, "If that's what you want," and something shot through her, a kind of violent excitement. She was wet, uselessly. This was not how she had imagined things would go. Her yellow blouse and red skirt looked dejected on the floor. What had she been thinking? It wasn't too late to put them on and start over, pretend that she'd just stopped by before her evening class. She bent over to pick up her clothes.

"God, Charlotte, what are you doing?"

Charlotte threw herself against the wall and returned to her original position, which now seemed like a child playing hide-and-seek in plain view. She would not turn around and look at him.

"I was waiting for you," she said. Fiercely and patiently, and for years and years.

"Charlotte, you are an unpredictable woman." Wilson stood there, and to Charlotte, it seemed the entire world shrank to the size of a postage stamp. Shame and miscalculation. The trees outside the window wagged back and forth. *Told you so*. Then she heard Wilson kick off his shoes. "You drive your own car in your own lane, I'll say that." He kissed the back of her neck, and the world in its grand, confounding splendor fell in.

Outside, Charlotte heard a sound like a gunshot, and maybe it was a gunshot, maybe some madman was running wild in the street. But now they were beyond all human concern, bulletproof.

Wilson draped himself around her. She arched up into him and he slid his hand around and down her belly. The shock. Charlotte did not move, and she did not breathe. Her insides were reconfiguring, and it was a wonderful thing to bear. There was the moment before this one, and there would be the moment after it, but in this beautiful interstice her life fell open, which until now had seemed to be of one long, impermeable piece. And though Charlotte couldn't let go of the fear she'd lose Wilson, she'd always know that once she'd been completely alive.

PART TWO

chapter thirteen
1990

Stay up until you must come down.

Wasn't that what Viva's teacher, Glenda Roan, always said? Glenda, a former dancer in the Merce Cunningham Company, taught advanced modern solo work, and she was full of directives: *Use your flesh to grab your bones, move like a noodle in boiling water.* Viva was trying to incorporate all three concepts when it happened without warning, one afternoon in late May, five days before her senior solo—her final college requirement. She was rehearsing in Traeger Hall when mid-leap she couldn't remember the next sequence, let alone the remainder of the dance—a dance she'd rehearsed for weeks in the studio, in the parking lot behind the studio when it was closed, and in the cellar of her dorm. Again and again and again. It was the last thing she thought of before she fell asleep and the first thing she thought of when she awoke each day.

Viva tried again, simply marking the steps this time, but in the exact same place, after the first transition and just before a stag leap, it was as if someone pulled the plug, and she landed clumsily on both feet.

Viva had never had great difficulty remembering combinations or complex choreography, although, on the occasion that she did, her loyal body would take over, muscle memory completing a sequence. But this wasn't about forgetting precisely, it was a sudden and complete inability to transcend the choreography, and without that her dance felt mechanical and pointless.

On her third attempt, she'd only completed her first combination when it happened once more—her movements became rote, her sequencing disconnected. Viva felt locked out of her own body. Maybe she was tired. Maybe she'd over-rehearsed. Viva packed up her things and walked to her dorm in a haze. She stopped to buy a large coffee and sat on a bench near the student union where she mentally rehearsed each movement of her solo, each pause, each breath. There, there it was. She could see it. She could feel it. Viva would try again first thing the next morning.

That night Viva told her roommate, Anastasia Bing, what had happened.

"Stage fright," Anastasia said, taking a swig of beet juice, which she drank for its antioxidant properties, and which stained her teeth, giving her the appearance of having guzzled blood. She wore her hair in three long intertwined braids, and her face bore a constant look of deep concentration, as if she was incessantly solving riddles. Anastasia was one of the best dancers in the program, and she and Viva often competed for the same parts.

Anastasia knew all about stage fright. She became so anxious before a performance, her throat would close and she couldn't swallow, let alone move. She'd been about to quit school when she learned about beta-blockers. Problem solved. She offered Viva a couple of Inderal, but Viva didn't take them. This wasn't nerves, it was something else.

The next morning, Viva performed her entire solo like nothing had ever happened. Once. But only once. Each subsequent attempt at a rehearsal deteriorated until she had to stop altogether. Who was this inner traitor who had so violently and swiftly overtaken her?

In a panic, she met with her teacher, Glenda Roan, who said, "Relinquish control."

"What do you mean?"

"When I danced with Merce, he withheld the sequencing of my steps until he threw the *I Ching* before my performance to determine them! See what I'm saying?"

But Viva didn't. Not really. She consulted her friends and other dancers—everyone had an opinion. Perhaps she was dehydrated. Perhaps she needed more protein. Perhaps it was stress-induced amnesia. Perhaps she didn't really want to graduate.

Jules Fado, the RA and a psychology major, told Viva her body was at long last expressing its grief over growing up fatherless. But what could Viva do about that now? Half the girls she knew had troubled relationships with their fathers, so really, maybe it was just as well she hadn't known her own.

But nothing anyone said could help her, because the real cause of Viva's problem, the one she'd tried so hard not to know, wasn't about something that she had or hadn't done. The real problem was that soon she would be competing with professional dancers, and she thought she wasn't good enough. This debilitating fear wasn't based on her actual ability, and yet she'd carried it within her secret self for years now, almost since the moment she knew she would pursue a path in dance, and despite progress, scholarships, and accolades.

Only weeks earlier, Glenda Roan, after watching Viva rehearse her solo, said she was "transported," that she forgot she was even watching a dance. She said Viva had "the ability to change the energy in the room." Surely that was a good thing? But later that night when Viva tried to recall her teacher's words, the initial hope and confidence she felt had all but disappeared. Something wary and obdurate within her, something she would pluck out if she could, rocked back to the old idea of not being good enough.

And now, in just three days, in her final performance before moving to New York to compete with a legion of dancers, her shameful secret would be on display for everyone to see.

Viva considered calling her mother, but what if she had been drinking? That would only make it worse. Besides, she hadn't talked to her for the entire past semester. The last time her mother called her, Anastasia had picked up and Charlotte regaled her with career advice for an hour. As if Charlotte had ever had a real career. Viva was deeply embarrassed.

Yet strangely, and while this made no sense to her, she felt her mother might have some special insight into her problem. Sometimes, she still felt as if she and Charlotte were the only ones who truly would ever understand each other's wiring. But she wasn't going to call her. Charlotte had sent her a postcard saying she was coming to her recital, but Viva gave it a fifty-fifty chance. Charlotte said a lot of things.

A bird was trapped in the hotel ceiling. Charlotte was sure of it. She called the front desk at the Silver Comfort Manor, the thirty-nine-dollar-a-night hotel near Viva's college, the cheapest one she'd found in the Yellow Pages.

"Please hurry," said Charlotte. "I don't think it can breathe."

The manager said they'd send someone as soon as possible, but they were busy due to the influx of visitors in town for graduation. Charlotte hadn't seen any other guests that looked like parents to her. Unless if by "parents" he meant hookers.

Charlotte paced the floor of her room, a discouraging arrangement of a bed, a desk, a bureau, and a window framed by dusty gingham curtains that faced a concrete wall. Green plaid bedspread. A competing plaid pillow in ghastly shades of maroon, a pillow with a permanent head dent. Charlotte heard a single plaintive chirp. It was enough to make a person smoke. And the person did, exhaling out a narrow window near the desk. Optimistically, she'd booked a nonsmoking room. She picked up the invitation to the recital she'd received from Viva a couple of weeks ago and reread it for the tenth time. There had been no accompanying note from her daughter, just the venue and time. It had been almost too late to book an economical flight, but she'd found one on People Express. Even if it was the aisle seat of the last row, diagonal to the restroom. Charlotte had arrived in New York that morning after flying the red-eye from California.

Once Viva left for college, Charlotte had moved to Glenalbyn, California, a tourist town where psychics sold spray tan products, and part-time contractors wrote diet books on the side. Tucked into the side of a mountain, "America's Black Forest" was forty-five minutes from Palm Springs and two hours from Los Angeles. It was rumored to have the strongest energetic field on the West Coast, and decades earlier, in an attempt to keep tourists out, residents chucked the town-limits signs. But the tourists continued to come.

Charlotte liked living in a place that required grit and ingenuity, what with the frequent wildfires, the endless shower of leaves and needles falling on everyone and everything, jumbo pine cones dropping from the sky like dead birds, and the fact that people had to hold down at least two jobs just to get by. Not everyone had the stamina for the place, and Charlotte was proud of the fact that she did. She got by on odd jobs—sample server at the local grocery store, part-time cashier at the gem and crystal emporium, and, most recently, a brief stint as a makeup artist at the local mortuary. Sometimes she drove to Palm Springs to participate in focus groups where she gave her opinions on video games she'd never heard of or beauty creams she would never buy. It was an easy hundred, and sometimes the companies provided lunch.

After Charlotte arrived at JFK, she took a shuttle to Grand Central and boarded a train north. She'd stopped only to call Viva from a pay phone to confirm her arrival and give her the name of her hotel. Charlotte hoped her efforts to travel cross-country last-minute would surprise and impress her daughter, make up for all that had gone before. Charlotte had to leave the message with her roommate, Anastasia, who sounded wary but said she'd pass it on. Once she checked into her room, she tried to nap, but every few minutes, a man in a golf cart sped up to the hotel dumpster and flung what sounded like bags of marbles into it. How did anyone get any rest? But maybe that wasn't the point of a place like this.

Since she couldn't sleep, Charlotte thought to call Viva again but didn't want to bother her, knowing that pre-performance concentration was a delicate thing. Then she changed her mind—she'd simply call to wish her luck. She doubted Viva would even pick up.

Things had been strained between them for years, and with a pang of regret, Charlotte recalled the night of Fender's arrest. After the carnival closed, she'd gone off with the Ferris wheel operator for a nightcap. Maybe two. Three tops. She was home by daybreak. But she'd missed everything. Viva was waiting for her. Furious. Somehow it was Charlotte's fault that Fender got arrested and spent three months in juvenile detention for dealing. Somehow it was her fault that after he was released his father sent him to a hard-core military school in Wyoming, and it was especially her fault that Viva never saw him again. But deep down, Charlotte knew she should have been there that night. In her final year before college, Viva's ambition became her weapon of choice, enabling her to receive a scholarship at SUNY Purchase. And then she was gone.

Viva picked up on the first ring, and she sounded foggy, as if she'd just woken up. Calm. Too calm. Not a good sign.

"Are you ready for your dance?"

"My solo."

"Yes, I know you're dancing alone."

"Why do you make it sound like that?"

"Like what?"

"Like I'm just dancing by myself."

"Isn't that what the word *solo* means?" Charlotte heard Viva sigh.

"Not everyone got a solo, Mother." The way Viva said *Mother* was familiar to her, the thud of the first syllable, the hard angry hook of the *r*. But beneath that, Charlotte could hear something else in her voice. Panic.

"Viva, what's wrong?"

"I've got to go." Viva sounded like she was on her way to her own beheading.

Charlotte thought she heard the bird rustle above her. Poor thing, trapped within the ceiling, which in its outward appearance was the texture of curdled milk.

She tried the front desk again, but no one picked up.

Charlotte sat on her bed. Stood up. She didn't want to wrinkle her skirt. She'd been lucky to find the salmon-colored linen suit at the local thrift store. It fit her perfectly. And the juice stain near the waistband wasn't visible if she didn't remove the blazer. Charlotte twisted her long hair into a bun and reapplied a new lipstick, one she'd bought for her daughter's dance recital. She inspected herself in the mirror. From time to time, people would ask if Charlotte herself was a dancer. Her slenderness and bearing, her aloofness that others sometimes interpreted as haughtiness, could give that impression. But Charlotte had no sense of rhythm. She'd discovered that in a childhood cotillion class when she simply could not locate the beat.

People didn't usually guess that Viva was a dancer. She had the height, but her posture was another matter. She'd always had a habit of hunching her shoulders, one she'd never been able to break completely. And yet, when she danced something snapped into place, a mysterious and powerful focus that allowed her body to move in a graceful assemblage unavailable to her in daily life.

There was a knock on the door and Charlotte opened it to find a maintenance man carrying a clipboard and a burlap sack.

"Where's the bird?" he said with the weary tone of one who has caught and removed one too many errant creatures—the spider in the suitcase, the dead mouse beneath the bed.

Charlotte pointed at the ceiling. There was a very faint chirp. "Oh God, it's almost dead," she said.

The man sighed, turned on his heel, and walked from the entry into an area that most charitably could be called a kitchen—a nook with a counter and a hot plate. He reached up toward the sloped ceiling and unscrewed what looked like a small plastic spaceship, something Charlotte hadn't noticed until this very moment. He pulled a battery from his pocket and replaced the old one.

How foolish. Charlotte put her hands on her hips. She felt like she was suffocating, but she would not take off her jacket.

"I'm here to see my daughter dance," she said.

The man looked at her and frowned. "Okay."

"She's quite good," Charlotte added. "Performing at the college this afternoon."

The man pulled a walkie-talkie from his utility belt and spoke into it. "Code 8," he said, a code that at this moment seemed to

Charlotte for her benefit alone, a code meant to clarify he was the maintenance man, not the conversation man. Embarrassed, she sat at the desk and pretended to study the room service menu until he left.

Charlotte realized she hadn't eaten since she'd nibbled the airplane breakfast hours and hours ago. The room service menu was broken into three main categories, Intro, Next, and End, mirroring the circle of life itself, it seemed, and the menu featured few items, one being *40-ounce regional beer*. Maybe something stiffer, Charlotte thought. But she caught herself. She hadn't had a single drink since she'd received Viva's invitation.

The phone rang, and when Charlotte picked up, she heard Viva, but she couldn't make out what she was saying.

"Viva, slow down."

"I can't do this."

"What can't you do?"

"I can't do this performance. I feel like I'm dying."

"What?"

"I'm going to completely humiliate myself."

"Where are you?"

"I'm at a pay phone outside the theater."

"Well, go inside and get ready. Can you do that? Can you just do the next thing?"

"I don't think so."

"Look, Viva, you've got to get a grip." Charlotte heard Viva begin to pant. "Viva, I believe you can do this."

"Why?"

"Because you're talented, and if you can't believe that right now, I'll believe it for you. Now, go in the theater, and I'll be there as soon as I can." Charlotte grabbed her purse. The performance didn't start for another hour and a half, but she'd be early. She'd grab a front-row seat if she could.

The first dancer, Viva's roommate, Anastasia, a girl with a fake gluey smile, began in a posture that to Charlotte looked like a drooping flower. It was hard to square her presence with the terse young woman who sometimes answered the phone when she called. Charlotte would imagine Viva perched on her bed listening as Anastasia reported that Viva had just stepped out. On occasion, Charlotte would try to engage Anastasia in conversation, but she'd cut it short. Anastasia swept to the side and spiraled at a diagonal. Her torso and legs seemed at odds, and her taped musical accompaniment didn't seem to have a melody. It was quite loud, though, and concluded in rapid ticking. At that point, the dancer ran to the far corner of the stage and marched in an exaggerated frantic fashion like a trapped wind-up toy. The end.

Some modern dance pieces did puzzle Charlotte.

The next dancer began in absolute silence, and this Charlotte recognized. She recalled a performance at one of Viva's recitals where the dancers sat in chairs facing the audience in complete stillness for what seemed like half an hour, at which point they fell upon each other, one after the next, like dominoes. She knew that type of dance was a concept, not a story, and that you shouldn't expect any slick steps from that kind of thing.

She returned her attention to the second dancer, who moved slowly and deliberately through a sequence that reminded her of someone trying to step around hot coals. She thought Viva had mentioned this young man as being one of the best in her class. Will? Danny? No, Danny was in Viva's high school class, the kid who got a full ride to Juilliard. Charlotte studied him carefully, and the muscles in his legs appeared impossibly powerful to her, almost equine. As his solo progressed, his movements became more sweeping, then unhinged, and his dance concluded with a series of deep lunges and falls. Charlotte thought he was quite good.

Viva was next, and Charlotte squinted at the program. Her solo was called "Quintessence," and the brief description of the dance said it was not just about the fifth element (even though most people thought there were only earth, air, fire, and water), it was about the distillation of human experience. There was something about alchemy, too. Charlotte had a hard time trying to picture what the dance might entail. The lights went down, and Charlotte leaned forward in her seat. The woman next to her began to cough. She didn't even cover her mouth. Charlotte had to all but grab her own hand to stop from slapping the woman on the back. No one was going to ruin Viva's moment.

But where was Viva?

The stage remained empty, and at first the audience waited attentively. A long pause at the beginning of a dance wasn't completely out of the ordinary. Charlotte had watched enough performances to know it built suspense. But there is a moment when suspense turns to only obligatory interest, and soon Charlotte felt a rustle begin to spread through the crowd.

She stared at the stage and willed her daughter to appear. What if after hanging up, Viva had left the campus altogether? She could be unpredictable that way, and with a stab of guilt, Charlotte realized she should have checked on her when she arrived.

And then Viva stepped onto the stage. She walked to the center, where she stopped and bent her head. She wore a long shroud that was made of a very dark green silk, almost black. Or maybe it wasn't a shroud, thought Charlotte, maybe it was a cloak. This kind of thing was always important. A cloak, she decided. Charlotte peered at her daughter and watched her flush from neck to head. Even the part in her hair was pink. A telltale nervous condition, one that Charlotte had witnessed many times.

Viva's music began, a cascade of notes that seemed to tumble down upon the stage, a modern piece full of bright cluster chords. The music quickened and swirled around the space.

Charlotte waited, and it seemed to her, the whole world waited. *Viva, please.* Charlotte had sweated through her blouse, and she felt perspiration run down her arm. *Just do the first thing.*

And then Viva lifted her head. Charlotte stared at Viva and saw something deep within her daughter settle and begin, begin before she even took her first step. Then she burst across the stage in a fierce, rushing combination of spins that prefaced an impossibly high, stop-time leap. Viva seemed suspended in midair. There was a hush in the audience, and when she landed, Charlotte could have sworn Viva looked directly at her. She was sure of it. Elation shot through her, because no matter how many teachers Viva studied with, they'd never share the frequency she did with her daughter.

The performance was over, and Charlotte was alone in the auditorium when it started—the faint, rhythmic clanging in her ear that sounded like a tiny person hammering metal. It continued for a couple of minutes, and then there was a brief pause, as if the person stopped to consider their work, to smoke a cigarette or drink a sip of tea. Charlotte looked around to make sure the sound wasn't coming from somewhere in the theater. She'd learned her lesson with the bird. But then it began again. Louder and this time more insistent. When it paused once more, Charlotte hastily left and rushed down the hallway to the reception area.

Viva was standing amid a group of dancers across the room. She looked luminous—there was no better beautifier than pure relief. The performers clutched each other, laughing and crying, some reliving key moments of their performances, arms loaded with roses and lilies and tulips. Flowers! In her haste to get to the performance, she hadn't brought any for her daughter. Well, there was nothing she could do about that now.

Charlotte edged closer to Viva and her peers, who stood surrounded by a larger circle of parents, friends, and teachers. Everyone was exclaiming and incredulous, some shrieking and whooping. It seemed to Charlotte that the audience members themselves were performing. And what a huggy bunch! Charlotte smiled vaguely at no one. She watched the girls flit about, intoxicated by accomplishment.

More people streamed into the reception hall. There didn't seem to be any air-conditioning. There was only an old, creaking ceiling fan, and the room became hot. Charlotte took off her coat and held her arm across her waistband in a Napoleon-like stance to hide the juice stain. Now Viva was talking to one of her teachers. When Viva turned her head, Charlotte waved, but Viva didn't seem to see her.

Charlotte tried to access the circle from another point. A nearby group burst into laughter and Charlotte chuckled weakly as if she'd heard the joke. She saw Anastasia Bing's mother present Anastasia with a bunch of gladioli worthy of a presidential funeral. Then the woman gave Viva a smaller but beautiful bouquet of tea roses tied with a lavender ribbon. How thoughtful. Not to mention tasteful. Charlotte felt completely inadequate. But hadn't she flown across the country to attend the recital? Hadn't she picked up extra shifts to afford it? And without her, who knew what the outcome of Viva's performance might have been?

Anastasia Bing's mother made a big production of photographing Viva and her daughter, fussing with the lighting and angles. Charlotte knew the woman had a fancy magazine job. Viva had mentioned it many times. Her name was something like her own daughter's name—Aurora? Albania? Charlotte grimaced as she watched the woman join the girls for the next photo, hugging them equally as if Viva was her own daughter. Viva gave her a peck on the cheek.

Charlotte felt a little dizzy. She realized she'd still eaten nothing since that morning. She spotted a banquet table at the other end of the room and made a beeline for it.

Nothing but plastic cups of red wine, from which she quickly averted her eyes — not opening that door today — and Ritz crackers topped with Cheez Whiz and pimentos. Good grief. The dance department was constantly sending her letters, pleading for donations, and now she could see why. But Charlotte was famished. She quickly loaded up her plate with the hors d'oeuvres, if they could even be called that. The Cheez Whiz felt like glue in her mouth, sticking to her teeth and gums. With a jolt of panic, she recalled the day she had her mouth wired shut. Sneezing and coughing had been impossible. She couldn't even cry, and she'd learned not to.

"Mother!"

Charlotte whirled around.

"Where have you been? I've looked everywhere for you!" Viva stood before her, clutching the bouquet Mrs. Bing had given her.

"I was here, Viva, right here!" Charlotte brought a cocktail napkin to her mouth to try to discreetly wipe off the cheese.

"Well, I didn't see you when I came out of the dressing room. Everyone else was there. All the parents. Did you even make it to the show?"

"Viva, of course I did. You looked right at me."

"When?"

"From the stage."

"You know I can't see anyone in the audience."

"But I helped you do your dance."

"What?"

Viva looked puzzled but also as if she might laugh, an expression that Charlotte had noticed she'd begun to cultivate since she'd left for college, an expression that Charlotte noted was her father's, through and through.

"It'll be our secret." Charlotte winked.

Viva frowned. "Have you been drinking?"

"Absolutely not." Charlotte set her paper plate on a nearby table and stretched out her hands like a child, flipping palms up and down. "See?"

Viva sighed. "Mother, you have a spill on your skirt."

Charlotte's arm flew to her waistband. "It's from before, from another event. In Glenalbyn. A gala event, actually. There were a lot of important people there."

Viva shook her head. "Do you have anything at all to say to me?"

Charlotte licked her right incisor, dislodging the last of the ghastly cheese. "About what?"

"About my performance!"

"It was very good. But you know that."

Instantly, Charlotte could see she hadn't said the right thing. But what was the right thing? She wasn't one to gush and gild the lily. Was that a crime?

Anastasia and her parents passed by on their way to the buffet table.

"Hello!" Charlotte called brightly.

Viva made no attempt to introduce Charlotte to them, but Anastasia waved half-heartedly. With a terrible clarity, Charlotte suddenly remembered calling Viva a few months ago when she'd had too much to drink. Anastasia picked up the phone, and she'd regaled her with advice. If only she could recall about what.

"Mom, I'll catch up with you later," said Viva.

"But I was going to take you to dinner." Charlotte had spotted a little café on her way into town. Although sometimes those small, unassuming places could be deceptively expensive. She would just order a salad if need be.

"Maybe later? I need to take care of some things."

"You're leaving?"

"Well, I have plans to meet up with a couple of my friends."

"Oh."

"But I'll catch up with you later. Okay?"

Suddenly Charlotte heard the strange noise again, and she brought her hand to the side of her head.

"Do you have an earache?" For a moment Viva looked genuinely concerned and Charlotte lit up.

"It's very strange, Viva, I was in the auditorium, and I heard something inside my head like a loud tapping, but I thought I'd imagined it because earlier today I heard a bird in the ceiling—oh, that was crazy, wait until I tell you *that* story!"

"What bird?" Viva frowned.

"Viva, we're taking the class photo," Anastasia called to Viva. "Come on!"

Charlotte thought she saw something pass between them. Was Anastasia making that up? Frantically, she looked around the room. Where was the photographer?

"Look, we'll connect later, okay, Mother? I'll call your hotel and we'll make a plan. All right?"

Charlotte said, "Sure, of course. Of course. Go on." She was aware of waving her arm like Lady Bountiful. Charlotte watched her daughter walk away and disappear into a crowd of well-wishers.

Viva's behavior was incomprehensible to Charlotte. Hadn't she sacrificed time and again for her daughter? Hadn't she made sure she had dance lessons? By hook or by crook! Sometimes by both. At least she gave Viva *something to push against*. To use Viva's own words. Charlotte roughly unbuttoned the top of her suit. She couldn't wait to get out of it. She'd never wear it again.

The room was almost empty then, and all the gaiety and high emotion of the previous hour seemed to have completely drained from the space. Charlotte watched a waiter dump what was left of the Cheez Whiz crackers into the trash. Good riddance. The other server began to collect the remaining glasses of wine.

"Wait!" Charlotte shouted. "Wait!"

She rushed to him, her heels clattering across the floor. Charlotte quickly grabbed two plastic goblets and made a beeline for the exit, where she stopped and turned. "One is for my husband," she called to the men, though no one had asked.

chapter fourteen
1993

Every day the same thing: Up at 5:00 a.m. Stretch for one half hour. One cup of tea. One teaspoon of milk. No teaspoons of sugar. By 5:45 a.m. Viva would be on the subway, traveling to class. If the second subway was late, Viva would run the many blocks to her dance studio, past fruit stands, and newsstands, and shopkeepers hosing down the sidewalk, past a church, a temple, a twenty-four-hour bail bond shop, and finally, past a Filipino bakery from which emanated the smell of fresh pandesal that enveloped and taunted her, but to which she would not succumb. Not at that moment, anyway. She would take two classes back-to-back, audit a third, and only then would she finally eat. One single roll from the bakery. No butter. The discipline, the rigor, the repetition, was a beautiful thing to bear. Purpose was its own drug.

Today, Viva awoke at four thirty. She had a callback for a new modern troupe in Brooklyn—Nexus—and before she left for class, she planned to practice. Only two other dancers had been called back, one of whom was her college roommate, Anastasia Bing. They both worked at the same bar, the Clink, and they often took the same dance classes. They both were ambitious, both talented. But they were gifted in different ways. Viva was more of a lyrical dancer, while Anastasia was more technically gifted. They told each other that no matter who got cast it would be all right. But as soon as she said it, Viva realized it wasn't true. She wanted the part. When she'd seen Anastasia last week in a class Anastasia said, "It's great you haven't had another episode like that time you froze up in college." She seemed sincere, but the mention of the incident immediately caused Viva to worry it would happen again without warning. It would be terrible if it happened at an audition.

It had been a challenging three years since Viva had arrived in New York, but she consoled herself with the thought that in the past six months she'd booked two jobs—one with the Zosia Lange Company, where she'd performed as a soloist, and another in a performance of Paul Taylor's *Esplanade*. Athletic and risky, the piece was based on a girl slipping and falling while running for the bus. Viva had been singled out in the *Village Voice* review as a "dancer to watch."

Viva put her teakettle on and began to mark the opening of the piece she would perform that afternoon. She was distracted by the thought of Charlotte. She worried about how her mother would continue to afford her place in Glenalbyn and she worried about her drinking. But she pushed her mother out of her mind. It was up to Charlotte to change her life.

Viva's tiny ground-level sublease, advertised in *Backstage* as a "charming wedge," had once been a maid's quarters. Low ceilings, a tiny kitchen, and a bedroom. Tub by the stove. But there had been fierce competition for it and the line of applicants snaked around the block.

To secure the sublet, Viva needed to pass an interview with the leaseholder, a dancer named Lark. Lark conducted the entire discussion sitting atop the back of a kitchen chair like an imperial mistress of ceremonies while she played with her hair, which was the color of fluorescent pee and arranged in a multitude of skinny braids that cascaded down her back. A friend told Viva that Lark was a former deb from Dallas and that if Viva wanted to get the apartment, she better not bring it up.

Lark flicked her gold-tipped cigarette that put Viva in mind of a party favor and solemnly asked a single question: Did Viva consider her approach to life to be linear or modular? Viva, not knowing which answer would put her in a better position, replied that her behavior was "situational."

Lark nodded and picked up a clipboard that revealed a list of forty or fifty names. Viva could see notes in the margins, although most of the names had lines through them and a few were completely obliterated by fat Magic Marker cross-outs. After a long silence, Lark said, "Well, you seem likable," and there was something in the way she said the word *likable* that seemed to indicate a certain small disgust. But Viva had an apartment, at least until the following summer.

It was too hot for an early May morning. Almost eighty-five degrees. Viva opened the kitchen window. The single light above the closed bodega across the street shone down in what seemed an almost theatrical way, as if the street were a stage and a show was about to begin.

She saw two men walking, one behind the other. Dark clothes. Walking unremarkably beneath the light, then past the light. Two dark figures nearing the corner when the second one suddenly rushed forward and hit the first one on the head. It seemed almost comic, like a moment in a slapstick film. The man crumpled to the pavement.

Viva ran to the phone to call the police, but by the time she got back, which couldn't have been more than three minutes, the second man was gone, and the first man no longer lay on the sidewalk. Vanished.

Viva stuck her torso out the window, looking left and right. The street was empty, and the light continued to beam, illuminating bottles of red soda and loaves of bread in the shop window. As if nothing had happened.

Viva realized she was shaking. What time was it in California?

Charlotte picked up on the first ring, and in a rush, Viva told her what had happened. She heard the ice in her mother's glass make its downward slide, heard Charlotte crunch on a cube. It would be two fifteen in Glenalbyn. "It happened so fast," Viva said.

"New York's a dangerous place," said Charlotte.

"You lived here."

"Yes, but I'm me."

"What's that supposed to mean?"

"It means I possess an exorbitant fortitude of spirit, Viva. Wait, inexplicable."

"Don't I have fortitude?"

"Yes, but you have the other kind." Viva heard her open the fridge. New bottle.

"What kind is that, Mother?"

"You have fortitude of will. The dogged kind. Not the transcendent kind."

Drunk logic. And of course Charlotte would make it sound like Viva had the dull kind of fortitude.

"Well, nothing to be done now, Viva. You called the cops. You did your bit. Tell me something new."

"I have a callback today. I think I have a decent chance at the part."

"You have great faith in your abilities. I'll say that."

Thanks a lot, thought Viva, but she didn't contradict her. She cradled the phone on her shoulder and quickly packed her lunch for the day—an apple, six saltines, and five figs.

"You know, when I was in New York, I might have had quite a career as a painter. If my hands didn't shake."

This was new. Sometimes she would have been a great painter if she weren't allergic to oil paint.

"I took a semester with Constantin LaSalle. Do you know who that is?"

"I don't, but I believe you. Can we talk about it later?"

Charlotte dropped her voice conspiratorially. "The thing was, I didn't like showing people my work. I was a very private painter."

Viva heard her mother throw Eddie a dog treat—the ping against the metal bowl, the mad scramble, Eddie's dog tags clanking. Charlotte threw another and another and another. Ping, ping, ping!

"You feed that dog too much."

"You eat too little."

Charlotte exhaled sharply and Viva responded with a loud inhale. They were at a familiar point in the conversation, the umbilical cord of the phone pulled taut between them.

"Get some sleep, please, Mother."

"Viva, you know the Huma bird?" Charlotte's tongue sounded loose in her mouth, and her words had begun to bob, disconnected, uninflected. "The Huma bird flies around all day. All day long. Damn bird can't land. That's you."

Viva looked at the clock. "Charlotte, I need to go."

"Why do you call me and just hang up! I don't do that to you."

"I called because I was scared."

"Then you need to stay safe! And if you ask me—" Charlotte abruptly stopped.

"Hello?" Viva waited. "Mother, are you still there?"

"For Chrissakes, Viva, turn down your music."

"What music?"

"What in hell are you listening to? Trombones and goddamn cymbals. Sounds like parade music."

"I'm not playing music. Is it outside your house?"

"No, it's not outside my house, Viva. Jesus Christ, it's driving me crazy."

Viva looked at the clock. She was almost fifteen minutes late and would need to take a cab to class. "Mother, take an aspirin and go to bed. Okay?"

Viva heard the freezer door slam, the crack of the ice cube tray against the counter. "Will you? Please?"

"Hey, Viva." Charlotte's voice drifted off. "Do you miss me?"

"Yes," said Viva. And she wanted to mean it. She felt a rush of guilt. "Of course."

"Well, give 'em hell today. And if you get nervous, just think of me. I'm your lucky charm." The phone clattered to the counter and Viva heard her mother shuffle away. Maybe she was finally going to bed, but Viva made a mental note to check on her later. Her sense of concentration and preparedness with which she'd started her morning had vanished. She hated being late, she hated that Charlotte made her late, and she hated the fact that she didn't know how to help her mother.

Viva quickly gathered her dance gear together and called a taxi. While she waited for it to arrive the city began to rumble awake, and she saw an old woman open the store across the street as if there hadn't been an assault there an hour ago.

As Viva would go through her day, she'd replay what she thought she saw earlier that morning, reframing it in different ways, and that was the problem with memory—the process of focusing on one thing necessarily required the exclusion of something else, and sometimes the something else was the most important part.

chapter fifteen

The Clink was hidden in the basement of a suburban mall forty-five minutes from Manhattan, and during the week mothers with children in tow, pinging from Big 5 to Macy's to Orange Julius, never suspected that beneath the graham cracker–colored behemoth that was the Kirkwood Galleria, there lurked on Friday and Saturday nights a secret social scene.

The Clink was not cleaned on a regular basis, if at all, and asbestos drifted through cracks in the ceiling like blue ash. The air was thick with the fragrance of cigarettes and coconut air freshener. It was a fire hazard. It was a health hazard. Gum wrappers, candy wrappers, condom wrappers, cigarette pack cellophane, and shredded cocktail napkins caught around girls' high heels like seaweed. The Clink served anyone over fifteen. Viva took the job, anyway. She was prepared to do whatever it took to cover her rent, audition during the day, and pay for dance classes. And tonight, it all seemed worth it because just before work, Viva got the phone call from the artistic director of Nexus. She was cast in their premiere performance of *Carpe Noctem*. Viva hadn't yet told anyone her news, but she felt as if tonight she could withstand any kind of rigor. She could work a hundred-hour shift if need be.

Viva punched in, hung up her coat, and put her purse in her locker. She tied her apron around her waist and marked the first steps of her audition piece with a deep retroactive pleasure. She'd fretted for a week about having flubbed a single step in the second half of her audition. After her mistake, the artistic director covered one eye with his palm while watching her—he was a slender cyclops who didn't say a word when she finished. Was that a good sign or a bad sign? It was impossible to know, and she'd talked herself out of thinking she would get the part.

Viva eyed the schedule hanging above the time clock and with a momentary irritation noted that a new hire, Daphne, would trail her that night. This was the third shift Daphne had shadowed her, and Viva didn't think she was going to make it. She mixed up orders, forgot to charge for drinks, and talked too much. Viva could cover for her only so many times. But the profound acceptance of the world that had descended upon her since Viva learned she'd been cast canceled out her annoyance. Even her commute to the Clink that night, one that involved a subway transfer and a bus trip, had seemed almost mystical, the city beneficent, everything conspiring to be part of some greater whole, and the overflowing garbage cans, the dead rat outside her apartment, the woman who clipped her nails on the subway, none of it could bring her down.

During prep time and before the Clink opened for business, the manager, Mrs. Nancy, played on repeat an Ace of Base song, "The Sign," with its admonishing lyric that warned the staff no one would drag them up into the light where they belonged. Fair enough, no one was looking for a handout.

There were the waitresses—Viva, Anastasia, Tiffany, and Jill. They weren't "the dates"—Sage, Julie, the other Julie, Pamela, and

Courtney. The dates were so young they chewed bubble gum while drinking whiskey. They wore mint, apricot, or mauve crepe dresses, hand-sewn by Mrs. Nancy and featuring long sleeves and sweetheart necklines—the type a choir girl would wear. The dates were there to entertain the guests but not have sex with them. "We are about respect," Mrs. Nancy would say. "Now get the shit out of your pants and sell some drinks."

The waitresses and the dates worked hard, and they were all saving for something—a sex change, equine veterinarian school, a preschool where children learned to whittle. In the first month alone, Viva socked away enough for three months of dance classes. The waitresses were practical, and they had moxie. They did not mind hoisting fifty-dollar fruit plates that featured two dollars' worth of fruit. They did not protest when uneaten fruit was scraped off the platter and saved for the next one. They especially did not protest when customers tipped off the bottle. They had goals, and they were getting the hell out of there.

Mrs. Nancy rushed past Viva wearing a green plastic visor, an unlit Tiparillo in her mouth, while the engine of her brain revved, her thoughts seeming to radiate fiercely and silently, like waves from a motorboat. The girls knew to stay out of her way when she had that look. They knew she was thinking about *the problem*. Not the usual ones, the big one.

The big problem was the egress, which Mrs. Nancy pronounced with a grand rolling *r*. Mrs. Nancy knew the compliance rules, even if she had no intention of respecting them. The Clink had no back egress, only a small door that opened onto the alley. If one was slender, one could slip through this door and crawl up to street level (Viva and Anastasia had tested it out one night), but it would never constitute an actual exit. The maximum capacity posted on the club wall was one hundred, but most nights Mrs. Nancy allowed in at least double and sometimes almost triple that number. During prep time, Mrs. Nancy sat at a little table, staring at blueprints, fooling with additions, sketching egresses here, there, and everywhere, but nothing came to pass.

It was the last weekend in May, and the bartender, Ed V, stood behind his bar, arms clamped to his chest, lizard eyes sliding back and forth. He looked disgusted, as if in attendance at a sporting event in which both sides were losing. Some said Ed V had "the goods" on Mrs. Nancy. Some said that Mrs. Nancy had "the goods" on Ed V. Some said he was her husband. Some said it was a green card thing. Mrs. Nancy said he was her "eyes and ears," and all the girls were careful about what they said around him.

Daphne sidled up to Viva, sweeping her long black hair into a ponytail. Daphne was in hairdressing school and saving for her own salon. "Did you know that people used to keep knives in their hair?" she asked.

"No, I didn't, Daphne."

"There's a lot people don't know about hair, for example, that it's primarily dead or that it can hurt you." Daphne briefly touched her index and middle fingers to her lips, a move that indicated she would like to stop her mouth but couldn't. "Ever hear of a hair splinter? If hair pierces your skin and you don't catch it, oh boy, big trouble."

"Daphne, can you fill the salt and pepper shakers?" Viva pressed her palm against the wall and stretched her right leg while scanning the room for Mrs. Nancy. Being the tallest waitress, she could easily track her whereabouts, and it had its advantages when carrying a tray full of drinks. Viva also had the respect of the other girls for being the best at handling drunks.

Viva considered phoning Charlotte with her good news but decided it would be best to wait until tomorrow morning. If she could help it, she never called past five o'clock in California.

"Viva!" shouted Mrs. Nancy. "Don't you have work to do?" Busted. The waitresses had to look busy every minute, even before their shift started. It wasn't especially hard since there were ketchup bottles to fill, silverware to sort. Once that was done, the waitresses strode around pretending to look busy, scribbling notes to themselves on check pads—*Buy toilet paper! Dentist?*

The dates did not have to keep moving. Viva glanced at Sage and Julie #2, lounging under an orange spotlight. Viva despised what she called "the hamburger light." You bet your ass she'd keep moving.

Anastasia passed by Viva on her way to the bar. She was beautiful with her small, upturned mouth, high forehead, and eyelids of a natural pinkish hue that made her look like she'd recently been weeping. But Anastasia's delicate looks belied her fortitude; she could work a double shift and knock out a matinee and evening performance the next day. She was also the best waitress at the Clink—she could memorize orders for a party of eight and got the best tips. Viva hated to admit she sometimes felt jealous of her.

"Hey, V, did you hear anything from Nexus?"

Until this moment Viva had forgotten that Anastasia also had a callback. "Um, did you not hear yet?"

"Crickets," said Anastasia. She grabbed a stack of cocktail napkins off the bar and turned to Viva. "Why? Did you?"

Viva felt her face flush. "I did hear from them, but I bet they haven't called everyone yet."

"What did they say?"

"Looks like I'm cast," Viva said, careful to mitigate her joy at the news.

"When did you hear?"

"Around noon."

"Oh." Anastasia's face fell. "Well, look, congrats. Can I take you out for lunch this weekend to celebrate?"

This was another thing about Anastasia and her near-maddening perfection—she was truly generous. Some dancers were kind only when things went their way.

"Definitely," said Viva. "And I still think you'll get a call."

"Viva! Anastasia! Cut the damn chitchat," shouted Mrs. Nancy. Abruptly, she turned off Ace of Base, cranked up the house music, and threw open the door.

And there they were—the mad stompers, the shufflers, the guy with a girl hanging off his neck, the guy with two girls hanging off his neck, the *Why did I come/I waited all week* ambivalent revelers, the pushy flashers, shy hopers, the chemically ecstatic and hardly awakes, the girls in six-inch platforms, falling all over each other like kittens. Music crashed through the speakers, a song that sounded like a huge heart thumping, interrupted only by the repeated zing of an electric cricket noise. The singer sang the same three-word indistinguishable plea over and over—*issa rhine wane?*

During the shift, no one could take a break, because Mrs. Nancy didn't believe in such a thing. "You break when you sleep!"

Hours later, when the going got rough, and it always did, what with customers jammed in every corner, smoking, drinking, and shouting, the experience seemed to Viva like being stuck on an airplane that would never land. Mrs. Nancy had just axed Viva's shadow, Daphne, and she had to handle her drink orders as well.

Finally, it was last call and Viva escaped to the utility closet where Mrs. Nancy kept boxes and boxes of check pads, and the shelves were stacked with pickling jars in which floated mysterious purple orbs. Were they exotic fruit, or pig's testicles, as Anastasia claimed? No one knew, and no one cared, because within the closet was a single folding chair on which a waitress or date might sit for a few minutes.

Viva brought a double vodka with her, one of Daphne's mistake orders, which she drank in quick, breathless sips. She didn't nip all night like some of the dates. She usually had an early-morning dance class—plus she couldn't justify the calories. But tonight, Viva would have just one, even if one was a double. To celebrate. She didn't have to worry about overdoing it, she wasn't her mother.

Viva had forgotten to eat dinner, but at this point she'd wait until she got home. She sighed and read the latest piece of graffiti. Written in tightly coiled script were the words: *I'm sick of this mid evil bullshit*. Viva coughed. Even the air in the closet was thick with cigarette smoke. When she returned home, she would have to hang her clothes outside before she could wash them. But this was of little consequence—she'd been cast in a professional production and she would be paid. She might even be able to cut back on shifts.

Viva took another sip of her drink and her mind wandered to something Anastasia had told her, which was that when the Mongols went on a long journey and ran out of water, they would cut open a vein in their horse's neck and drink its blood. This thought fortified and inspired her in some mysterious way. Viva finished her drink and stepped out of the closet. It was three in the morning, the last drink sold, the last date fished out of the sunken sofa in the ladies' room where she had fallen asleep after drinking too many Jack and Cokes, jumbo gum pack clutched in her hand.

Ed V began to hand-wash each glass with the dreamy, satisfied look of a child stringing beads. Viva and Anastasia sat in the largest circular booth and totted up their tips, whispering, "One hundred, two, two fifty . . . three," like nuns at vespers. There was no off night at the Clink.

When they were done Anastasia bought Viva a shot of whiskey. "Kudos on the gig. Drink up!"

"Thanks, but I shouldn't." Viva already felt tipsy from her first drink.

Anastasia lifted her glass. "Come on, Viva. This deserves a toast."

"What the hell," said Viva. They clinked glasses and Viva knocked back the shot.

Mrs. Nancy, her Tiparillo finally lit, ran toward the booth and clutched Viva's arm. "You. Help me." She removed her green visor and ran her fingers through her hair.

"Will it take long?" said Viva.

"Not long," said Mrs. Nancy. She shooed everyone out the front door and locked it. Ed V had already fled after executing his final act of the night, which was to dump a garbage pail full of ice into the back alley, a thing he did with great savage gusto.

"Come," said Mrs. Nancy.

Viva had never stood that close to her, and something was disorienting about it. Mrs. Nancy had sad brown eyes, and she held one arm across her stomach as if cradling a problematic organ. "You fix cats?" she asked.

Mrs. Nancy had mixed up Viva with Jill, who was not yet enrolled in equine veterinarian school because she still needed another year of college, and even though cats were not horses, and even though Viva was not Jill, she said yes. Why not. The drinks she'd had made her feel loose and magnanimous, magically inflating her heart. Besides, if the show was a success, she probably wouldn't be working here for much longer. It was the least she could do.

"Follow me." Mrs. Nancy set off down the narrow hallway that barely accommodated two people abreast, and the floor dipped to the right. They passed by a small door that led to the basement, a place only Mrs. Nancy and Ed V were allowed.

Mrs. Nancy's office was not as Viva had imagined it. It smelled like lavender, and lo and behold, there was a dish of actual lavender buds on her desk, above which hung a signed Ace of Base poster. Pens and pencils were aligned on her blotter by descending height. A jaunty ceramic frog paperweight squatted on a neat stack of bills.

Next to that was a shoebox, and inside of it was something swaddled in a blanket.

"This cat, she has the feline disease." The cat looked small and crumpled like a gray glove. But she was breathing with each weak lift of her midsection.

Viva looked at the cat, which didn't even lift its head. She picked up the box and weakly the cat cried out.

"Doesn't eat, doesn't sleep." Mrs. Nancy sighed. "Take it."

"Wait. What?"

Mrs. Nancy swiftly left the office and disappeared down the basement stairs.

Clutching the shoebox, Viva stepped out of the club and into the night. Her first breath of fresh air was intoxicating, as it always was after inhaling smoke and sweat and liquor for eight hours. It was much cooler than when she'd arrived, and she smelled rain in the air. She made a mental note to pick up milk. And cat food.

Then something happened that she would replay in her mind many times in the years to come, something that required the perfect intersection of unexpected events. Or maybe that was the definition of an accident, but if the front door hadn't been locked and Viva hadn't had to use the alley door, if Ed V had tossed the ice behind the dumpster as he usually did instead of right outside the door, and if she hadn't been carrying a tiny sick cat, she wouldn't have slipped.

The pavement seemed to fly up at Viva. A single cube shot from beneath her foot and clattered down the alley. One single ice cube. Amazingly, she did not drop the cat. Viva balanced herself on her left palm and slowly stood up. Everything was fine except that her right knee felt like it was stacked on her ankle. What was that song? — *The ankle bone connected to the shin bone. Shin bone connected to the knee bone.* Something had disconnected.

chapter sixteen

Through her open kitchen window, Charlotte heard the world rush in—a single plane shearing the clouds, cars streaming down the 10 Freeway, and wild parrots that had recently descended upon Glenalbyn after a pet store in Palm Desert burned down.

But then, out of the blue, there was the other sound—the mysterious noise, the sound like a tiny person hammering metal in her ear, the thing that signaled the other thing—the music. It had disappeared a few months ago, but in the past two weeks, suddenly and without warning, she'd become her own private jukebox, albeit one with an endlessly shifting playlist that played for hours or seconds. It had scared her enough to stop drinking. For now.

It was impossible to know whether in the next second she would hear the stuttering symphony, the tinny, looping calliope music, the minor-key canticle, or the elevator Muzak that seemed to squirt directly into her brain. Charlotte tried to ignore it, and sometimes, for a few days, the music vanished. But then it would begin again when she least expected it.

The previous day she was relieved to discover that the music she suddenly heard blaring came from a car radio. That was, until it morphed into mad parade music. But Charlotte had a plan. She was going to will it away. Mind over matter, and she was starting today.

Charlotte didn't expect Viva, who'd been convalescing at her cabin, to be up for hours. She'd gone to bed early the previous night, and Charlotte worried about the amount she was sleeping. Still, Charlotte treasured this time alone. Being cooped up with her daughter in a 550-square-foot cabin for the past three months had created a continual static in the air. Charlotte stepped outside and surveyed her plants.

Charlotte ran a no-kill garden. No beetle murders. No aphid massacres. No ladybug slaughter. Forget the thrips. She'd never even gone after the crickets, not when they got into her garage and took up residence in her cache of empty garden pots and not when they somehow migrated to her cabin and mysteriously made their way up a flight of stairs in an overnight silent siege, invading her cedar closet, popping every which way when she opened the door. If they brought good luck, as some believe, Charlotte had a great deal coming to her.

But sometimes saving a thing involves killing a thing.

Today Charlotte planned to salvage what was left of her poor skeletonized *Brugmansia* tree, its leaves, or what was left of them, lacy with holes. Small green caterpillars no longer than an eighth of an inch had arrived the previous week during days of strange, fretful, hot October winds. At first, Charlotte had painstakingly picked them from her *Brugmansia*, put them in a bucket, and relocated them to her compost pile—a relocation of epic decadence if there ever was one. But she couldn't stay ahead of the caterpillar carnage, and because she had no privacy, because her daughter swanned around in a perpetual state of mourning, because the music was starting to drive her crazy, today something snapped.

She would kill them. She would kill them all.

Charlotte filled a spray bottle with tap water, adding two table-spoons of blackstrap molasses and one teaspoon of Joy detergent. She was always careful to keep her dog Eddie from the *Brugmansia*, since the blossoms were hallucinogenic. As she sprayed the leaves, she remembered drinking *Brugmansia* tea one day long ago, in fact, what seemed like a hundred years ago. The last time she'd ever spoken to Wilson.

Wilson. Lately, he'd been on her mind a great deal. She tried to remember what he looked like and could truly recall with great clarity only a scar on his back, from a time in his youth when he'd run across the lawn and fallen on garden sheers left carelessly in the grass. Just below his right shoulder blade. Jagged, it turned purple when he showered. He'd teased her when she first saw it, telling her he'd been knifed, and she'd believed him. Wilson had been so confident, and it terrified her.

Charlotte stepped over Eddie, a wolf dog, collapsed on his side in the grass, his legs sticking straight out before him. Lying perfectly still, he looked like he'd fallen from the sky. Despite being on the somnolent side, Eddie often got into vicious fights with other dogs. Charlotte was forever paying off neighbors' veterinarian bills. But he was a true and faithful companion, one she called her dog husband.

Charlotte wondered if Wilson was one of those people whose assurance evolved into arrogance with age. She imagined him as a photography professor at a college somewhere, a group of young women clustered around him, hanging on his every word. But he'd always been on the laconic side. She couldn't really see it. Would he have a family? Doubtful. Was he dead? Charlotte felt a wave of sorrow when she considered she'd left him before he could ever leave her. Something she was certain would happen. It was painful to have such little faith in oneself. Certainly, Wilson must have wondered what had happened to her and why she never returned his calls. Sometimes she thought about trying to contact him.

———————

The coffeepot was a concession. Milk was nonnegotiable. Charlotte didn't allow it in the house, citing it as a throat chakra inhibitor. Never mind that the liquor cabinet was fully stocked, although Charlotte told Viva she was on the wagon. After months of Viva's begging, Charlotte finally purchased an old percolator at the thrift store. When Viva turned to plug it in, she crashed into the side of the stove, stubbing her toe. Though she'd been off crutches for a week, she and her body were in serious disagreement, and they had been since the accident.

The diagnosis was a severely torn medial meniscus, and when it first happened, the doctors said her cartilage was floating and migrating, which sounded menacing to her, like an uncharted pirate ship. That was just one of the problems. She'd also done damage to the bone and to the anterior cruciate, the ligament that controls stability and movement.

Viva picked up a postcard sitting on the kitchen counter. From Anastasia, it must have arrived that morning.

> *Dearest V,*
> *I escaped the Clink! Touring Spain for three months with Calyx. Madrid is divine. Let's have dinner when we both return to NY. Heal quickly, friend!*
>
> *Kisses, A.*

Viva flipped the card over and stared at a photo of the Royal Palace. Anastasia had drawn a stick figure of a dancer atop the building. She stuffed the postcard into the back of a cookbook.

The TV was blaring in the living room, but Charlotte was nowhere to be found. Everyone in Glenalbyn had jerry-rigged cable stations, no one paid for them, and the viewing options were not standard fare. There was a twenty-four-hour survivalist channel, endless infomercials for wondrous plastic blankets that could be tucked into a wallet, and late-night ads for a sexual enhancement drug called Ching-a-Ling. Viva swiftly turned it off. She prided herself on never watching television, and now on top of everything else she had to hear this garbage. It seemed a cruel irony that though Charlotte finally had a place of her own, Viva felt no comfort there. Her days stretched out before her—no classes, no auditions, no job. She was careful to not look at the clock, which seemed to mock and mark her lack of purpose.

Viva returned to the kitchen and started her coffee. While she waited, she placed her hand against the refrigerator and began her flexion-extension exercises. Three sets of twenty, three times a day. In the beginning, she could barely do two. She'd worked hard to build the quadriceps and calf muscles that supported her knee, and she was much stronger. Everyone said so. But not strong enough to pursue a performing career. Not ever. Her former agility was lost to her, and no longer a master of space, she constantly bumped into things, broke things, and misgauged her own dimensions. The one thing she had always been able to control, her body, refused to listen to her. Viva even had trouble standing still, as if her inner moorings had broken free. Anger, fear, and a bitter hopelessness sloshed around inside her.

The old Sunbeam began to percolate, making a rough gurgling sound like a death rattle. Viva turned it off, poured a cup, and stared at the oily liquid. Swiftly, she grabbed a bottle of whiskey from the liquor cabinet and poured some into her coffee. Viva felt a stab of guilt. What if she hadn't been drinking the night of the accident? But there were other factors, she consoled herself. Still, she'd never know for sure. Fuck it. She blew on her coffee and drank it. At least she'd saved the cat and found him a home before she left New York. Through the kitchen window, she spotted Charlotte fiercely raking the oak leaves that blanketed her backyard. Charlotte wore an old army jacket that hung mid-thigh and an ankle-length brown woolen skirt. Her long brown hair blew every which way in the wind. Abruptly, she turned to stare at Viva. Charlotte always had the ability to sense her daughter's presence, even from a distance.

Charlotte waved her outside. "Grab a rake, do yourself some good."

Charlotte began to drag her blue tarp full of leaves toward the woods that bordered her yard.

"Let me help," said Viva.

"No, you work your own pile," said Charlotte. She grunted as she hauled the tarp behind her. The bottom of her skirt got caught in the tarp, and she kicked it free without even breaking her stride. Eddie trailed behind her.

Viva chose a spot adjacent to where her mother had worked and began to rake, slowly and carefully, creating small piles that she planned to combine.

"Rake *with* the wind, Viva!" Charlotte called to her. "With the wind!"

Viva ignored her and continued to work, holding her legs in the position her physical therapist had shown her for a task such as this, one leg in front of the other, knees slightly bent. She actually had to review the position in her mind before she did it, something she would have found laughable a few months ago.

Charlotte returned and began to rake again, working twice as quickly as Viva. "Did you hear the Gillettes' music last night?"

Penny and Paul Gillette were Charlotte's new neighbors, to whom she'd taken an instant dislike.

"I didn't hear anything," said Viva.

"I went to their door first thing this morning and told them to knock it off. They said they weren't even home." Charlotte began to rake faster, the metal prongs of her rake clattering against the earth.

"Maybe they weren't." Viva paused to rest.

"Are you saying I'm a liar?"

"No, Charlotte, I'm not."

It appeared they were going to beat their own record for first quarrel of the day.

"Don't lean in when you rake," said Viva.

"What?" Charlotte continued her assault on the lawn.

"Try a scissor stance and keep your chest up."

Charlotte stopped raking and put her hand on her hip. "This isn't a dance, Viva, this is good old-fashioned work, and not everything has to make a pretty shape."

"It's not about the aesthetics, it's about the future pain you might cause yourself."

"You're worried about my future pain?"

"Yes, of course I am."

"That's rich, because it seems only one of us can be the queen of pain."

"What does that mean?" said Viva.

"It means you act like the world should come to a stop because you had an accident."

"What?"

Eddie started barking and ran in circles around them.

"Sorry, but that's the truth—maybe it will give you something to *push against*. Want to write a letter to someone about it?"

Viva gasped. "Are you happy I'm hurt?"

"For fuck's sake, of course not." Charlotte scooped up a pile of leaves and hurled them into a bin.

"Maybe you are. Maybe it makes it easier for you."

"What's that supposed to mean?"

"Now you don't have to be jealous of me."

"I'm *not* jealous of you." Charlotte reddened and savagely swept her hair into a bun. "I have *never* been jealous of you! Why would you say such a thing?"

"My life is ruined!"

"Tell it to the Greeks and get back to me!" Charlotte shook her rake in the air.

"What is wrong with you? Why are you so angry?" shouted Viva.

"Maybe I've got my own health problems, all right? But I take care of myself, I always have, and I don't expect others to do it for me."

"That's not true, Mother. I've taken care of you plenty of times."

Charlotte shook her head like she had water in her ear and grimaced. She turned from Viva.

"What's going on? Is there something wrong with—"

Charlotte spun around and shouted, "You know, you're not the only one who's ever wanted something."

"What did you want, Mother? Tell me. What did you want? You were never a real artist. You don't know what it's like to put in the time. Unless you count the art of drinking."

Charlotte went completely still, then she straightened her jacket and patted her hair.

"I put my time into you."

"Sometimes you did."

Charlotte's right eye twitched, as far as she ever got with crying.

"Certainty is a killer, Viva," said Charlotte, her voice breaking. "But since you're so goddamn sure about everything, I think it's time you got your own place and your own job and your own life. I'll expect you out in a week." Charlotte threw down her rake and strode back to her house, slamming the screen door behind her.

chapter seventeen
1968

Someone wanted to do it through the eye, like Cleopatra, who used *Brugmansia* tea to dilate her pupils, but that would require eyedroppers. Besides, it was much easier to drink it.

Crowded into Wilson's Lower East Side apartment, Charlotte brought the pewter chalice of hallucinogenic tea to her lips and almost gagged. Only moments before the cup had been stuffed with pens, paintbrushes, and clarinet reeds. Had anyone even washed it beforehand? No one seemed to care.

Most of Wilson's friends were successful painters or writers or comedians. Another one was a concert pianist. Wilson had already had a gallery show with another in the works. He and his friends traded inside jokes that were impossible for Charlotte to contribute to and bantered in a mock-self-deprecating way that seemed to her only to reveal how seriously they took themselves.

When Wilson told the group he'd bought the dried *Brugmansia* flowers ("Orange Rapture") from an old woman in Sunset Park, Charlotte mentioned they grew wild in the backyard of her childhood home, their trumpet-shaped flowers the size of dinner plates. No one responded, but Wilson's roommate, Ben, gave her an indulgent smile. Dressed in full Revolutionary War regalia, he'd just returned from a play rehearsal. Ben handed the mug to Charlotte again and she took another swig. She looked at Wilson across the room and tried to catch his eye, but he was busy making another batch of tea, deep in conversation with his friend Linda Burl.

That morning, when Charlotte awoke in Wilson's apartment, she'd found him organizing photos for his upcoming show on the kitchen table, a series that featured hands. He told her he planned to show only eight portraits. Wilson was big on not overhanging. He wanted to let the photos breathe. He showed Charlotte a black-and-white photograph of a hand—no thumb, no index finger. The owner of the hand had worked as a brakeman on a train. Wilson said the man seemed proud of his injury and told him that most brakemen lost fingers, some lost limbs.

"Look at this," said Wilson, holding up the next one, a photo of a palm with only the faintest of lines. "The guy said the last time he was arrested, it took the police five tries to get a print."

"These are great," said Charlotte. It intimidated her that Wilson was a working artist while she only studied the history of art.

"Thanks. Are you ready to meet the gang today?"

"Looking forward to it," said Charlotte, even though she wasn't, even though she'd hoped to have Wilson to herself. She gave him a kiss and went to take a bath. Charlotte was so small she often sat in the tub not lengthwise but crosswise, arms clasping her knees. Wilson had photographed her in this exact position the previous week.

Wilson had other photographs of women in this same tub, some in other tubs. One perched on the edge of his kitchen sink. He'd shown them all to Charlotte. Nothing to hide. After all, if he was going to become a great photographer, he had to shoot all the time. Wilson had told Charlotte that portrait photography was an exercise in unearned intimacy, but she thought that in quite a few cases he'd probably earned it.

When Charlotte looked at the photos, she made a point of complimenting something about each woman—her hair, her eyes, her lips. When she looked at her own photograph, she kept silent. Later, when Wilson turned his back, she slipped the photo into her purse. She wasn't going to be another trophy.

After her bath, when Charlotte joined Wilson in the kitchen, he asked, "How's your painting class going?" Charlotte had recently enrolled in a course—to better understand the artistic process, she'd told him. But Charlotte loved painting and secretly she would much rather be making art than studying it.

"The professor said I had an intuitive grasp of chiaroscuro."

Charlotte didn't tell him that she sat in the back of the room, never talked, and never willingly offered up her work for critique. She told herself it didn't matter since really she was an art history major, not a painter. But she was terrified to show her work, an act of exposure that brought her face-to-face with her overwhelming inadequacy.

And yet in her class the previous night, quite unexpectedly, Professor LaSalle had plucked her painting off her easel and presented it to the class, commenting on Charlotte's use of light and shadow. The painting portrayed a lone woman staring into a cup of coffee. Charlotte was surprised the teacher didn't notice that basically it was a rip-off of Hopper's *Automat*, and beneath that she felt ashamed she was unable to summon a completely original image. When she relayed the incident to Wilson, excluding her inspiration, he said, "Can I see it?"

"Oh, I don't know."

"Come on, please?"

"I don't have it with me."

"Isn't that your portfolio?"

When she'd arrived last night, Charlotte had set her blue leather portfolio atop the refrigerator lest it touch a drop of water. Made in Spain, she'd paid for it with two weeks' worth of grocery money. She carefully retrieved her painting and presented it to Wilson.

"Well, look at that," Wilson said. He held the painting at arm's length and squinted.

"Do you think it's good?"

"Sure, except for her hand. It's not to scale. Unless that was intentional."

It was not. Charlotte glanced at the woman's right hand, and it appeared to her like a big floppy paddle.

"But you've got a good eye, you do." Wilson grabbed Charlotte's hand and kissed it. But Charlotte knew she didn't, not really, and she knew she didn't possess the rigor to develop it or the confidence to show her work once she did. It was an awful thing to acknowledge, and she put it out of her mind as quickly as possible.

Charlotte trailed behind the group as they crossed the street and headed into the meadow near West Seventy-eighth Street in Central Park. A breeze sluiced through the field, creating lateral rows that looked like grass steps. Ben led the way with the confidence of an actual Revolutionary War general, halting traffic to allow the group to pass. His girlfriend, Minka, clung to his side. Ben kept a sex diary about their exploits, which he regularly left open on the coffee table. Minka was an usher at Lincoln Center, and because she was not an actress, a dancer, a painter, or a writer, Ben considered her to be pure and above reproach. He'd told Charlotte he was a "self-hating artist," but that acting had chosen him. Prior to this, Charlotte had never seen Minka in the light of day, only Ben leading her down the hall in the dark—stealthily, urgently—a woman with a pixie haircut wearing a black skirt and blazer. His diary was surprisingly dull. Good sex with Minka. Great sex with Minka. No sex with Minka.

Charlotte paused in front of a small shop that advertised the repair of zippers and umbrellas. She caught her own reflection in the window, a fractured and incomplete image, partially hidden by an awning. No jaw. No mouth. Her hand flew to her face.

Charlotte continued, dragging a wagon in which sat a gigantic watermelon. It had seemed a great idea when she thought of it, but now it made her feel childish, younger than the others. Which she was. And far less accomplished than the others. Which she was. Then three blocks from Wilson's apartment Charlotte realized she'd forgotten to bring a carving knife, and Wilson ran back to get it. Charlotte hoped he'd hurry. She pulled at her turtleneck, which, too hot for the day, was strangling her. If only she and Wilson were going to the park by themselves. If only the day was over. But Wilson had said he wanted her to meet his friends. Not that all his friends seemed to want to meet her.

Charlotte caught up with the rest of the group and fell in behind Linda Burl and her cousin Phyllis Hoyt, swinging a picnic basket between them, their rear ends swaying in companionable counterpoint. Phyllis shot a quick look back at Charlotte, and she imagined that they were talking about her. She was fairly certain Wilson had dated Linda and maybe Phyllis, too. Linda Burl was an artist who created large-canvas mixed-media works. She'd recently caused a stir with her new series that included beads, buttons, dead butterflies, and Spackle. Charlotte thought her work was atrocious.

Charlotte licked her lips, and she could still taste the tea, which was pungent like a radish.

Her wagon caught on a rock, and she stopped to free it before continuing. Disgusted, she thought the flower tea was no more hallucinogenic than Twinings. She didn't feel a thing.

Except that without warning her right hand and wrist seemed to have worked free from her body. When Charlotte turned, she saw her arm encased in red wool, her fingers wrapped around the wagon handle. But she had no feeling in them. Her arm was like a joke arm, the type that hangs out of a mailbox on Halloween. She was very, very thirsty, and when she inhaled the air felt thick. When she exhaled, for a moment she thought she saw her breath hang in the air as it would on a winter's day. Other than that, she felt perfectly fine.

But where was Wilson? For a moment she considered he'd ditched her. Then suddenly Wilson was next to her, and she realized that perhaps he had been walking alongside her for some time.

"Are you all right?" he asked, and the features of his face, as he turned to her, swiftly shifted and realigned—Wilson as painted by Picasso.

The important thing, Charlotte thought, was to not react. She was determined to hold her own with Wilson's friends, who, for all she knew, drank a different hallucinogenic tea every night of the week. She could hear herself breathe and the world seemed to have gone still. Ahead of them, the group stopped, settling in an area near a stand of elm trees.

"Picnic," Charlotte said to Wilson. With relief, she had recalled the word, which seemed to roll down a tiny chute deep within her mind, directly into her mouth. What a word, *picnic*. The wrong word for what it was. A picnic should be a sewing accessory, like a bobbin or spindle. This needed to be resolved. Immediately. Her brain accelerated and she told herself to remember the thought. Then she told herself to remember to remember.

"Charlotte?" Wilson held her bloodless hand, the one attached to the arm that did her bidding but offered no sensation. She and Wilson were located somewhere just above the earth. It wasn't like they were floating, it was as if they were standing on jelly, beneath which she could see the dirt and grass, for which she felt sudden and great sympathy.

Ben walked past them, murmuring, "So new, so nice." He was referring to the entire universe, she could see that quite clearly, and she realized for the first time how truly wise Ben might be.

Phyllis and Linda threw a blanket on the ground and pulled things from their picnic basket—a wedge of Fontina, saltines, green grapes, and two bottles of T.J. Swann Appleberry, which they arranged with great deliberation. Charlotte looked at the watermelon in her wagon, but the idea of moving it to the blanket seemed overwhelming. She noticed that Phyllis's skirt had caught in the top of her stockings, and her pale blue underpants peeked out haplessly. No one told her, and no one would. An amazing acceptance had washed over the group.

"You need to tell me if you're all right, Charlotte. Are you all right?"

Charlotte stared at Wilson, and his face snapped back together. There were his thick eyebrows, there was the chicken pox scar on his right cheek. Charlotte felt like she had been released from being held underwater. Her brain was a knife that in one single moment cut away all that did not matter.

Ben stood on a rock and began to reenact a scene from the film *The Blood of a Poet*, the part where the statue comes to life. The others listened to him, slowly nodding like tired cows. Minka sat on a blanket, back arched, gazing at the simmering spring sun. Her posture seemed to indicate she might summon it to full boil. Charlotte thought she saw her exchange a glance with Wilson. Was it possible that she'd slept with him, too?

Fred Neil's "Everything Happens" playing on a nearby radio floated up around them, and Wilson took Charlotte's hand. She pressed close to him and slowly they began to dance. Over Wilson's shoulder Charlotte saw a curious sight—a family eating fried chicken, fractal style. It was not unlike looking through a kaleidoscope, and she recalled a long-ago summer afternoon, just after her jaw had been wired shut, lying on her bed, pointing a kaleidoscope at her bedroom window, watching the sky and a lilac bush endlessly turn, shatter, and reconfigure.

They danced for a few minutes or maybe an hour when Wilson kissed her neck and said, "Let's take a walk."

Charlotte wasn't sure if he meant an actual walk or something more fun. They had been trying different places, most recently an empty carrel on the upstairs floor of the St. Agnes Library. Instead of seeming frivolous or wild, there was something serious about it, as if they were paying respects to their true animal natures, approaching some elusive primordial truth that could be illuminated only by fucking. Wilson stared off into the distance and tucked his shirt into his pants. Maybe he actually meant a real walk.

"What do you say, Charlotte?" he said softly.

He squinted and lifted his chin. She studied the V-shaped vein on his forehead, which, almost imperceptible in this light, became visible when they had sex. His eyes were big glass marbles, and a wavering light seemed to radiate from his head.

"Charlotte!" Wilson shouted and pulled her arm. With fierce determination, Charlotte willed her feet to move. Long shadows began to creep across the park, and they were momentarily alone.

Except for the woman standing on the Seventy-seventh Street Balcony Bridge, peering at them. Then the figure began to move in their direction, heels snapping on the pavement.

For a moment Charlotte thought she recognized her as a girl with whom she had attended high school, a girl named Martha May.

But this was not Martha May.

Wilson smiled slowly as the woman approached, and she was almost upon them when Charlotte recognized her from Wilson's driveway all those years earlier. Leila Greenleaf. Silk dress the color of an egg cream, long legs, and knees that appeared to spin like miniature airplane motors. Oh, no. Charlotte willed the tea to wear off, but it would not accommodate her wish, and suddenly she felt thrust back in time, still that girl leaning out her bedroom window, watching Wilson kiss Leila goodbye, mouth locked, fingernails digging into her thigh.

A sound escaped Charlotte like the single pluck of a guitar string—a tiny, mournful sound. She covered her mouth. Too late. She was still thirsty, and she needed to use the bathroom.

"Leila, this is Charlotte," said Wilson. Charlotte frantically tried to remember something she had read about the order in which two people should be introduced. The name of the more important person should be spoken first. Or was it the other way around? What did this mean that he had said Leila's name first? And how was it that Wilson seemed barely affected by the tea? For a moment Charlotte considered that he'd played a trick on her. She realized she was still standing there while Leila extended her hand. The beginning of a terrible headache crawled up the back of her neck.

The three stood in silence. Then Wilson said, "The bridge looks so beautiful in this light."

"I've long admired the quatrefoil cutouts," Leila said in a manner that would indicate she'd selected the design herself.

Something was vibrating between Leila and Wilson—Charlotte could almost hear it. She was a mass of yearning and want, and she thought they could see it. Even worse, her mind jumped to an afternoon in the previous week when she had stood naked, clutching a doorframe while Wilson knelt before her. She had power over him, and she knew it, and in her mind, she used the word *dominion*.

Leila and Wilson spoke about his photography, about the Nikon F he'd bought this week, something he hadn't mentioned to Charlotte.

"Nikon F," murmured Leila, like it was the name of some sexual spaceship. Charlotte strained to understand.

Better they should have done the tea through the eye, the original aperture.

"Do you shoot things, too?" asked Leila.

"Charlotte is an art history major," said Wilson.

"Oh."

"Might go to Rome," Charlotte heard herself say. Her school offered a semester abroad, not that she'd ever entertained the idea of going. She searched for something further to say that would impress Leila, but her mind went blank.

Leila canted her head to the side. "She's lovely," she said to Wilson.

Anger swept through Charlotte's body, and she began to shake a little. Charlotte considered Leila's age. She might be as old as thirty-two. Old enough and experienced enough to not be overcome with lust and fury and blurt out the first thing that came to mind.

And where was the public restroom? Charlotte didn't want to ask. It was embarrassing that she needed to go so often.

"Well, I better run along," said Leila. "I need to meet my rep."

Charlotte and Wilson continued to walk, Wilson just ahead of her, hands jammed in his pockets.

"Who is Leila?" Charlotte asked, even though from her bedroom window she'd studied this woman's every move for three years, from the way she carried her purse to the way she crossed her legs, because what Charlotte really meant was *Who is Leila to you?*

"My ex." Wilson said it with no more weight than if he had said *That is my coat,* or *That is my lunch.*

Wilson lit up a cigarette and she thought she would gag.

"She's my ex," Wilson added, "but I sometimes see her. As a friend."

"Go to hell," she said, immediately regretting it.

"Oh, Charlotte," Wilson said. He rubbed a small circle on her back. She was fast returning to her earthly body, which did not care for complexity. Charlotte kissed him in confusion, her desire and good sense colliding.

It was almost dusk. Scraps of laughter and conversation wafted through the air, which seemed unseasonably warm and dry. The leaves on the trees chafed against each other conspiratorially. A nurse crossed their path, pushing an old man in a wheelchair. He stared at them unabashedly, and it was clear how much he hungered for something he thought they possessed.

Charlotte looked at the man, and suddenly she felt seized by an awful clarity she'd worked hard to evade. There was so much for her to try to not know—that she was pregnant, that she suspected Wilson was a man who could never really be married. Charlotte knew there would always be women, none of them wives, some of them more important to him than others. It took incredible effort and will to not know these things, and beneath them lay the worst realization of all, the one she could no longer ignore—Wilson didn't love her as much as she loved him. He never would, and there was nothing she could do to change it. She might as well try to change the color of her eyes. Wilson would always have power over her, there would always be an aching deficit. And in that moment, Charlotte decided she would not tell him. She'd change her phone number and take a friend up on an offer to come to the Jersey Shore for the summer. She'd figure out what to do after that.

Wilson took her hand and led her into a stand of maple trees across from the bridle path. They were no more than fifteen feet from the trail, and Charlotte saw a teenager on a red bike whiz by. She simply lifted her skirt and leaned against a tree. In a fury, she kicked off one of her shoes. Dominion at all cost.

PART THREE

chapter eighteen
1995

The campus of Findley Academy entrapped decades worth of girls' secrets—girls who leaped across the quad with big, unsorted dreams of the future rolling around in their heads, girls who cried behind bushes and pillars that failed to hide them, and girl after girl after girl who stood before the gaping mouth of her coffin-like locker stuffed with schoolbooks, love letters, and messages to self, single words of hope and despair that read *now* or *never,* not to mention the girls who scrawled on the inside of their locker doors cryptic and nasty fuck-you symbols amid the detritus of makeup, packs of Marlboro Lights, the good-luck voo-doo doll lying on the tiny mattress of a half-eaten peanut butter sandwich, and jumbo spray cans of knockoff designer perfumes like the Opium impostor Ninja and an Obsession fake called Confess, which they applied on the sly, inexpertly, like bug spray. Too much!

And that was the thing about these girls, they were too much, even the quiet ones like Calla Fortuni, who kept an extracted tooth, a fang, really, in a velvet box inside her locker, each of them serving out their sentence, roaming the halls of Findley Academy loaded up with so much emotion they might as well have had explosives strapped to their backs. Girls were dangerous, and girls were good, and girls would never be this way again.

Viva had been hired at Findley Academy to teach modern dance to young women whose curious, ridiculous, wanton energy flew out of them at all the wrong angles. It seemed to her she was hired to help them tamp it down, batten the hatches, close their mental loopholes, and do whatever it is people do when they try to get young women to focus.

She'd been working at the school for almost six months. When Charlotte kicked her out Viva told her mother she'd return to New York. But in the end, she couldn't do it—New York now only represented the end of her performing career. So here she was in Los Angeles, only an hour and a half from Charlotte but far enough away to start over. Maybe Charlotte had done her a favor, forcing her to move on with her life. Viva told herself that at least her job was related to dance. But it was hard. Some of the dancers were only six or seven years younger, and the ambition of the best ones reminded her of herself not so long ago. Here she was in the prime of her dancing years, teaching a bunch of privileged kids who spent more on their dance bags than she'd ever spent on a year of dance clothes. Even if they were terrible dancers. And the worst part was that some of them felt their money would buy them a career. Their entitlement and her own despair were daily hurdles to overcome. Beyond that, there was something she hated to admit, since she was the teacher and not a student, but sometimes the girls made her nervous. Their alliances made her wary—the whispers, the laughter—and she would recall the Tituses' inside jokes and unfathomable rules.

Viva turned up the long driveway of Findley Academy. Today was the Great Shakeout, the yearly earthquake preparedness drill. More than 24 million people, including 9.5 million in California, had agreed to duck under their desks at 10:17 a.m. local time to drop, cover, and hold on. Planning for an unplanned event was not a simple matter, and some of the teachers at Findley Academy requested that the drill be changed to 7:25 a.m. so they could be done with the exercise before the school day began.

Maisie Lomax, the principal, declined the request, saying they needed to be in accordance with the State of California, and at the most recent school assembly, she distributed a pamphlet to all the girls, which cautioned them that in the event of a real earthquake they were to note if anyone went missing.

Calla, Viva's favorite student, raised her hand and said, "But what if I go missing?" Calla was very pale, and her long white-blond hair hung like limp curtains on either side of her face. When she angled her head, her features disappeared except for her nose. The first time Viva met her she was struck by her resemblance to a long-ago girl—Kate.

The principal said, "Stay where you are, and we'll find you."

"What if no one knows where that is?"

"Calla, please," said Mrs. Lomax. "There will be further instruction in the case of an actual earthquake."

Calla began to urgently bite her nails, every one of them, out of sequence, but neglecting none. Calla, who was a scholarship student, lived in a small green house near Findley Academy, and after school Viva often saw her walking her ancient mastiff, his heavy dog head just skimming the sidewalk. When a car or skateboarder passed by, the dog rumbled to life, barking at everyone and everything. Calla would shout "Ignore, ignore!" and it wasn't clear if the command was for the dog, herself, or perhaps the entire world—a directive indicating that there are things we must fail to consider if we want to get along in life.

It had been a year since the day Viva learned that her knee would never be the same again. *Ignore, ignore.* But despite her best efforts, she found it impossible to let go of what might have been.

Earlier that morning, Viva had received a phone message from Anastasia Bing. Anastasia was touring with the Pilar Broom Company and performing in Los Angeles for two nights. Did Viva want a comp? Anastasia the quick and powerful. Anastasia with the rickety ankles that seemed incapable of supporting the powerful machine that was her body.

A feeling came over Viva that was not unlike the first symptoms of a cold, recognizable and unwanted, something she would wish away if she could. Envy. If she hadn't hurt her leg, she might very well have auditioned and been accepted into the company herself. It was too painful to consider going. Viva deleted the message.

Viva could still teach. She did teach. She would become an even better teacher. And Viva took consolation in the fact that she covered her rent, supported herself, and not once had she relied on others for a place to live. She made a mental note to send a check to Charlotte. They hadn't spoken for a month after their showdown, but then one day Charlotte called, penitent and in a panic because she was going to get evicted. Viva bailed her out with her first paycheck. Since then, Charlotte seemed to be doing a little better and had a new job as a stock clerk at the drugstore.

Viva sped up the driveway, which, built in 1911, hunkered amid jacaranda trees that wagged back and forth in a rogue Santa Ana wind, recklessly showering the entire lawn with purple petals. Viva passed the carved Findley Academy sign and the reflecting pond in which the morning sun wobbled. She was late. Viva was never late, but this morning she was hungover.

Insomnia. It started the week she was hired at Findley Academy, and she'd begun to drink at night to help her sleep. It was a temporary measure, a medicinal measure, she told herself. But it was becoming a necessary measure. This would have been shocking to her a year ago, before her injury, when a disciplined lifestyle was second nature, when abstemiousness was a gift in itself—the purity and rigor. Viva planned to quit cold turkey at the first of the month. She'd seen enough alcoholic behavior to last a lifetime, and she didn't want to become her mother. Atop the school sat a cupola that featured two bay windows, which appeared like all-seeing eyes, and this morning they seemed to peer at her in judgment as she turned up the driveway of the school.

Findley Academy was an expensive school, highly rated, and yet the original structure had seen better days. But that, too, seemed part of the school's prestige. Its creaking, crooked, stained wooden floors presented a vague idea of old money that appealed to people in Southern California, where most of the "old" architecture wasn't more than a hundred years old.

The school espoused a teaching philosophy called Perimeters and Parameters, some of which was oddly progressive. If a girl needed a tampon, she simply shouted for it—in the middle of the lunchroom, in assembly, in the classroom, and yet she wasn't to clamor for one in the courtyard. That was an example of establishing a Perimeter. When Viva first started at the school and expressed her confusion to Sherry Stedman, the physics teacher, Sherry told Viva to just think of Perimeters and Parameters as Borders and Boundaries, to think of the Double P as the Double B, but that hadn't helped, either. Beyond that, and despite the school's seemingly liberal stance, there was an entire Findley-speak guidebook for Viva to memorize, one filled with antiquated formal jargon and high-minded mandates worthy of a British barrister.

Viva turned right at the quad and drove parallel to a blue glass–ceilinged hallway, which ran like a central vein within the white clapboard body of the school. Separating the junior and senior high schools, the hallway had been added in 1985, the gift of a distant cousin of Ethelette Findley, the founder of the school.

Viva saw Walter McKinley striding down the corridor, and though she waved as she drove by, he didn't see her. Walter McKinley, a passionate recycler and popular civics teacher at Findley Academy, possessed an easy confidence that spread to everyone in his vicinity like a most delightful flu. The fact that there were no male students at the school logarithmically increased his allure. Viva was flattered that he took an immediate interest in her when she was hired, and they'd started dating not long after. Viva was stricken to remember that she was supposed to meet him for dinner the previous night. But after a couple of drinks, she'd fallen asleep. She'd make it up to him tonight.

Viva pulled her Ford Falcon, a car she'd bought from an ad in the *Recycler* for a steal due to its Ajax-colored paint job, into her parking space. It wasn't much wider than a queen bed. Findley Academy was an exclusive school with a tiny parking lot, and parents didn't seem to mind the fact that they had to park at the bottom of the hill and hike up to attend choral events, recitals, and field hockey games. It required effort, and effort of any type was highly prized at Findley Academy. She cut the engine and the car made a strange gurgling noise. She needed to get that checked.

Viva ran up the steps of the school, passing a large piece of cardboard, a remnant from the science fair, jammed in a trash can that read:

What is going to happen is the carrot and fork are going to be balanced on the water glass. The carrot will start to roll off the glass because of gravity. The roundness of the carrot is no match for the cylinderness of the glass!

She pushed open the heavy oak school door and was immediately enveloped in 2 Live Crew's "Me So Horny," which blared from the school speakers. Each week a different student had the opportunity to be the school disc jockey. In support of the school's Parameters, the student DJs were allowed to play any kind of music they wished, and they did.

Maisie Lomax strode toward Viva, pretending to not hear the lyrics, her head canted to the left as if it was simply too full of thoughts and commitments. And certainly, the Great Shakeout. Her shoulders appeared stuck in a permanent shrug—a posture that said *If I don't do it, who will?* She swerved and stopped in front of Viva. "Ms. Devlin."

"Yes?" Maisie was inches from her face. Viva had meant to use some Visine before she came to work. She stepped back from the principal.

"I've received your monitor report and you need to sign your six-month review within ten days. Check your inbox."

All new teachers at Findley Academy were reviewed by the most senior teacher in their discipline. The school's dance program offered ballet, modern, jazz fusion, highland step dance, and tap, which was taught by none other than Greta Tinker, who had graduated from the academy twenty years ago. Viva thought back to Greta, standing stone-faced in the back of the dance studio the previous Friday, clipboard in hand. Viva had taught a good class but recalled losing her temper with one of the students. "Of course, I'll be sure to sign it," Viva replied.

Viva continued on and almost bumped into the school janitor, Zeke, sweeping the floor in broad, strong strokes. The way Zeke swept, he might have been harvesting a crop, and a small circle of sweat appeared on his back. It was rumored that he once had a young daughter who drowned in a pool, and it seemed particularly painful to Viva that he should work in a girls' school. One time, late on a Friday afternoon when she was the last teacher left in school, he offered her a beer, and they stood behind the school and drank it, sharing a cigarette.

"Viva, your mother called. She says it's urgent." Last month Zeke had offered to let Viva use the phone in his custodial closet, which was across the hall from the dance studio. But now Charlotte had taken to calling Viva there.

"Urgent? It always is. I'll tell her not to call that number. Sorry."

Two of Viva's students were draped around the dance studio door. There was Sienna Beckett, one of her strongest dancers, standing in passé, sucking on a piece of grapefruit leather. In her choreography, Sienna favored tight, thinky dances and was constantly palming hard-boiled eggs into her mouth to increase her protein levels.

Leaning on her shoulder was her deceptively demure younger sister, Nicole, who, the previous year, in a moment of fury almost shot a girl in archery class. Though fierce, Nicole made frequent, obvious displays of her gentleness, whispering her answers in class, slinking around corners, and, during study period, hunkering into a willow tree in the quad, where she wrote in her journal with a daffy feather-tipped pen, as if to make sure everyone knew she would cause them no harm. But she could. And they all knew it. Sienna and Nicole were both very thin, with long, beautiful arms made for dance. But they were particularly unkind to Calla, and Viva thought of them as the Skinny Meanies.

Sitting on the floor near Sienna and Nicole was Taylor Dale, who rolled her neck from side to side, breathing from her abdomen deeply and loudly as Viva had taught them. Beside her sat a small white bag inside of which there would be a blueberry muffin for Viva. Taylor smiled constantly and always volunteered to collect the dance props after class. But Taylor was uncoordinated and had a terrible time remembering combinations. Still, Viva accepted her into the group because of her pure, dogged will, which, if it were her only talent in life, would not be the worst thing.

Viva worked hard to locate something within each girl—a fierceness, or sorrow, or anger, and wake her up to the fact that she could use that energy as a vehicle. But then there were the girls who just wanted to get it right—the movements, the counts, and the combinations—while completely absenting themselves. They were girls who either didn't believe that they had an inside or didn't think it was a valuable task to locate it. What good was an inner life if no one could see it?

When Viva opened the door to the dance studio, she almost stepped on Madeline lying against a wall of dance bags and backpacks, an anatomy book on her chest.

"The groin is in the eye, right?" asked Madeline.

"What? No," said Viva. She motioned for her to get up.

"But the eyes are like the groin of the face," said Nicole.

"Sexcellent!" said Madeline. *Sexcellent* was a term they all used to describe everything but sex. Shoes were sexcellent, scones were sexcellent. Sex was crafty. Craftwork was oral sex, which they were all obsessed with learning or describing or pretending to have had or given. Except for Calla.

"Where's Calla?" asked Viva.

"Late again," offered Sienna, and Viva could see the pleasure this statement gave her. "If she's late again, she can't audition for the spring showcase," she added. And it was true, Viva had made the rule herself. These girls knew trouble and liked trouble, and they could spot a brewing conflict at fifty yards. Throughout the day grievances and impassioned requests were issued and retracted with alarming rapidity, like stocks the girls invested in, tracked, and cashed out, sometimes all in the same afternoon.

Then there was Calla, slapping down the hall in her loafers, which seemed two sizes too big. Her energy flew in all directions, and her long hair whipped every which way. More than once, Calla had accidentally tucked her hair into her pants, and that was one of the things Sienna and Nicole teased her about. Cruelty was a lozenge permanently lodged beneath their tongues, savored but never swallowed.

Calla rarely sat, and her body seemed to vibrate with a surfeit of tension. Her hands, long-fingered and delicate, shook when she became excited. But once she focused her energy, it was a thing to behold. She danced as if she was trying to rip open space. As Calla walked toward them, she traced a dance in the air with her finger. Viva had taught her this method, even though it wasn't useful for everyone.

Viva waved her in, and the girls fell silent. She demonstrated the first series of steps in a new combination, which started with a bold tipping move. She repeated the movement, then clapped it. "What is the beginning of this dance trying to do?" she asked them.

Taylor, as always, bowed her head and observed before committing to a single move. Nicole clapped faintly and just behind the beat of Viva's clapping. Calla stood completely still, but Viva could see something working its way through her like a slow-moving electrical charge.

Viva said, "This dance is an abstraction about what endures and what disappears." She continued with the next part of the combination—three steps backward, a turn to the side, then a quick revolution into a halting high contraction. Viva told them to imagine themselves standing on the edge of a cliff.

"As a performer, you need to create a situation from the inside," she said.

"The inside of what?" said Sienna.

"Yourselves!" Viva said. "We're displacing gravity," she added, "and I want you to think about the idea of space supporting you."

They nodded and considered, a couple of them tried it, and Nicole clicked her tongue, which indicated she was about to perform the move with her usual exacting surety.

Calla looked like a girl standing in a field just before a thunderstorm. She appeared lost and puzzled. Then she threw herself to the side so abruptly it seemed she'd fall to the floor, but she didn't. She held the position and looked at Viva for approval.

"Good, Calla, that's it," said Viva.

"Sexcellent," murmured Nicole, and this was a less common but no less impassioned usage of the word—as a denigration.

Viva shot Nicole a look. The girl turned away and rummaged through her dance bag for her pen and pretended to sketch the move. For all Viva knew, she could be tracing the trajectory of an arrow to Viva's heart.

She told the girls to practice and glanced at the clock. Already ten fifteen. Two minutes until the Great Shakeout, two minutes until a kind of terrible electric mooing would blare through the loudspeaker. Viva quickly poured herself a cup of tea and made a mental note to call Charlotte. Zeke had left a note on her door that she'd called twice since that morning.

Sun sliced through a large window above the piano and fell across the studio wall. It brightened and glowed, and all extraneous sound—basketballs smacking the outside court, feet shuffling in the classroom above them, the whoops and giggles and cries of girls echoing through the halls—all that fell away. Viva looked at her students, each of them completely absorbed in the task of learning this new dance, and beneath their sass and bluster, beneath their casual cruelty, beneath their desperate distaste of childhood, she could see in each of them, like a personal pilot light, their wonder.

chapter nineteen

Walter McKinley put Viva in mind of one of those Renaissance men, the young swain type, depicted in paintings leaning against a tree, eating an apple, or plucking a lute. Slouching against the doorway to her living room, he wore a pressed white shirt, pressed black pants, and expensive black leather flip-flops. He looked like he'd just taken a shower, and the tips of his curls were still wet. Viva stared at him.

"Can I come in?"

"Of course." Viva suddenly felt awkward. Walter was the first man she'd dated in Los Angeles after dating no one in Glenalbyn. During college she'd never had time for a real relationship. She had to focus on dance. There were a few dates with a mirthless abstract painter and a brief fling with a visiting dance teacher, but Viva felt she lagged behind most women her age when it came to relationships. Dating Walter was, in part, an effort to remedy the problem. That, and something she didn't like to admit—Walter came from wealth, and unlike Viva, he'd lived in one place his entire life. She was drawn to the idea of his upbringing, the predictability and ease of it, perhaps as much as to Walter himself. He sometimes reminded her of Anastasia, who also had grown up with privilege, the easy expectancy of good things on the horizon, and an unquestioning belief that one parlays one success into the next.

Walter walked into her living room, halting midway. He put his hands on his hips and peered at the Elsinore Hotel through her window.

Built in the 1930s, the Elsinore was a tall, narrow hotel covered in dark gray stucco. A squat turret arose from the right corner, its paint flaking off, revealing another, paler shade that in certain lights caused the stucco to resemble mottled elephant skin. When Viva's apartment manager showed her the apartment the first time, he told her a famous artist had overdosed at the Elsinore. A famous rock star, too. Not to mention the writer. It was that kind of hotel. Two medieval-style lamps hung from chains outside the entrance, which was built to look like a drawbridge. Viva loved the building's baronial appearance, its just-this-side-of-grim demeanor, which contrasted sharply with the candy-colored more popular hotels that flanked it on either side.

"That place gives me the creeps," said Walter.

"I think it has character," said Viva.

"Oh, that it does," said Walter.

Viva's phone rang, and looking at her caller ID, she saw Charlotte's number, one that in its skinny arrangement of ones and sevens, numbers with no real meat on them, seemed to describe Charlotte's physicality and loneliness.

She could picture her mother at her kitchen table, coffee in hand, Eddie at her feet.

"Hello?"

"I need to talk to you about something," said Charlotte.

"Can it wait?" Viva rubbed her neck and waited for Charlotte's response. She'd slept poorly the night before and her entire upper back was stiff.

"No," said Charlotte. "It can't."

"Okay, I've only got a minute, but go ahead."

"Are you with Scooter?" Charlotte knew his name. She'd met him briefly and declared him a milquetoast.

"Yes, and I can't talk for long."

Walter checked his watch and frowned.

"Mother?" said Viva. "Mother?" The phone had dropped out. Or Charlotte hung up. Viva called her back twice but got a busy signal.

It was Easter, and they were going to Walter's family home in Tustin. Viva slung her purse over her shoulder and picked up the hos-tess gift for Walter's mother, a bowl she'd recently bought at a farmers market. She'd heard about Walter's previous girlfriend, Phillipa—how she and Walter's mother had gotten along so well it took Walter an extra year to break up with her. Viva had spent too much time shopping for the hostess gift, a present that in her imagination would never compare with the one Phillipa would have selected.

"And away we go!" said Walter, clapping his hands. His enthusiasm, the effects of which were legion at Findley Academy, suddenly seemed outsized to Viva within the confines of her apartment.

As they cut through the courtyard of her building, which featured Moorish arches, terra-cotta tiles, and a grand but non-working fountain, Viva saw her neighbor Lukania Moravec, who lived in one of the coveted rent-controlled apartments, standing before his open window. Smoking a cigarette, he stared at her in a strangely intimate way, as if he knew something deeply personal about her.

Luka had the physical bearing of a fairy-tale woodchopper— slow-moving, impassive, his shoulders straining against his suit jacket, which he never appeared to remove except perhaps when he went to sleep. When he wasn't working as a driver, he parked his limo in front of the apartment building, and even though it took up two spaces, most tenants didn't seem to mind, since it gave the impression that a celebrity was being picked up or dropped off.

The day Viva moved into the building, she'd struggled through the courtyard with an antique mirror. Luka, who appeared to be coming home from a shift, helped her carry the mirror into her apartment, where he set it on the floor in the corner of her living room. When she passed before it, she could see only her feet and calves. No knees. Viva preferred it that way. She meant to hang the mirror; she meant to hang it any day.

Luka continued to look at Viva and lifted his chin a fraction of an inch in greeting.

"Friend of yours?" asked Walter.

"Him?" said Viva. "No." But as they walked away, she turned to look at him and saw Luka still gazing at her.

As they neared their destination, Walter became increasingly agitated. His right eyebrow, which he often lifted in bemusement as he strolled the halls of Findley Academy, reached toward his left in mutual consternation. He began to whistle, a tuneless, blatantly reactionless, anti-whistle of sorts that mysteriously bloomed in his mouth when he was in the throes of stage-one distress. Was it possible that he was anxious about visiting his family? Viva worried that it might have something to do with her, but before she could ask, Walter pulled into the driveway of his childhood home. Bird-of-paradise flowers, nestless and eggless, savage in their pointy-headedness, clustered around a large bay window through which Viva could see Walter's family peering out.

"Shall we?" said Walter. He was sweating a little above his lip.

Viva stepped out of his car into bright sunlight and immediately realized the long flowered dress she wore must be see-through in this light. She'd meant to wear a slip. Awkwardly, she tried to walk with her palms covering her thighs as they strode up the front walk between two rows of Easter lilies captured in gold pots, their medicinal fragrance potent and cloying.

Alexa, Walter's sister, threw open the front door. Wearing chunky gold earrings that tugged at her earlobes and a matching cuff bracelet, she firmly clutched Viva's wrist like a holiday gladiator. She introduced her husband, Mr. Jim, and waved them in.

Behind her, Viva didn't notice Walter slip out of his flip-flops, and as she stepped into the house and onto lush wall-to-wall cream-colored carpeting, she saw before her cream-colored walls, a cream-colored baby grand, and a cream-colored sofa that resembled an enormous sunken meringue.

"No shoes! Please!" said Alexa.

"Oh, of course," said Viva. She quickly untied her espadrilles and couldn't help but feel that not only was she leaving her shoes in the foyer but something essential to her ability to navigate the afternoon. A familiar queasiness overtook her as she remembered trying to divine senseless family customs and rituals—the first order of business for a professional guest. Sheila Titus kept a cabinet full of expensive hand towels no one could use, especially not guests. Then there was the three-sheet-maximum toilet paper rule, the silent Sundays, no phone after five. As a child, Viva prided herself on being quick to please and blend into the situation at hand, but now her knee-jerk accommodation response felt like a personal betrayal. But not enough to keep her shoes on. She carefully set her espadrilles next to Walter's flip-flops.

Evie, Walter's mother, swooped into the room, clementine crepe swirling around her hips. She hugged Viva warmly, then grasped her shoulders, and said, "Just look at you!" Though she smiled, Viva thought she could see Evie remorsefully superimpose the legendary Phillipa's face upon her own.

Walter palmed a pale yellow Easter egg into Viva's skirt pocket, where it poked out like a weak, misshapen sun. They were hidden behind the chimney of his parents' house where no one could see them, though they could hear everyone racing around the backyard, particularly Alexa, who yelped over every egg she discovered.

It was clear to Viva that the Easter eggs had been hidden in the same places since Walter and his sister were children, and when Walter's mother shouted, "Begin the hunt!" Viva panicked. Across the yard, she'd watched Walter easily retrieve eggs from a coiled garden hose, an empty terra-cotta pot, a hole in a stump.

Seated in a lawn chair, Walter's father, Thomas, made a motion with his hand that seemed to indicate there would be plenty of eggs to find if only Viva would venture farther into the yard. At least he was trying to be helpful. When Viva first met Walter, he described his close relationship with his father, and she felt a familiar inner drop, a sinking feeling of inadequacy. In a rush of envy, she told him her own father had been a lawyer who died of a stroke.

The clammy spring heat and wafting wrist corsage that Walter gave Viva earlier that day, a lather of pastel ribbons embroiling two gardenias, was contributing to her disorientation. That and the fact she'd already drunk two mimosas. It was past noon, and they'd yet to be offered any food.

Walter was whistling again. He rubbed a lavender egg against his shirt as if to polish it, then he turned Viva's palm upward and placed it in her hand. "Two is more realistic."

Evie called everyone to lunch. They stepped out from behind the chimney, and as they turned the corner of the house and crossed the lawn, Viva held the lavender egg aloft in her left hand, the pale yellow in her right. But really the jig was up, everyone witnessed her not find a single one. Miserably, Viva thought of her mother's words — *We're not joiners and we never will be.*

A buffet table cloaked in a white linen tablecloth appeared to strain beneath the multitude of food placed upon it. There was a ham, a chicken, salmon, a plate of cold cuts, a platter of cheeses, two bowls of pasta, two kinds of bread, deviled eggs, green salad, bean salad, and one that involved seafood. A silver tower, displaying olives and nutmeats. A tray of miniature quiches. In the center of the table, a jumble of paper bunnies and ducks stared pop-eyed at this great abundance. Place cards stuck in tiny china eggs ringed the table. Viva was so hungry she almost swooned.

Walter's sister and brother-in-law joined them and took their designated seats. Evie stood at the head of the table, hands gripping a folding chair.

"Walt," Evie said, indicating that he should sit next to her. When she pronounced his name, it sounded like *walled*, and it seemed to Viva that the exuberant Walter she knew from school was rapidly vanishing.

As she sat before a place card marked *Vera*, she remembered she'd left her hostess gift in Walter's car. He left to fetch it, and as Walter walked away, she noticed two round spots of sweat appear on the back of his shirt like beseeching eyes.

Thomas, who sat not at the other head of the table but to the side of his wife, sliced a single piece of ham and chewed it contentedly. For a moment, Viva flashed on her mother flying down a grocery store aisle. Only Charlotte could nick a ham like it was a pack of gum. Viva smiled at Thomas, and he looked at her carefully. Walter had told her his father was a heart surgeon, and he possessed a certain precision in his movements, a stillness that made it easy for Viva to imagine him before an operating table. His eyes were an odd flat blue, the shade of lake water when a cloud passes over it.

"So, you're a dancer," Thomas said.

"*Was* a dancer. I teach dance now."

Viva poured herself another mimosa and drank half of it. She was so famished she was fairly shaking. She took a helping of salad and a slice of chicken, and as she reached across the table for the miniature quiche tower, Alexa pushed it toward her with both hands like a big pile of poker chips.

"Dance for us," said Thomas. He put down his fork and knife.

Was he kidding? Did he want her to prove she knew what she was doing? Viva felt a kind of bemused antagonism ping around the table. She scanned the yard for Walter but there was no sign of him. The crick in her neck, which had only worsened since this morning, suddenly leaped to her left shoulder blade. The family stared at her, and she felt the ghost of Phillipa hover. What would Phillipa, the best girlfriend in the world, do? Perspiration streaked down the inside of Viva's arm.

"I'd like to see a dance," said Alexa.

"Right now?" said Viva.

"Yes," said Mr. Jim. He smiled ruefully and devoured an entire deviled egg in a single bite.

Viva took a gulp of her mimosa. "All right," she said, willing her neck and shoulder to relax. Viva rose and stepped to the side of the table. A sharp pain swiftly pinballed from her ankle to her knee, a pain that had begun not long after her surgery. But Viva would get through this moment.

Alexa began to hum an odd, insistent melody. Was this meant to be her musical accompaniment? Viva scanned the yard for something she could use to spot. She saw what appeared to be a pink ball in the crook of a sycamore tree. She squinted. Not a ball, an egg. An egg that not even those in the know had discovered. This fact gave her a small burst of fortitude, and squinting, she lifted her right arm in a wide scooping motion.

"What are you doing?" said Walter, tapping on her shoulder. Tapping. Just as she'd seen him once do with a student who threw a Twinkie wrapper on the ground. It wasn't until this moment that she realized how much she hated that tapping.

Clutching Viva's hostess gift to his chest, Walter looked miserable and confused. He reeked of weed. He leaned in to Viva and whispered, "Are you drunk?"

"They *asked* for a dance!" she said, and looked to Walter's family for confirmation. No reaction.

Awkwardly, Viva and Walter sat down, and he poured her a large glass of water.

"For you, Evie," Viva said, handing her the present.

Evie passed the package to Thomas, who withdrew a pocketknife from his jacket and sliced it open in one swift move. Viva thought of him cutting open a chest with equal ease and enthusiasm and unabashedly staring at a person's most private heart.

Evie picked up the bowl and inspected it. Viva noticed a rough patch on the side of the pottery just as she was sure Evie saw it, too.

"It's high-fired with a raku glaze," said Viva.

"At the grocery store," said Evie, "they were giving away similar bowls with the purchase of ham." She laughed. "Of course, this isn't the same bowl."

At her side, Walter carefully folded, unfolded, and refolded his linen napkin.

"Excuse me," said Viva.

Viva fled to the house. She opened the back door, grabbed another mimosa off the kitchen counter, and walked straight into the living room, forgoing the oversize cream-colored sofa covered in adamant family butt prints. She perched on a narrow piano bench and reached for the phone on the end table.

Charlotte picked up without saying hello and before Viva even heard it ring. This happened often, though neither of them ever mentioned it.

"Mom, what did you want to tell me this morning?"

"Listen, Viva, they shot my Eddie."

"Who? Who shot Eddie?"

"The police. He attacked the Gillettes' terrier."

"For heaven's sake, why did they have to shoot him?"

"For his nature, I suppose."

Charlotte sighed, and all Viva could think of was how ridiculously proud Charlotte was of the fact that Eddie could catch flies in his mouth.

"It's a dark day, Viva, a dark day."

Viva stood and looked out the living room window past the cluster of bright orange bird-of-paradise that in the late-afternoon sun appeared to ignite. Beyond them, she could see Walter and his family. Something had happened since she'd left the table, a kind of energetic reconfiguration, and she couldn't help but feel that it had to do with her departure. Alexa put a napkin on her head, and they howled.

"Are you still there, Mother?" Viva heard Charlotte smoking.

"Listen, there's another problem."

"What?"

"I'd rather talk about it in person."

"Can you give me a hint?"

"No," Charlotte said. "Have fun with Scooter and the bourgeoisie. Happy Easter, and don't forget I'm the one who hatched you."

"Wait—" said Viva. But Charlotte had hung up.

Through the window Viva watched Walter and his family head out for a walk. Were they not even going to wait for her? Viva considered how much it would cost to take a taxi from Orange County to Glenalbyn. A lot.

chapter twenty

The crickets were back, and the news was bad. The first thing seemed to signal the other if one were to look for signs. Earlier that morning the sun lay on the horizon like an egg that didn't break right, and all day it had threatened to rain. Blown by wild winds, bougainvillea piled up outside Charlotte's front door—a snowdrift of pink petals. She kicked at them with her blue rain boot, and two crickets sprang from the pile.

Charlotte let herself into the house and, out of habit, looked for Eddie. But of course he was gone. She'd buried him early that morning near a little stream that bordered her property. It wasn't legal in Glenalbyn, but she didn't care.

Charlotte picked up the remote, turned on the television, and cranked up the volume. Her head was hot with music. If only she could unscrew it and dunk it in a pail of cold water. After disappearing again for almost half a year, the music was back, and this time it was relentless. She knew she should see a doctor, but what if they told her she was just imagining it? What if she was just imagining it? When she was a girl, she'd gone to doctor's appointments for two years straight after she broke her jaw—enough to last a lifetime. She was afraid of doctors then and still was. She didn't think anyone in her family had ever experienced something like this, but she had no way to check. Her sister, Ardel, being a Christian Scientist, never went to doctors. In the last five years of her life, she prayed her way through arthritis, pneumonia, shingles, the West Nile virus, and then simply died one day while taking a nap.

It was becoming impossible for Charlotte to concentrate. At least her most recent part-time job, addressing envelopes for Save the Whales, didn't require her to make contact with other people. Sometimes, in an effort to appease this strange and frightening condition, Charlotte sang along with whatever symphony or pop song or jingle appeared on the crazy set list in her brain. But nothing made it abate. If she drank, the musical hallucinations became insidious and unending. If she blasted her television to drown it out, it worked for only a few minutes. She'd tried massive doses of bee venom. She'd tried massive doses of vitamin C. She'd paid the Wiccan down the road fifty bucks for a health spell. No dice. The music box in her head went where she went.

Charlotte heard thunder (a real sound!) and it began to rain. Viva would be here soon, and she needed to tidy up. Due to the constant musical distraction, she hadn't been able to keep up with cleaning. Charlotte would wash her kitchen floor. Hurriedly, she gathered her supplies, and kneeling on the terra-cotta tiles, she sprayed white vinegar on the grout. She poured baking soda atop it and watched as a frothy stream ran between the tiles. Charlotte began to scrub the grout inch by inch with a toothbrush, and it gave her a strange seething satisfaction.

On this afternoon's musical menu, she heard bits and pieces of a jingle from her childhood—a gum commercial. The local radio station played it constantly the spring when she broke her jaw, a mocking song, it seemed, given that her mouth was wired shut. She'd hated it then and she hated it now. It began, *Hey, kids, whaddya say?* The melody continued, but the lyrics were jumbled. Something about chewing your pain away. What was the gum called? Big Mouth? Mouth Full? Big Stuck? The words *Whaddya say? Whaddya say?* circled around in her brain.

Charlotte sat back on her haunches and wiped the perspiration from her brow. As if she'd flipped an invisible dial, the music quickly changed to a Fred Neil song and Charlotte remembered Wilson and her dancing in a park. They had once danced in a park, hadn't they? Or did that not happen? Memory was incredibly efficient at being inefficient. A car door slammed. Someone was coming up her driveway. Through her kitchen window, she saw a red umbrella. Then a face. Viva. She walked with determination, clearly preoccupied. Something in the way she held her head—the bend of her neck, the deep concentration—reminded her of Wilson. In her increasingly rare occasions of silence, ones in which Charlotte almost stopped breathing for fear the music would start again, she'd begun to hear a different kind of radio station—regret—and in those moments she thought she should have told him.

———

Viva was late. And it was Anastasia's fault. Or it seemed that way. This morning, as she was about to run out the door the phone rang. It was Anastasia, who wondered why she hadn't returned her message about the upcoming performance. Anastasia, whose feathery voice, so perfect for a dancer, became hushed when she told Viva she was concerned. *Given your injury. Given what you must be going through.* She paused. *But* you *are a survivor.* In an effort to cut the call short and not feel worse than she already did, Viva told her she'd attend. And even bring a guest.

Viva rushed up the driveway past Charlotte's old VW. It still ran, if not especially well. The passenger-side mirror was duct-taped to the van, and the right door was pitted in a way that brought to mind acne scars. Still, people offered to buy it with surprising frequency. Viva caught sight of her image in the fractured side mirror—she looked exhausted. She hadn't slept well the previous night. Walter had insisted on driving her home, as if to prove that he wasn't the type of guy who would abandon his own date. Even though he had. Though she hated to admit it, she was glad her mother needed her.

Viva knocked on the door and waited, standing next to Charlotte's near-life-size Kuan Yin. Kuan Yin, goddess of mercy and compassion, whom Charlotte once said heard the "inner sounds of the world," the secret sounds of people silently yearning. Viva cradled a bouquet in her arm, one she'd picked up to commemorate dear old Eddie. She could tell Charlotte was heartbroken, but beyond the loss of her dog husband, Charlotte had sounded frightened. Viva was frustrated that she wouldn't tell her what the problem was on the phone. She thought that maybe Charlotte was in serious financial straits. Anticipating this, she'd brought her checkbook.

She knocked again. No response. Viva opened the front door and stepped into the living room. Her mother was in the kitchen, scrubbing the floor in her raincoat. The TV was blaring.

"Hello? Charlotte? I brought you some flowers."

Her mother continued scrubbing.

"Your favorite—lavender roses."

Charlotte appeared in the doorway, drying her hands on a pot-holder. She'd lost some weight in the past year and stopped cutting her hair, which, undone, almost reached her waist. Most days she wore it in an imperious, high chignon. Occasionally, people in town mistook her for a former model or a retired priestess. Charlotte was still beautiful, still tough, as if part of her essential being was not human blood and tissue but something inert and inviolable, like wrought iron.

"Would you like to take off your coat, Mother?"

"If I wanted to, I would have."

Viva set the bouquet on the coffee table. She knew Charlotte wouldn't put them in water until she left and would save them for weeks until they dried, at which time she'd put them in a drawer with the other bouquets that Viva had bought her.

Viva turned off the television, removed some of the books and magazines stacked on Charlotte's sofa, and gingerly sat down.

"I'm so sorry about Eddie," said Viva. "I know how much you loved him."

"He was a very good boy," Charlotte said. She grabbed his leash off the wall and threw it into the closet. "The goddamn Gillettes didn't need to call the police on poor Eddie. And that cop didn't need to shoot him. They're so desperate for action up here, they killed my dog! Fuck!" Charlotte flung herself on the sofa and sighed. "Now look, Viva, there's something I want to talk to you about."

"What is it?"

Charlotte squeezed Viva's hand, and Viva noticed the line of freckles that ran across her right hand had multiplied into entire galaxies.

"That thing is back and it's much worse."

"What thing?"

"The music. I feel like my head is strapped to a fucking radio."

"What music? What are you talking about?"

"I get these songs in my head, sometimes whole songs, sometimes pieces. I can't think. I can't sleep. It's driving me crazy."

"How long has it been going on?"

"It feels like forever—it comes and goes, but it's been hard-core the past few weeks."

"Why didn't you tell me before?"

Charlotte slumped in her chair and grimaced. She looked up at her daughter, and Viva saw anguish and helplessness in her eyes.

Viva grabbed the phone book off the coffee table. "What's the name of that hospital in Palm Springs?"

"No!" said Charlotte. "You're not calling anyone. I'll take care of it."

"How will you take care of it?"

Charlotte put her hand to the side of her head and frowned. "This stupid gum commercial. Why can't I make this stop?"

"You have to promise me you'll call a doctor. *Tomorrow*."

"I'll make an appointment, I promise."

Viva stood up and went into the kitchen. She would make Charlotte a cup of cinnamon tea, her favorite beverage since she'd at last given up clove cigarettes, or so she said. Viva thought she smelled them on her. Viva put the kettle on to boil and looked around Charlotte's kitchen, at the jumble of canned vegetables on the counter, discount brands of dish soap and milk, boxes of crackers half-opened. She had a bad feeling about this mysterious illness. And if her mother needed serious help, who would take care of her but Viva? She quickly pulled an airplane bottle of Smirnoff from her purse. Didn't open it. Was she becoming her mother? Impossible to consider. Viva drank the bottle and threw it into her purse. She'd extend her quit date out another week.

Viva brought Charlotte her tea and blew on it for her. "I'm not an invalid!"

"Sorry."

"How was your big date with Scooter?"

"Awful. We're done."

"I could have told you that was in the cards." Charlotte rubbed her temples and frowned.

"How's that?"

"He's not your kind."

"And what kind is that?"

"People who put on airs. He's just like Anastasia, and I don't know what you saw in her, either."

"You didn't really know her."

"She's a phony. We don't like phonies."

"We're not the same person, Mother."

"You like phonies?"

Viva knew that Charlotte was picking a fight because she didn't want her to leave but was incapable of asking her to stay. She did this every time.

An hour later, the sun had disappeared over the hill, and Charlotte's living room was becoming chilly. They'd just finished dinner and Viva grabbed an old *Glenalbyn Gazette* to start a fire in Charlotte's potbelly stove. "I could sleep over tonight. We'll call the doctor first thing tomorrow morning."

"You're going to hit traffic if you don't get on the road."

"Will you promise me you'll call?"

"I promise," said Charlotte. "I'm very tired. And don't frown, Viva," she added. "You're just like your father, the muller. Always mulling." Charlotte sighed and closed her eyes.

Viva knew better than to bite. The Great Man of Mystery had been mentioned and it was duly noted. Sometimes Charlotte didn't mention him for a long time, and sometimes she went on jags where she mentioned him frequently and casually, as if he'd just walked out of the room. Years ago, she'd told Viva she thought he'd been dead for some time.

Viva tucked a quilt around her mother's slender body and walked around the cabin, checking that Charlotte's windows were locked. Then she stood there for a moment, listening to her mother breathe. Charlotte sometimes cried in her sleep and even laughed, although Viva knew she wasn't asleep at all. Charlotte wasn't big on goodbyes.

As Viva pulled her car out of Charlotte's driveway, she narrowly missed a pine tree that stuck out into the narrow passageway. Its branches brushed her car as she slowly backed up, past the gleaming, eerily smiling Kuan Yin, past Charlotte's padlocked mailbox, where Viva paused and looked up to see Charlotte standing motionless in her darkened bedroom window, watching Viva leave as she always did.

———————

Charlotte saw Viva's headlights bounce up and across the shrubbery in front of her house as she backed out of the driveway. Her daughter began to drive away but then stopped. Was she coming back? No. Charlotte felt a familiar stab of loneliness.

She sat down at her desk, and even though it was a cold night Charlotte opened the window. She needed to stay sharp. Charlotte pulled a piece of paper out of the drawer and picked up a pencil. She never did like to write in pen. She hated her own penmanship—the fierce slashing quality of her words like exit wounds on the paper, the superloopy *m*'s and the *t*'s crossed not precisely but too far to the right.

Dear Wilson,

Many times I've almost written you. After a while, it seemed too late. Time is a bitch.

I hope your life turned out the way you wanted. You once said I was a dame who'd flourish with time, but age has not brought me wisdom. Age has brought me Tom Jones belting "Delilah" in my brain until I think my head will explode. And that's between gum commercials. On a good day. But that's not why I'm writing you.

I remember waiting for you in your apartment one long-ago August. It was so hot, but I would have waited all day for you. I didn't become pregnant then—it wasn't until two weeks later—though, in my mind, it was that day. I've never used up this memory, no matter how many times I've relived it.

Those were shaky years, and more times than one fear has almost sunk me. Sorry I ran. Wasn't sure you'd ever be all in. Sorry I

Charlotte stopped and stared at the piece of paper. Would this make any sense to him? She needed to get to the point: daughter, twenty-six, Viva. A phone number.

Charlotte felt a kind of inner jolt. It was not unlike the feeling one might have the moment before sleep. That feeling as if you've put out your foot, but where oh where is the step? The music in her mind started up and she could barely think straight. Charlotte was suffocating in sound. Abruptly, she finished the letter and signed her name, the last few letters trailing off, wispy and exhausted.

chapter twenty-one

Viva was late for school. Again. Her Falcon wouldn't start, she needed to find a ride to work, and if she didn't get her car towed in fifteen minutes, she'd be hit with a street-cleaning ticket.

Yesterday, Viva had taken her mother to the doctor—not willingly. At the last minute, Charlotte insisted she didn't need medical help, that she wanted to try a healer. Certainly, Glenalbyn was crawling with healers. But Viva talked her out of it, and by the time they got to the appointment, Charlotte was already trying to silence a phantom bout of Muzak. Viva stayed to make her dinner, and by the time she returned home it was almost midnight. Her old car, after valiantly making the four-hour round trip, refused to even turn over.

Viva would take a taxi to school. She'd have to eat the ticket. Viva grabbed her dance bag, locked the car, and spun around, colliding with her neighbor Luka. Just minutes ago, she'd seen him ease into an impossibly small parking space behind her, his limo gleaming like some aquatic creature.

"Trouble?" he asked.

Viva told him she'd just had a tune-up, but when she turned the key it didn't click. Luka didn't look at her. Instead, he looked at the car as though it might tell its own side of the story. He popped open the hood with ease, even though it had a tricky release gizmo that gave most mechanics pause. He stared into the guts of Viva's car without judgment and with a kind of reverence. Viva stepped aside to give him room to work. He smelled like sex. Also, oranges. His girlfriend, Dusty, was always walking their dog, a partially blind, ancient poodle that listed down the street on long legs, shaking her curly head like she was dispirited by the world. Dusty could be heard coaxing her along, and she constantly ate oranges, happy to tell everyone in the building that it wasn't because of the vitamin C, even though nine out of ten people might think that—it was because oranges were natural antidepressants.

After ten minutes of peering into Viva's car and fiddling with things, Luka extracted himself from beneath the hood. "Try it now." And that was the single time he looked directly at Viva. A rush went through her. Luka's eyes were dark gray, like the underside of a rock, and he had an impenetrable gaze that indicated he'd just about seen it all.

Luka slammed her hood. Her car started on the first try. Luka nodded and walked away. He hadn't even said goodbye.

Calla Fortuni didn't seem to care that the girls were watching, and the girls were judging—girls whose lips were sticky with pomegranate lip gloss, or Vaseline, or coconut oil, or in the case of Nicole Beckett, rimmed red with Robitussin, the magical red elixir she slurped when she thought no one was watching.

This month some of Viva's students had gone on a mirror fast—no looking at themselves. And yet, during the warm-up, the girls canted this way and that, taking secret peeks at slivers of neck, and thigh, and calf. They preened and scrutinized, and with merciless precision made final appraisals of their strengths and deficits. Sometimes a girl would plunk to the floor, cry, and shake, and be done with it. Some, like Sienna, favored postponed punishment—the dinner of two raisins followed by three hundred sit-ups. Some, like Nicole, who squinted at her square torso, reacted as if to an unexpected death, a death of hope made audible in gasps, sighs, and indelicate grunts, which escaped her viscous lips.

Today, they were doing a workshop on extemporaneous dance, and Viva told the girls to find something they wished to be rid of, to put it in a part of their body and then release it. Calla spiraled across the dance studio floor, and there might as well have been flames shooting from her head. She came to an abrupt stop, and Viva could see her try to express something, something that seemed stuck within her. Then she began again, cutting across the floor in a zigzag pattern as if the floor was tilting, as if the ship was going down.

Silence in the studio. The girls were watching and the girls were judging.

Calla reversed her direction and leaped past the group clustered by the barre—Sienna, her sister, Nicole, who lurked behind her, pointy chin resting on Sienna's bare shoulder, and Madeline, who stood en pointe, always en pointe, if possible, because she preferred ballet to modern and because she could, despite frequent and false laments about her "banana feet."

Nicole furtively pecked at her top lip with her tongue, disappearing one last bloodlike drop of cough syrup. The three didn't flinch as Calla leaped close to them, and bemused reprobation emanated from them like a vapor that traveled across the studio floor, enveloping Madeline, who lit up with a fake, moony smile. The effort with which they didn't acknowledge Calla's talent was fierce, pure, and more powerful than anything they exhibited in their own choreography.

Taylor Dale, who wished to be Viva's favorite but wasn't, sat by herself in a chair across the room. Knees bouncing, legs shaking, her entire body vibrated like an idling car. She brought the back of her wrist to her nose and inhaled deeply.

It was frog dissection week in Biology II class, and the new biology teacher, Phil Dykstra, allowed them to daub their wrists with Vicks VapoRub to stave off the stench of formaldehyde. Wrists slick with ointment, the girls sniffed and snorted the mentholatum not only in bio class but as a general gesture of protest, indicating that Findley Academy with its gauche aromas of cafeteria goulash and wintergreen air-freshener strips secreted above the bathroom doorways offended their delicate sensibilities.

Calla tipped on one leg and snatched at the air, greedily grabbing handfuls, and this was the thing about Calla, there was something rapacious in her movement and abandon. She executed a final jump, landed, and stretched out her arms, execution-style. She had a far-away look in her eyes, as if she had completely left the confines of her physical body.

"Look at her shitty line," murmured Sienna.

Calla's extended arms concluded in fingertips that reached awkwardly skyward.

"Relax your hands," said Viva.

"Please," said Nicole.

"There are no straight lines in nature," said Viva, shooting a look at Nicole. It was true her line needed improvement. But it was also true that her talent ran deep, and it wasn't true the girls didn't know it. As she looked at Nicole, her features blurred a little bit. Viva grabbed a Coke and took a swig. She was still hungover from the previous night, though she would fight not to show it. Being hungover at school was different from being hungover anywhere else. It engendered in her a feeling of weightlessness and an increase in her patience toward the girls. That is, if you didn't count the shame. She had extended her quit date to the fifteenth of the month.

"Don't hold your breath when you leap. Stay up until you *must* come down. Do you understand what I mean, Calla?"

Calla nodded and waited for her further comments. She always wanted more critiques. Viva had been the same way. Anastasia, too. It was the mark of a good dancer. Viva thought back to her phone conversation with Anastasia the previous week. Why had she agreed to attend her show? Today in the teachers' break room Viva had picked up the newspaper and seen an article about the Pilar Broom Company, featuring a photo of Anastasia. She looked luminous, and her features, always lovely, had shifted somehow. Staring straight into the camera, there was no trace of the girl who needed to take beta-blockers before she performed. She had crossed a threshold, one that Viva would never be able to approach. Worse, Viva couldn't say Anastasia didn't deserve her success.

Calla tried the leap again, and this time she flung her arms above her head, revealing large sweat marks under her arms. Sienna giggled, then her sister joined her. They both made a show of containing their laughter, only to have it overtake them again.

Madeline and Sienna had complained to Viva the previous week that Calla needed to use deodorant, that it compromised their creative concentration. The next day Sienna thrust a Neiman Marcus bag filled with Dial extra-strong deodorant soap into Calla's hands as she stood by her locker.

Calla didn't look in the bag. Calla had been given bags before. The bag of worms in first grade and the bag of worse in fifth.

Viva clapped her hands and shot a look at Nicole and Sienna. "Quiet." She turned to Calla. "That was better. I want everyone to pair off and try the combination we learned yesterday. I'll be right back."

Viva walked to the rear of the studio, retrieved her dance bag from her closet. She pulled out her thermos and poured a cup of orange juice mixed with vodka. She drank it quickly—her back wasn't turned for more than a few minutes. But the instant she turned around and joined the girls, she became aware of something silent, something riotous that slithered through the air and whipped around the room like an invisible electrified snake. And yet, no one had moved. But something was humming within these girls, something that said *get her get her get her get her get her.*

There they stood, staring at Calla, each one holding her wrist to her nose.

"Rank," said Nicole, grimacing.

Calla stood very still, arms limp at her sides, face mottled except for a patch of angry white skin where she clenched her jaw. The other dancers drew closer, eager to see what would happen next. Whispers rippled through the studio. A nervous cough. Calla and Nicole faced each other and the air seemed to thicken with anticipation. Viva stepped between them. "This kind of behavior has no place in dance class," she said. "If you want to be professional, act like it! Or we can stop right now." She looked around the room and glared at the girls. Her sense of forbearance had completely evaporated.

Nicole and Sienna swapped smirks. Calla stared straight ahead as if she were in a trance. Viva looked at her watch. Fifteen more minutes. Maybe she'd have them stand at attention until the bell rang. Nicole elbowed Sienna and they both looked at Calla. Sienna pretended to cough into her hand and snorted like a pig. An eruption of laugher.

"Sienna, what was that!?" Viva demanded.

"Nothing," said Sienna. She had just enough time to feign a look of innocence when suddenly Calla leaped from behind her, seized her slender freckled arm, and bit her wrist. There was a stunned silence before a horrifying shriek. "Oh my God," shouted Taylor, and she jumped back as if she might be next. Sienna was wailing, clutching her arm. The other girls quickly circled around her. Calla stood to the side in a daze. "Calla! Go to the principal's office," said Viva. "Taylor, run and get the nurse." Sienna dropped to the floor and locked eyes with Viva. She thrust her arm in the air, presenting the red bleeding bite to Viva, and in her eyes was a look of implication.

It was just after four when Viva was summoned to Principal Lomax's office. Calla had been there since one, waiting for the principal to return from a trustees' meeting. Viva quickly locked up the dance studio, and as she did, she worried that Sienna or one of the other girls had complained about her behavior, about her frequent disappearances from class. With a stab of regret, she recalled spilling her thermos in front of two of the girls.

On the door of the dance studio was a Post-it from Zeke that simply said *Mother*. She'd call her as soon as she got home. Charlotte hadn't seemed like herself at the doctor's appointment. She struggled to answer a couple of the doctor's questions, later telling Viva it wasn't because she didn't know the answers but because she couldn't concentrate. Earlier that week, she told Viva she'd run out of her house in an effort to escape the mad music, but of course it made no difference. Viva would call her as soon as she got home.

At the principal's office, Viva saw Calla sitting on the big antique oak settee, the hot seat, a Gothic-style chair featuring wide flat arms into which were carved ghoulish monkeys. Calla's toes just touched the floor. She hadn't been allowed to return to class for her shoes. Viva caught her eye and Calla brightened.

Maisie Lomax looked weary. The trustees were notoriously difficult to deal with—half of them were as old as Ethelette Findley would have been if Ethelette were still alive, and the other half were new-money types treated with great suspicion by those who'd served on the board for decades. The principal plopped her egg-plant-colored shoulder bag, a sad, misshapen thing, onto her desk. She didn't offer Viva a seat.

"Calla, we do not accept feral behavior at Findley Academy. We do not accept biting, spitting, or base emotional indulgences. We have a code of conduct. You yourself signed that code of conduct, and this is a breach of that contract. You will be suspended for ten school days, and you'll be required to re-sign your code of conduct upon your return." Principal Lomax sighed. "Calla, do you understand the reason for this disciplinary action?"

Ten days. Calla would miss auditions for the spring showcase.

Viva watched something surge through Calla's body, an anger that shot from her toes to her torso and slammed into her shoulders, which lifted in a brief, violent shrug before she murmured, "Yes."

Viva said, "The girls may have provoked Calla's behavior," and she chose her words carefully, since Findley Academy was big on self-control. The school espoused the idea that the actions of others, no matter how unkind, need not cause reactions—a behavioral mandate based on a kind of inverted karma.

Principal Lomax reached into her desk drawer for a glucose pill, which she lolled around in her mouth, clicking it back and forth between her teeth. "Explain," she said.

To explain it, Viva would have to say she lost control of her class. To explain it, she'd have to say she was hiding in the back of the room drinking a screwdriver at ten in the morning. Viva began to perspire.

"I bit Sienna because she had it coming," said Calla, grasping both arms of the wooden chair.

Maisie Lomax stared at Calla blankly. She licked her forefinger and swiped at a smudge of mascara beneath her eye. The expression on her face said that the hour of diminishing returns had arrived and that dealing with a biter was more than she could bear. "You need to write an incident report, Viva."

Findley Academy rules stipulated that if a student was placed on suspension, she needed to be picked up by a parent or guardian, as if a girl might walk out the door and keep right on walking, never to return.

Viva escorted Calla to the lobby, and they stood before the arched floor-to-ceiling window that overlooked the grounds of the academy. Viva glanced at the sky, which was a troubling Brillo-pad gray. A thunderstorm was predicted, a great rarity in Southern California.

"You see lightning before you hear thunder because light travels faster than sound," said Calla.

"You can't bite people, Calla."

"I know."

Calla absently rapped her knuckle against the window a single time, then shoved her hand into her jacket pocket.

"Your improvisation in class today was very strong."

Calla stared at the floor. "My line was bad."

"We'll work on it."

Calla nodded and squinted at an old car winding up the academy drive. In profile, Calla's countenance was both resigned and determined, and even standing completely still, Calla seemed to waver, as if she worked very hard to contain the emotional turbines that spun within her.

"What did you wish to be rid of, Calla?" said Viva.

"Myself," she said. A patch of red on Calla's cheek became a developing country.

They heard the rumble of a car engine, and Calla's older sister, Gwen, pulled up to the entrance in an old burgundy Cutlass Supreme. A high school girl who on occasion appeared at Calla's recitals, she had the dutiful and distant mien of a public servant who longed for retirement. Calla's younger brother, Maurice, jumped out of the car, clutching a Crown Royal bag full of marbles. He stood there and shouted her name.

Calla didn't move, and she didn't look at Viva when she said, "I want to be like you. I want to be you." Awkwardly, she clutched Viva's arm.

"Calla, would you like to go with me to a dance performance next month?" asked Viva. It would be good for Calla to see a dancer of Anastasia's caliber. Viva didn't admit to herself that she couldn't bear to go alone.

Calla frowned. "How much does it cost?"

"It's free."

"I have to ask my mother. When she gets back."

"Where is she?" Calla bit her lip. "Can you ask your sister instead?" Viva asked.

Gwen violently honked the horn, and Calla ran out of the school and down the granite steps, her long, tangled hair flying behind her. Outside of the dance studio, Calla seemed unremarkable and gangly, still childlike. It was almost impossible to square her talent with the girl who piled into the Cutlass and slouched in her seat as Gwen peeled down the driveway.

Viva headed to the teachers' parking lot, taking the shortcut through the blue glass–ceilinged hallway. At this hour, with no sun to illuminate it, the corridor was cold and full of shadows. She thought she heard laughter toward the far end, but she wasn't sure.

Viva flew around the corner and came upon Nicole and Madeline huddled together, sharing a cigarette. They immediately flew apart, and Nicole tried to hide it behind her back.

"Sorry, Ms. Devlin."

"Sorry." Madeline quickly folded her hands prayerlike in false obeisance.

"You know the rules," said Viva. "No smoking."

Nicole smirked. "What about drinking?"

Madeline stifled a laugh.

"What did you say?" asked Viva.

"Just kidding," said Nicole.

"Take it outside and extinguish it. Now. Or I'll need to write you up."

Viva followed the two girls through the exit door and watched as Madeline ground the cigarette beneath her heel. Quickly, they walked away from her, hands at their sides, and the fact that they didn't speak did nothing to hide their condemnation.

chapter twenty-two

Viva felt like her head was filled with electrical cobwebs, wafting and sparking—the start of a migraine. It began on the drive from work, and she couldn't wait to get home. Viva sank into her sofa without taking off her coat and thought about the news she and her mother received that morning. Charlotte had been diagnosed with something called musical ear syndrome. The neurologist said it was very rare and that it might be caused by a lesion on the brain. But they didn't really know. He advised Charlotte to get an MRI as soon as possible and told her she shouldn't travel or drive farther than the grocery store. And she should check in with her daughter twice a day. Charlotte balked at the directive even though she usually called more than that. When Charlotte asked the doctor if there were further precautions, Viva saw her eyes light up. Meaning, could she still drink. They got into a fight about it on the way home, despite Charlotte's assertion it was the farthest thing from her mind. But Viva knew better. Better than her mother might guess. When she dropped Charlotte off, her mother slammed the car door and said, "Don't worry, kid, I'm tough as old boots." Viva waited while her mother walked to her door, and just before she reached it, she gave her a funny kind of backward wave, an imperial dismissal.

There'd been a mandatory faculty meeting after school, one that dragged on for hours. Ironically, the topic was brain-based learning. Fritz and Cynthia Zale, a costly husband-and-wife consulting team, were flown in from Tucson to conduct the seminar. What would Charlotte make of such a thing? She'd never held academics in high regard, and Viva knew her mother would have a few choice words about brain consultants. Besides, what did anyone really understand about the intricacies of the mind, how without warning a brain can suddenly turn on itself? Viva thought how Charlotte used to say they were wired the same way, but now her mother's mysterious circuitry had run amok.

The first hour of the seminar was spent parsing the differences among pedagogy, andragogy, and heutagogy. Viva's butt had gone numb in the orange plastic cafeteria chair, one of thirty that comprised a "brain-friendly" horseshoe shape dictated by the Zales. When she stretched her leg, her knee clicked—a new and disturbing development.

The school provided refreshments at the break, pretzels and apples for the faculty, a more lavish spread for the Zales, who awkwardly turned their backs on the famished and wilting teachers as they guiltily filled their plates with chicken salad, Brie tarts, and chocolate-covered strawberries.

The seminar concluded with a brain exercise, and to demonstrate, the Zales paired Viva with Walter. They hadn't spoken since the disastrous Easter visit to his family and avoided eye contact whenever they passed in the hall. Reluctantly, they stood before the group, arms crossed.

The Zales instructed them to stand a few feet apart and throw an apple back and forth. Nice and simple. Surely the brain could handle that.

Walter pretended to do a big windup before he threw, and Viva laughed. They smiled at each other and threw their apple back and forth carefully, overly solicitous. But when Viva dropped the apple and it rolled beneath a table, neither of them retrieved it. For a moment, she considered pulling him aside to tell him the news about Charlotte, but no. She'd seen how he looked at her mother the single time he'd met her, how he indulged her in an obvious way that did little to cloak his disdain.

Some of the teachers refused the exercise altogether and remained in their seats, where they glumly bit at their apples. By the end of the seminar, Viva felt as if her poor brain was swelling within her skull like a foot in a too-tight shoe. What would she do if things got worse with Charlotte? She didn't have insurance. She didn't have savings. Viva had already received the first doctor's bill.

After the seminar, Viva checked her mailbox before leaving school. She found nothing but a document titled *New Teacher Personal Review as Administered by Monitor for Consideration by the Board and Committee on Professional Development.* Below that was typed a single sentence:

Seemingly passionate about dance principles, teacher appears to lack professional patience.

The initials *G. T.* were scrawled in minuscule, flowery script and dangled off the end of the sentence. Was that all Greta Tinker, her monitor, had to say about her? After all that loud and dramatic notetaking? And what did she mean by "seemingly"? So what if Viva had reprimanded Madeline rather strongly that day? Madeline wasn't paying attention and clunked across the floor in chassé as if she'd never danced a step. Viva's childhood teachers had employed much stricter correction methods. One slapped Viva's back to fix her posture. Another would take her cane and hook Viva's ankle as she performed an extension and lift skyward until she couldn't breathe. Greta Tinker wouldn't have lasted a second. Viva thrust the paper into her purse.

As she rushed out of school, Viva bumped into Walter. "Hey, can we chat?" he asked. Walter had a new haircut that was a structural masterpiece, and his forelock, stiff with gel, hung at a rakish angle.

"Sure," said Viva.

"A couple of the girls were talking about you. Saying some things that concerned me."

"What things?"

"They say you might be starting the party a little early some days."

"What?"

"You have to think about appearances, Viva. You have to think about how you're perceived. Perception is everything. My mother taught me that."

"Well, if your mother said it, it must be true." Viva picked up her pace. They walked in silence until they reached the end of the hall.

Walter smiled earnestly and said, "I'm here for you, Viva." He left the building, passing by a group of adoring girls whose attempt to not react to him was evident nonetheless in the eyes that cut his way, the giggles and shy waves. Walter nodded at them and flashed a wry smile, as if he, too, was in on the charade, as if they should all just recognize his irresistibility and get on with things.

Viva willed herself off the sofa and finally took off her coat. Charlotte was right about Walter.

Charlotte. Viva glanced at the red message button on her answering machine, which blinked like a single accusing eye. Three messages.

She played the first one from her mother.

*I want to tell you something, Viva, and this is very impor-
tant. The human challenge is to try and stuff a big soul into
a puny human body. It's tough stuff. Tough but true.*

Viva smiled. Sometimes Charlotte did hit the nail on the head.
She thought her mother sounded better this afternoon. But Viva
would need to drive to Glenalbyn to check on her this weekend.

Viva picked up her mail and opened an envelope that contained
two tickets to Anastasia's performance. She poured herself a glass
of vodka and swiftly drank it.

She looked out her window at the Elsinore and heard a strange
sound float up through the floor vent, which served as a kind of
radio for the private noise of the building—the human sound station. It wasn't talking, which she often heard, though never clearly
enough to make out what people were saying, and it wasn't crying;
she'd heard that plenty, too.

Someone was singing. Someone was singing a bad song. It had to
be Christina Britten, who was a soprano in the Los Angeles Master
Chorale. It seemed that she was practicing a modern piece, which
began with a long atonal note and words Viva couldn't quite make
out. Christina repeated the phrase again and again. Excruciating.
Viva wondered if this was what it was like for Charlotte. No, probably
much worse.

There were two more phone messages, but before Viva could
play them, she heard a knock on her door. Then a sheet of paper
shot from beneath it.

*I need a favor about going to court. For something I did a
long time ago. I thought you could help being you are a
teacher. Lukania Moravec*

P.S. We can talk in the hall.

Viva undid the original flip lock on her door, the one from the twenties that was more decorative than protective, then the cheap chain lock, and finally the Schlage lock, and as she did so, she became aware of a presence on the other side, a kind of heat. A hit of aftershave. Pungent, sexy.

Lukania Moravec. She'd seen him park his limousine in front of the apartment building an hour ago. Viva opened her front door and beheld Luka standing there in the hall, his arms folded across his chest. She could imagine him standing in an early-morning alley, waiting for a client. Certainly, she thought, he must wait a lot.

"Can you help me?"

Viva looked at him and for the first time noticed a scar near his ear. He straightened his tie, and his suit looked a little rumpled.

"What do you need?" she said, and at that moment Viva realized he was older than she'd originally thought. Probably in his fifties. Why hadn't she noticed that when he fixed her car? She thought that being a neighbor meant seeing people regularly but not as they really are. Sometimes people were less good-looking up close, or once you heard their voice, every assumption you'd made about them changed. To know a neighbor meant to view only a little piece of someone's life, usually the same piece over and over, like Dusty walking her dog. From time to time, Viva would wonder about Luka and Dusty, what kept them together. Once, Viva had seen them slow-dancing in front of their living room window. It almost seemed like they wanted people to look at them, as if they were on a stage.

"I need you to write to the Los Angeles Superior Court, 1954 Hill Street. Please tell them I helped you with your car."

Viva looked at Luka. Her headache was blooming, and she heard her phone ring.

"Do you need to get that?"

"No, I don't." She heard her machine click on and record a hang-up.

Luka smiled like he understood the situation, although there was no possibility that he could. A window at the end of the hallway suddenly flew open, and the smell of jasmine poured in. For a moment the hall was suffused with bright spring light.

"Why do you have to go to court?"

Luka sighed and clasping his hands behind his back, looked at the floor.

"A passenger trashed my limo, and I kicked him out. He claims I gave him mental distress."

"You must meet a lot of different people in your line of work," said Viva.

"You know from hello what they'll be like." Luka unclasped his hands and leaned toward her, or maybe he hadn't even moved.

But something inside him had moved. Viva was sure of it. Viva steadied herself against the doorframe.

"Viva, do you feel like yourself?"

There was something in the way he asked this, a concern and simple kindness, and Viva felt something within her unhook.

"I'm very lonely." And this was not what she meant to say.

Luka took her by the arm, and his palm was very warm. Although Viva knew he must escort people to his limo on a regular basis, perhaps in this very same manner, there was something about the way he encapsulated her wrist, held it so gently, that made her turn and pull him into her apartment. Her door slammed shut behind them.

"What happened here?" Luka traced the scar on the back of her arm with his finger.

"I punched a window when I was a kid."

"Fierce," Luka said, and laughed. Then his tone shifted. "I saw you sleeping in your car Monday night. "

And it was true. Not for long, but she had. She'd had some cock-tails with the AP French teacher and the principal's secretary. Too many cocktails. Someone had rapped on her window. And that someone was Luka, which she recalled only this very instant.

"Maybe you need a driver."

"Maybe I do."

They stood facing each other, and Viva thought she'd never seen a man go so still. "I'll write your letter. I'll say you're good," said Viva. Even if she drank too much, she took some small pleasure in the fact that he'd asked her to be his character witness.

"I am."

Something jumped between them, and Viva felt a swift abandon roll through her. It felt like the moment after a plane takes off when it hurtles recklessly upward—a nonnegotiable, *nothing can be done now* feeling.

Luka looked at her mirror on the floor, still in the exact same spot where he had set it months ago.

"What do *you* need?" he said.

Had Luka said that? Did he mean in return for the letter? What would she even say in this letter? And then it swiftly came to her—she would say he was *stalwart*. Remarkably, her headache had vanished, and something within Viva seemed to snap into alignment. She picked up her vodka, which she'd hidden behind the sofa. No need to hide anything in front of Luka. No need at all. She finished her glass and noted that she'd never felt less drunk in her life. She thought. Her poor old brain had slipped free of its tight shell and seemed to float somewhere above her head. Time was bending, just a little.

"You need to take care of yourself," said Luka.

Viva stepped out of her dress. "Take care of me now."

Viva awoke on the sofa. She'd dreamed of having a clock in her mouth. It was dark outside, and naked, she was covered in an afghan. No Luka. A new headache replaced the old one. There was a note on her dresser:

I know a guy at the Elsinore—Boris. He owes me a room.
Next time. If you want. Luka

Viva was very thirsty. Across the room, she could see her message machine blinking and blinking. She'd never listened to her second two messages last night. She struggled out of her blanket, padded across the floor, and pressed play.

Silence. Probably a wrong number. Then she heard someone singing, indistinctly at first, and then more clearly. Charlotte.

When you don't know what to do, gum is here to help you through
If your pain is here to stay, grab a stick—whaddya say?

Viva skipped to the next message.

...whaddya say? Chew Big Mouth minty gum—

Silence. Viva was about to delete it when she heard her mother sigh, then begin to sob.

Viva, call me. Make it stop. Make it stop. Help.

chapter twenty-three

Charlotte surveyed the beach, which was deserted, and the tide, though low, looked cranky. It swirled and jerked, pulling this way and that as if Poseidon himself had issued wild and conflicting commands.

That morning, she'd been consumed by the idea of driving straight to San Diego. No stops. Straight to the ocean. Against doctor's orders. Too bad. If she drove fast enough, maybe she could escape the music. She'd skip breakfast and simply reheat last night's coffee in the microwave. But Charlotte couldn't seem to remember how it worked. Which number did a person press? There were so many. Too many. She pushed the help button again and again, but the mysteries of the microwave refused to reveal themselves. Fuck it. She'd forgo food or drink—she was on a mission.

Charlotte drove south, the phantom DJ in her head playing a new and unrelenting tune, a nameless film score, lugubrious and sticky, with its wavering, weepy reverb and grand unending glissando. Somewhere around Temecula, that quit. Then

Charlotte heard her own self, singing to Viva the lullaby "Ding Sally Shinepath."

There was a warning sign at the top of the stairs that led down to the beach, but its cautionary words were unclear. Most had been baked off by the sun. Charlotte peered at the sign for a moment, which looked like an incomprehensible message in a dream—most likely rules and the consequences of disobeying them. Charlotte never did have much truck with rules, and she didn't plan to loiter, grill, or shoot off firecrackers. No Eddie, so, no dog. What could she possibly be fined for?

Charlotte passed a deserted green beach shack and picked her way across the sand, careful to step over and around things coughed up by the ocean—a deflated inner tube, a ketchup bottle, a child's sandal. She kept going until she reached a stone jetty. Waves crashed along one side of it, throwing spray in the air. Charlotte would walk to the very end of it, and there, finally, she would hear silence. She was sure of it.

Charlotte was halfway down the jetty when she stopped to rest on a rock that resembled a huge toad. The rock was slippery with lichen that was not green but yellow, and if she squinted, it almost looked like a patch of buttercups. Charlotte closed her eyes and listened to the ocean creak and groan, and beneath that she thought she heard something high and fine, a bright whistle. The red sun set the waves aflame. All doors flew open to her, none of them wrong.

And that was it. A wave abducted her—a sleeper, a rogue, a runaway—pulling her off the jetty. Charlotte thrust her arms into the air reaching for something, anything. The water felt like a thick blanket in which she was completely entangled. Charlotte tried to kick, but her legs were useless broken scissors. She corkscrewed in an unknown direction, fast becoming bodyless.

She was flying, and she was falling off a horse, and the sun burned the waves. She was pulled under and over, and there was her life—the bright, hot pull of sex, the silence of a mouth, the scorched iron, cold soup, squeezing Viva's hand, sticky with pine sap. Falling asleep in a big pile of leaves, and a man shouting, "Little girl, are you dead?"

Once, when Charlotte was in high school, she left in the middle of math class, got in her car, and drove as fast as she could. She was that kind of girl. Driving fast, going nowhere. Why? And some things would never be explained, like why geraniums smell like pennies and bean sprouts smell like pubic hair. Dear God, life was brilliant.

And why did she kick the game of Monopoly across the room that time? The thimble and the ship spinning through the air. She and Wilson were playing and they stopped for sex. "You drive your own car in your own lane, I'll say that," said Wilson. One thousand lips ago. Why had she run from the person she so desperately wanted? Why had she been so afraid?

And did she stamp the letter to Wilson? Did she? Too late now. Charlotte had gone very far, very fast, and in that last and final brightness her big soul burst free of its human cage.

Then finally—*quiet*.

Too quiet. The water wasn't even wet. What a thing. If only she could tell Viva.

chapter twenty-four

Dead Not Dead was a game Charlotte played with Viva as a child. Creatures to consider: spiders, lizards, snails. Horseshoe crabs. Dead-like, but not dead. You had to guess. Easy to be wrong. Their neighbor's dog froze to death in a snowbank but looked like he was only sleeping.

Charlotte was everywhere in her absence.

The previous day, Viva thought she saw her mother run a red light. Or, to be specific, her mother when she was thirty years old. The woman had the same bearing as Charlotte—imperious, urgent, driving like her life depended on it, and Viva flashed on her mother driving down the suicide lane on the Cape. But of course it wasn't Charlotte.

It had been three weeks since her mother was declared dead. Even though her body hadn't been found. Dead, not dead. A rescue crew searched until nightfall before calling it off. The police told Viva that the fisherman who saw Charlotte drown was the final witness to her life. He thought she was waving at him, and when he realized she wasn't, it was too late. Since Charlotte's death the world had taken a tilt. Small things like a person's shoes appeared in hyper-relief, and large things like buildings appeared one-dimensional and borderless—a kind of terrible intoxication.

If only Viva had listened to all her messages when she came home. When she thought of her mother in her final moments, she almost couldn't breathe. And Luka. What a terrible mistake. Viva was suffused in guilt and shame. She needed to stop drinking. Tomorrow.

Viva slid into a booth at the Elsinore Hotel and ordered a vodka tonic from the bartender. The bar looked like it hadn't changed much over the decades—blue flocked wallpaper, thick, murky carpet. The air felt dense and suffused with the countless number of interactions that had surely occurred there over the years—confessions, rebukes, and come-ons, apologies extended, accepted or not. Charlotte would have liked this bar.

There were only three other patrons—a couple and a man by himself. The couple appeared to be in their eighties. The elderly man wore an ascot and a rumpled jacket. The woman wore a loose caftan that might have been a bathrobe. They sat erectly, holding hands, staring into the middle distance as though they were on the deck of a slowly sinking ocean liner.

Across from them, the single man swirled the ice cubes in his drink. With his free hand, he brought his phone to his ear and frowned. "Listen, you fuck," he said, "I don't use math."

Viva sipped her drink and avoided eye contact.

When Viva had spoken to the police, they gave her information about where to pick up Charlotte's van, which, parked near a beach in Encinitas, had been impounded due to unpaid parking tickets. Viva's name was on the insurance, which she paid for Charlotte, despite her claims that she'd never need it.

Viva had tried to be a good daughter. But then she considered the many times she'd fled from Charlotte, beginning in high school.

Once, when she saw her mother walking home after work at her real estate job, she hastily got on a bus going the other way. And then she'd moved across the country. Yet how many times had she come running when her mother needed her? But not the time she needed her most.

Viva considered ordering another drink, but tonight was Anastasia's performance, and she needed to pick up Calla beforehand. When she'd called earlier no one answered.

Well, maybe just one more. Lately, after two or three glasses of white wine, after changing to red, she would start counting from one again. Charlotte's policy. Except that her mother's practice, more liberal, extended to a change in liquor as well. Viva ordered a gin and tonic.

Yesterday, while cleaning out Charlotte's cabin, Viva stood before the one expensive piece of furniture in the house, a tall mahogany hand-carved bureau with twenty-one brass pulls that Charlotte removed twice a year and polished. A hulking, kingly piece, not feminine in the least. Her mother never used the top three drawers because she couldn't reach them, and she didn't use the large bottom drawer once her back began to give her trouble. Viva had offered to buy her a more functional dresser, but no.

Atop the bureau sat a sterling-silver hairbrush her mother had owned since childhood. Viva picked it up. Surprisingly heavy. There was a dent in the back where Charlotte once threw it at Ardel, missed, and hit the wall. A few pieces of her long gray hair were tangled in the brush. Viva had removed them and put them in her pocket.

And then Viva saw it—a small animal in the partially open top right drawer. White fur. A rat? A dead rat? She stepped closer, and it didn't move. Viva rapped on the side of the dresser. Nothing. She opened the drawer and saw not an entire animal, but part of an animal.

Tiny toenails. A rabbit's foot. Something Viva was strictly forbidden to have as a child. When she'd saved up to buy one, Charlotte took it from her.

But it was already dead, Viva had shrieked.

That's not the point, Viva. It was an animate thing. And here she'd kept it all this while.

Viva cautiously reached her hand into the far back of the drawer, which was empty except for an envelope. She pulled it out, and there, gazing through the envelope window, Viva saw her mother. Hair swept high atop her head in a wild tangle. Dark, untamed eyebrows. Her crooked smile and defiant gaze. That inimitable, puzzling smile that said *Try me.*

Viva pulled the photo from the envelope and studied it. Charlotte was sitting on the edge of a clawfoot tub, legs dangling, small feet tucked one over the other like wings. Pale nipples. A visible scar on her abdomen where she'd had her appendix removed as a teenager. Charlotte's hand is stretched out as if to say *stop*, but it's clear from the look in her eyes that stop means go.

Behind her, Viva could see the reflection of a man in the medicine cabinet mirror. His face was almost completely obscured by the camera. Dark hair. A strange feeling came over her, a kind of recognition. It was simple and quick, like the passing of a hand over the back of her head.

The bartender served her drink and Viva lifted her glass. To Charlotte. No matter how hard she'd tried, she'd never been able to fathom the mysteries of her mother. Charlotte, who once called herself a drinking artist. Charlotte, eternally on the precipice of something exciting. If only she'd been able to take her wildness and willfulness and channel it into real art.

Viva settled her bill and stood up to leave but suddenly felt like her legs couldn't carry her. She sank into the leather banquette, closing her eyes, and in that moment a memory from the summer on Cape Cod came to her, one she'd all but forgotten.

The sky looked poured out, lacking crease or cloud. Viva and Charlotte were walking the pier when they saw a group of campers gathered near the end focused on something in the water, a frenzied energy radiating from them. When they drew closer, they saw a strange spectacle—hippies diving for coins in the water. There were at least a dozen of them, and they swam singly or in pairs, all of them naked. The crowd stood above them, pitching coins. Two boys in the ocean shoved each other as pieces of change flew toward them. One disappeared beneath the surface and triumphantly reappeared with a fifty-cent piece, which he held aloft before tucking it inside his already bulging cheek.

Charlotte gave Viva a few quarters and placed her palms on her shoulders. Viva peered at the bobbing heads, naked breasts, palms waving. "Come on, sweetheart, over here!" a redheaded girl shouted. She clapped her hands. "Poppy," she said by way of introduction. "Right here!" Viva stared at her. The girl was probably only a couple of years older than she was. Wild. Untamed. Money in her mouth. Viva wanted to throw her coins, but her arms remained dead at her sides.

Charlotte pulled Viva close, leaning in to her, and for a moment Viva felt like she was carrying her mother on her back. Poppy swam up to the pier in front of Viva and Charlotte and flipped in the water. Viva glimpsed her bare bottom before she surfaced and stared at them. Like an imperious mermaid, the girl locked eyes with Viva as though she could see deep within her and see that Viva was frozen with fear, incapable of speaking, throwing her quarters, or taking any action at all. The girl clung to the dock and shouted, "What are you *so* fucking afraid of?"

There were countless things Viva was afraid of: being electrocuted, peeing her pants, having a bird land on her head or, worse, shit on her head, getting her teeth pulled, bleeding to death, nurses, rectal thermometers, poison, pinchers, bad boys.

Never knowing her father.

Then suddenly Viva was in the sea. Waves slapped at her, then submerged her, and for the single instant she was able to right herself, she heard Charlotte scream, "She can't swim!"

Viva twisted and scratched at the water. Someone had snatched the sky, and no matter which way she turned, the ocean captured her. A bright pink beach umbrella taunted her from the shore. Then it was gone. Time became elastic, and the more she thrashed the slower it became. People shouted things at Viva, jumbled directions and commands that mixed and distorted in the air. Incomprehensible. Useless. She opened her mouth to scream and salt water flooded in. Why had Charlotte pushed her into the ocean?

Then Poppy grabbed her shoulder. A slice of sun. The world flipped right-side-up. A boy grabbed her leg, and someone else pushed her from below. It felt like they were helping her climb out of the water. It reminded Viva of an illustration she had once seen of Jacob's ladder, an image of millions of bent souls lumbering up, one after the other, rung after rung. The souls at the top of the ladder appeared to be vacuumed up into a shiny cloud, and this was how she felt now, as though an unknown force directed her body, and all she had to do was give herself over to it.

Then Viva was lying on the pier. It was a shock to be in her body once again. Finite, limited, human. But that glimpse of a self, if it could be called that, a self with no start or stop was a revelation.

Charlotte pulled Viva to her feet. She was crying and her makeup was smeared. She tried to wrap a towel around her daughter, who shoved her away.

"Why did you push me?" Viva shouted. "What is wrong with you?"

Charlotte grabbed her by the shoulders and shook her. "Viva, I didn't push you—you jumped."

Someone was shaking Viva by the shoulder. "Miss, are you all right?"

"What?" Viva opened her eyes to see the bartender. "Of course I'm all right." She looked at her watch. She'd be late for Anastasia's performance, and first she needed to track down Calla. Viva gathered her things to go, but she wanted to linger. She could almost feel Charlotte right there beside her. Almost. But the person whom she'd defined herself against was gone, and the society of two was now one.

chapter twenty-five

Viva pulled up to Calla's house, which, once painted a spruce green, was now blanched gray by the sun. On the patio was a disemboweled TV set, a tricycle, and an old surfboard piled high with socks drying in the sun. The curtains were closed, and it appeared no one was home until Calla's old mastiff sprang to life behind the gate. Viva rushed to the door and knocked. She'd drunk three Cokes before leaving her apartment and now she had the jitters.

Gwen, Calla's sister, opened the door a crack. "We're not buying," she said.

"I'm here to pick up Calla."

Gwen opened the door, frowned, and gave Viva the once-over. She looked much older than a high school girl and radiated the low-level menace of a drugstore security guard. It was impossible to consider that she and Calla were sisters. Except for the shared wariness.

"Who are you?"

"I'm her dance teacher. Viva Devlin. I'm taking her to a show."

"A show?" she asked, as if Viva had said was taking Calla gambling. "What show?"

"A dance performance. It's a professional company, and I thought Calla—"

"Calla isn't here. Took off three days ago and I haven't been able to find her. But if you see her, tell her to get her ass home." She closed the door before Viva could say anything further.

When Viva arrived at the theater the parking lot was full. She circled the area twice and unable to find a space, paid the valet twenty dollars. She ran into the theater and found her seat only minutes before the show started. She hadn't attended any professional performances in almost two years. It felt strange to be in the audience rather than backstage, but she'd deeply missed the hush that fell over the crowd and the sense of anticipation in the air.

The lights went down and the first and featured performer, Anastasia, appeared upstage. Slowly, very slowly, almost as if she was floating, she made her way down to the lip of the stage, where she teetered, appearing to blow in a nonexistent wind. Her gossamer style was on full display, and for a moment, Viva thought she locked eyes with her. But she knew that was impossible. Blue and green lights began to flash, and four dancers swept in from the wings, lifted Anastasia, and elevated her prone body above their heads. The group began to spin like a pinwheel, faster and faster, until Anastasia was almost a blur. When they came to a jerky stop, two of the dancers pitched Anastasia forward, where she landed once again on the edge of the stage. It was a beautiful, nervy opening to the piece, and despite her envy, Viva felt something that had all but abandoned her—inspiration and longing.

After the show, the lobby was packed. Viva spotted a couple of the principals exit the stage door and skirt the crowd. But

Anastasia had told her to wait. Next to Viva, two fast-moving weather fronts of competing perfumes enveloped her. Nauseating. The two women had been seated behind her in the theater and chatted nonstop during the performance. Viva detested this kind of audience member—the type who had plenty of money for season tickets but little respect for the performers. "No," shrieked one of the women. "This was *before* I married that asshole Finnish hand surgeon!"

Why had Anastasia asked Viva to wait if she didn't plan to make an appearance?

Jacob Johansen, a dancer Viva recognized from her New York days, strode through the lobby. He hadn't been a strong performer when they were in class together. But here he was, dancing with the Pilar Broom Company. Viva considered that she very well might have been part of the troupe were it not for her injury. She made a beeline for the concession stand and bought another glass of wine. She'd already had three. Fifteen dollars for three or four ounces. What a rip-off.

But this one did the trick. As she drank, she felt the familiar magical overlay begin to descend, the one that hovered just above the ordinary instant, making it melt around the edges, deepen in the center, and become full with possibility. For a fleeting moment, everything seemed all right. She would congratulate her friend. She would go home and get to bed early. Because in some small part of Viva, the performance had enlivened her. Maybe she'd spend some extra time in the studio tomorrow. Maybe she'd work on a new dance she'd been thinking about.

"Brava," shouted one of the women as Anastasia swept into the lobby. She stopped and dipped her head toward the woman as if she'd thrown roses as well. Viva waved but Anastasia didn't see her. Instantly, she was swallowed up in a crowd of well-wishers and other dancers.

Viva wended her way through the crowd toward Anastasia, rehearsing what she wanted to say. Because if she didn't, she feared she'd say it was excruciating to watch Anastasia's beautiful and moving performance, that it was incredibly hard to be so close to something she missed so much. That she'd give anything for one more chance to push her body as far as it would go for a single moment of transcendence.

Then suddenly Anastasia was rushing toward her, arms outstretched. "There you are!" she exclaimed, as if it were she who'd waited almost an hour for her friend. She looked at Viva and began to tear up. "Oh, God, I'm sorry. I've missed you *so* much!"

Viva immediately tried to feign a similar expression but felt her face turn to stone. "Anastasia, you were a relevation!" she said, too loudly. "I mean revelation." She was slurring a little. "I mean, really. You were so good. So good!"

Anastasia smiled ruefully—she'd always been modest—and said, "Look who's talking." But what could she have been talking about? Only Viva's past.

"So how are you? Really. How is it teaching at that school?"

"Wonderful. Really wonderful," Viva added, painfully aware of how flat her voice sounded.

"Do they know how talented you were? Do the kids love your choreography? I bet they do. I mean, how could they not?" Anastasia spoke very rapidly, but Viva chalked it up to post-performance adrenaline.

Viva mustered a smile. "Some of the girls are quite good." She thought of Calla and how she would have loved the performance. Calla. Where could she have gone? She'd call her sister first thing in the morning.

"Well, they're lucky to have you. I mean that. I really do." Anastasia clutched Viva's hand. "I was so sorry to hear about your mother."

"Thanks."

"I mean, even if you're not close with a parent, it can be devastating once they're gone."

"I was close with my mother."

Anastasia tilted her head and squinted. "Well, sure, right, I know you would have liked to be close with your mother, but she made it hard for you with her drinking and her crazy ways and her . . ."

Viva frowned, and Anastasia trailed off.

"Look, Viva, I'm sorry."

"Anastasia!" A man interrupted them and gave Anastasia a peck on the check.

"Viva, I want you to meet someone—a terrific L.A. choreographer. I told him all about you," said Anastasia.

Viva flushed and finished her wine.

"Donovan, this is my dear friend from college, Viva," she said. "Well, also my fiercest competition."

"Was," said Viva, and she considered that Anastasia said this to her only now that she wasn't a threat. Anastasia laughed nervously and Viva noted again that her energy seemed to be cranking in a way she hadn't seen before.

Viva and Donovan chatted for a minute before he said, "We'll see you later, Stasia. Nice to meet you, Viva," he added.

"Viva, listen, are you okay?"

"Of course."

Anastasia looked at Viva and Viva thought she saw pity in her eyes.

"Hey, do you want to come out with us tonight?"

"I'm pretty tired."

"Well, I've got just the thing for that."

Maybe it wasn't just after-show adrenaline causing Anastasia's exuberance.

"So will you join us?"

Viva felt determined to show her that she wasn't someone to be pitied. Yes, Viva would join them, and yes, she'd be the life of the party.

The rest of the night was a blur—drinks at two different bars and then an after-party downtown at Donovan's loft. Music blasting. Everyone dancing. Some girl topless on the kitchen counter. Anastasia drinking champagne out of a toe shoe. Viva thought she remembered making out with someone on the balcony. Jacob Johansen? Maybe. The room spinning. She'd done a bump before driving home at daylight. There would be no time to sleep even if she could sleep. She needed to shower and dress and get to school early. But first she needed to make a stop.

It is wrong to go to a liquor store at six in the morning, a liquor store above which a neon sign blinks the words *Pip's Cheap*. Too late. Viva heard a faint sizzling noise in the quiet. She looked up at the sign and abruptly the *C* sputtered and blew.

A security guard lurked inside the doorway, a woman with short, black hair who contemplated Viva, clicking her high school ring against her teeth before allowing her to pass.

A small radio sat near the cash register, and Karen Carpenter singing "Superstar" ribboned its way through the quiet of the store. The first and only album Charlotte had ever bought for Viva was *Close to You*. And they were close, weren't they? Despite what Anastasia thought. Viva picked up a fifth of vodka and set it on the counter next to a display of condoms and glow-in-the-dark key chains. She made her purchase and quickly left.

Viva was unlocking her car when she heard a commotion. Screaming and shouting, wild kids descended on the parking lot in a tangle of arms and legs. Two boys shot into the liquor store. The others, laughing and whooping, ran to the side of the building and waited. And though it was semi-dark, one of them moved in a very familiar way.

"Calla?!" shouted Viva. "Calla!"

The boys came flying out of the store clutching a case of beer, the security guard chasing after them. The kids took off down the alley.

It was Calla, wasn't it? But maybe Viva was only imagining that. She started her car. For once, she'd be on time to school.

chapter twenty-six

There was solid ground beneath the car, and then it was gone. It was not unlike the quick-jerk start of an amusement ride. No going back. Mr. Magoo driving off a bridge. Her dashboard rattled and exploded. The glove box flew open, her car clock cracked. Viva was *driving down stairs*, and she needed to back up immediately, needed to turn this situation around, but her car was heaving like some kind of mad metal whale. Nuts and bolts flew everywhere and all at once, ringing as they clattered off the pavement.

Viva had taken a wrong turn at the quad and driven down a concrete staircase. There was something about the sight line that day—a late May afternoon when the air was so gray and murky, she might as well have been driving through the ocean. Still, with a seizing clarity, she knew she was in the wrong.

As she flew past the parking kiosk, she saw a man in an orange vest. He lifted his arm as if to wave, as if to say, *Everything is okay, all is well. Stop!* he meant. *Stop!*

She remembered a boy from Encinitas named Nick Fleck.

Fender's buddy. Nick went drag racing out by the state mental hospital and drove off the side of a hill. It was rumored they never found the corpse. Some said his body fell into an open garbage truck in the next county, was crunched, spun, and sucked up into the ether. The kids drew secret pictures of it in art class, wheels spinning in midair, a boy with a big open mouth and the word *Noooo!!*

A hubcap flew off, bouncing hard and fast like a gigantic fat quarter. Viva could smell burning rubber and much worse, coffee cake air freshener, which they'd sprayed at the car wash without her permission.

When Nick Fleck drove off the hill, it must have felt like he was flying, and maybe he was overjoyed at being thrown into the sky, thick with black clouds, and maybe for a crazy moment, he thought they would catch him as he fell. Nick Fleck was sixteen, and he should have known better. She should have known better. It wasn't too early for shame—never too early for that—and her car hadn't even hit the ground.

The word *velocitation* flashed in her mind. A driver's ed term. *Velocitation*: Going so fast, you don't know how fast you're going.

Then her car came to a quick, hard stop—like a door slammed, like an argument ended. The entire drive down the steps couldn't have taken more than six seconds.

Viva may have been the only person in Los Angeles to get a DUI without driving. She was, however, sitting under the influence when the police arrived. She was taken to the station, where she was booked, fingerprinted, and given a summons to appear in court.

The next morning, Viva was called to the principal's office. Maisie looked at her for what seemed like an eternity, then said, "People in the arts have a predilection for substance abuse, but in your particular art form things can get very dangerous very quickly." She took a deep breath and twisted the top button of her blue blazer, winding herself like a watch.

Viva should have known the minute Maisie seated her without closing the office door. Behind her in the hallway, Viva heard Shawna Klinger, the youngest girl in her dance class, a pretty girl who smelled like baby powder and farts, exclaiming her way down the hall. Shawna was just over four feet tall and in a permanent state of astonishment. She twirled past the open doorway of the principal's office and proclaimed, "I'm so excited, I think I might sweat!"

Viva and Maisie exchanged a smile, and for a moment Viva felt herself back in Maisie's good graces. After all, she was a very good teacher, and her students loved her. They sometimes slipped notes into her dance bag, ripped notebook paper scribbled on in turquoise or lavender ink that declared: *You are an estrella—that's Spanish for star!* and *No matter what, stay the way you are!*

Viva loved that they lived in a world of possible, instant malleability, where one could actually fear slipping into a new persona overnight. And it wasn't completely far-fetched. She recently read in *Limn: The Chronicle of Secondary Teachers* an article that stated it was possible to change the structure of one's brain, the actual layout. It seemed that hundreds of taxi drivers had been tested, and the longer a driver drove, the larger his hippocampus, the part of the brain that stores spatial information, became. It had to do with relying on navigational skills in response to environmental demands. Viva was briefly comforted by the thought that perhaps her own hippocampus was larger than most. Not that it was the kind of thing one could brag about, but dancing did require spatial skill. And yet, if she was wired like Charlotte, as her mother often said she was, might her own circuitry go haywire down the road? She quickly dismissed the thought.

Shawna squealed with wild laughter that abruptly ended. The moment passed and Maisie's face fell. Viva could see this meeting was not easy for her. Maisie peered at Shawna over Viva's head and spiraled her wrist in a move-along motion.

A single tear leaked out of Viva's right eye. She remained motionless in the hope that Maisie did not see it, but already she was offering her a tissue from the Lincoln Continental of Kleenex dispensers.

Maisie leaned in and said, "Can I tell you something? Because I think you'll understand."

Viva braced herself and considered that this statement was not always a compliment. Maisie quickly inhaled and looked Viva in the eye. "I am in love with Kit Stockbridge. No, I am sick with love for Kit Stockbridge. It is *like an addiction.*"

Kit Stockbridge taught an AP junior class called Into the Woods: On Personal Inquiry, featuring the works of Thoreau and Emerson. He detested wasting water and wore wrinkled white shirts that did not seem completely clean. It could be argued he was a man of great passion.

"What do you think I should do, Viva?"

"I think you need to head directly toward it."

"You do?"

Maisie looked stunned at the simplicity of the directive. She got up from her seat and reached out to hug Viva, not quite putting her arms around her.

It was suddenly clear to Viva that Maisie had meant only to scare her, only wanted to make her feel what it would be like *if* she was asked to leave. Viva had been spared.

"So can I stay on?"

"Oh, no, Viva, you're fired."

"Look, Maisie, what I did was wrong, but it was a one-off, and it won't ever happen again," said Viva. Immediately, she thought that of course it wouldn't happen again because how many times can one drive down stairs?

The word *one-off* shamefully hung in the air. She never used that word and had no idea why it had flown out of her mouth. She needed to take a different tack, and quickly.

"Maisie, I could talk to Kit for you, drop some hints, see if he seems interested."

Maisie looked disgusted. A kind of internal resolve seemed to overcome her, stiffening her posture, and she squinted at Viva. The look in her eyes said this wasn't the first time someone had tried to pull a fast one. Maisie hadn't made it this far as an emotional traffic controller of whiny teachers, petulant parents, belligerent coaches, and drunk dance instructors without a certain kind of moxie.

"Viva, I will pray for you."

Viva went to gather her things, and as she walked down the corridor, she passed a group of field hockey girls. They fell silent as she approached before continuing on like a multiheaded beast—whispering, snickering, dragging their sticks behind them like so many wooden tails. She took a right at the end of the hall, and as she passed the open door to the Latin classroom, she saw two lines written in green chalk on the blackboard:

> *Lacrimae rerum: the tears in things*
> *Please refer to "the tragedy of life," p. 55*

As she came around the corner, she almost bumped into Zeke polishing the floor. He looked up, looked down. He wouldn't be offering her a beer today. He knew. They all knew.

chapter twenty-seven

Viva put her palms against her living room window and looked at the Elsinore Hotel, above which a milk-tooth moon lingered in the sky. Standing slumber seemed possible. Some of the hotel windows were dark tonight, plain and simple black, the black of serious shoes and unmade choices. Other windows were lit by the blue fires of television. She watched them flame, brighten, and vanquish. Hotels were wonderful places. Joy was possible — people jumping, and loving, and throwing each other like toys in the air. She's seen them, or she thinks she's seen them.

Viva thought the thing that drew people to hotels, the thing that people were really after, was the secret ingredient, sleep-infused air. So many sighs, chortles, and pants — and the softest of all, dream breath. Who isn't innocent then?

It had been two weeks since Viva was fired. Two lost weeks. She felt slightly melted around the edges. Viva recognized this particular hangover — Hangover of the Tender Sorrows. It made her miss her mother even more. It made her miss people she hadn't seen in years, miss people she had yet to meet. Bad songs seemed better. Strangers appeared kinder. People she encountered during the day, for example, clerks stocking grocery store shelves, seemed like novitiates in their dedication and attention to their work. Hangover of the Tender Sorrows caused her to donate money to all sorts of causes, generally ones on television—Red Cross, dog shelters, Sally Struthers. She thought of Charlotte, queen of the hard stop. How did she do it? Not that she always succeeded.

Oh, for a knuckle of sleep. Her mind felt like a distant doll head on gyro. For hours she'd lain awake, shoveling breath, awaiting the word rest from the invisible human engine room that stays open from birth to death.

Viva's license had been restricted for thirty days, and she had to attend three months of court-ordered "alcohol safety school." In addition, she was required to pay eighteen hundred dollars in fines. The program was located in an old building off Cahuenga Boulevard that rented to the odd business—Dizzy Daisy's Crochet Creations, JBL Flag Emporium, Quake Secure, and one dentist's office, which seemed disturbing given the general run-down quality of the building. In the lobby, a humpback whale–shaped crack extended along the wall from the revolving doors to the water fountain, which was filled with candy and snack wrappers.

There was no counseling at alcohol safety school. There were "activities." An activity involved watching a movie about drunks, and each activity cost one hundred dollars. Viva was required to attend twelve activities. If she missed an activity, she would be charged double for the makeup activity.

So far, the class had watched *Clean and Sober*, *Days of Wine and Roses* (twice), *Leaving Las Vegas*, *The Lost Weekend*, *Drunks*, and a PBS documentary called *The Hijacked Brain*. The "counselor," Ricky G, would stride into the room without making eye contact, slam a tape into the VCR, and vanish. As always, he wouldn't turn off the fluorescent overhead lights, as though that, too, would teach them something. Afterward, Ricky G would take five minutes of questions. Half the time people asked things like *Does Richard Lewis still act?* Because no one, no one, wanted to appear that they needed to be there.

There was the man who wore a zipped-up windbreaker to every activity and spent the entire time loudly shuffling papers, a woman who whipped out nail polish the second the counselor left, a high school kid who did his homework. Today in class, Viva sat next to a dental hygienist named Kaley who spent every activity studying an atlas. She said she was memorizing the world. Without shifting her eyes from Uzbekistan, she told Viva to eat a stick of butter before drinking. And if Viva should end up in a more serious court-ordered alcohol safety school, such as one in which the activities involved taking a urine test, she said to swallow a few pennies beforehand. If a person actually wanted to stop drinking, this was the last place they should go.

And how does a person change? Viva recalled reading an article that said a person could change in twenty-one days. Or maybe it was thirty-six. Or maybe it was twenty-one for simple things like learning to chew with your mouth closed but thirty-six for replacing cigarettes with archery. What is the conversion rate from bad habit to complete and total change when you factor in genetic hesitancy?

Viva looked at her clock. It was 3:00 a.m., and even if she could fall asleep, she had no plans for the next day. Viva missed the routine of her early-morning modern class, where she usually found Calla and a few of the others half asleep outside the studio door. They, at least the serious ones, were there because they loved what she loved, and what she loved about dancing was the slicing through air, the impermanence of posture, throwing her heart to the sky. How often did anyone get to do that with good cause? Good cause, and good pay, because after all, she was paid pretty well at Findley Academy.

In front of the Elsinore, a bank of white irises shook in the wind. Viva's eyes traveled up the side of the hotel to the penthouse. And then she saw him—a man in the top window, watching her. Viva squinted. Luka? Same broad shoulders, same stillness. She remembered him saying his friend could get them a room. Was it Luka? Viva couldn't completely make out his face, but she thought she saw him gesture to her. And even from this distance, Viva could sense his lack of judgment, his complete understanding of her. She grabbed her toothbrush and wallet and left for the Elsinore Hotel. The Elsinore Hotel, where one could disappear into the discreet chapters of days, the click of the key card in the lock.

chapter twenty-eight

An ambulance streaked by the Elsinore, and up in the hills, the coyotes went off. Yipping, yowling. They were everywhere, waiting. Nearby a searchlight looped in the night sky, and the fragrance of night-blooming jasmine enveloped Viva. She rushed past the doorman and entered the lobby.

"How can I help you?" The woman behind the hotel counter, whose name tag identified her as Sophie, wore a vaguely nautical uniform, and the way she asked the question indicated it had been a long night.

"Could you call your penthouse guest and let him know I'm here?" Viva asked.

"Penthouse guest?"

"Yes."

"We don't have a penthouse."

"Isn't the top floor of the hotel the penthouse?"

"We have a presidential suite, if that's what you mean, but no penthouse." Sophie gave her a wonky, exhausted smile that said even the ignorant must be tolerated.

"Then my friend is in the presidential suite."

A slight pull at the side of the woman's mouth, no more than a twitch, because information had been provided, and why did some people have to push it? "No. That isn't possible," she said. She peered at Viva's blouse, which she'd buttoned crookedly in her haste to leave her apartment.

"Look, is . . . ?" She tried to remember the name of Luka's friend. "Is Boris on tonight? He can straighten this out."

"Boris? There's no Boris employed here."

A supervisor joined them. He wore no name tag. No name, no one to assail about the bad bed, the extra charge for the extra Coke, the tub that's too big, too small, too blue.

"I'm just trying to meet my friend," Viva said.

The man placed his palms on the counter and sighed. "The presidential suite is being used for storage, *okay*?"

"What are you, the junior senior manager?" Viva asked.

The man turned on his heel and disappeared through a narrow door behind the desk, a door that may have existed solely for this type of encounter.

Sophie returned her attention to her computer screen. She typed and paused, typed and paused, stared into the monitor as if it was an aquarium filled with exotic fish. "Room 232, nonsmoking, two kings . . . ," she murmured to herself.

Viva was being dismissed. She stepped out into the city street, and even though it was almost four in the morning, the air was still hot and humid. She felt like she was walking into a human mouth. The doorman looked at her but didn't make direct eye contact, and Viva noticed for the first time that he was wearing an earpiece. Perhaps Sophie was speaking to him that very instant.

"Don't worry, I'm leaving!" Viva shouted.

A deep plum color began to bleed through the dark night sky. Viva was exhausted. She was thirsty. As she approached her apartment building, she saw, parked at an angle, Charlotte's van, which she'd picked up a week ago. Viva's Falcon was totaled. She walked through the open security door, which, despite urgent notes from management imploring tenants to keep it closed, was propped open with a car battery.

The hallway was a weird netherworld, unmoored from hour or season, the gray-green overhead light weak and wavering. Viva hurried down its length, avoiding the jumbled bowling shoes in front of apartment 101 and the ever-increasing stack of newspapers outside apartment 104.

And there he was—Luka, standing by his door in full chauffeur regalia. Probably an early-morning airport run. Viva felt as if he somehow knew everything that had just happened. She thought she saw a flash of warmth before his face snapped shut, expressionless and remarkable in its lack of recognition. Viva felt nauseated, and as she rushed past him, she saw Dusty, standing in their doorway in a baby-doll nightgown. Dusty flinched, turned her head, and spit on the hallway floor.

Viva fled up the stairs. This night had to end. How could she have been so stupid to think Luka was waiting for her? How could she have totaled her car? How could she have lost her job? She was ashamed for drinking again after she'd quit. Again. The light was out on her floor, and when she approached the landing, she stumbled near the top step. She flew around the corner and almost crashed into a figure standing outside her apartment door. Thin, still, one hand gripping the banister. Viva couldn't quite make out the features, but she would know that posture anywhere.

"Calla?"

The girl whipped her head around.

"Are you all right?"

"I don't know."

"How long have you been here?"

No answer. Calla was shivering, and she clamped her arms across her chest.

"Come on, come inside." Viva stuck her key in the door only to realize she'd left it unlocked.

Calla followed Viva into her living room and stood there stiffly, studying the floor. Viva was shocked to see her transformation. Gaunt, her hair was now cut short. She was wearing dirty orange cutoffs, a green crop top, and black lace-up boots. Calla's hand fluttered to her lips, and Viva noticed three red rubber bands circling her right wrist before she jammed it into her pocket. She lifted her head, and she was so pale, it was hard to imagine blood pumping through the veins beneath her skin.

"Calla, sit down." Viva threw her keys and purse on the coffee table and went to the kitchen to put on a teakettle. She quickly swallowed three Tylenol and drank a glass of water. She checked her fridge—when was the last time she'd bought groceries? They'd have to settle for some crackers and raisins. She grabbed a sweatshirt off a chair and returned to Calla, who stood exactly where she'd left her. When Viva handed her the sweatshirt, she could see the momentary pleasure it gave Calla to contemplate wearing it. Very carefully, she pulled it over her head, and as she did so, Viva saw a bald spot near the part in her hair—a sign of anorexia. Calla quickly covered it with her palm.

"Calla, your sister said you ran away. Are you okay?"

Calla perched on the edge of the sofa. "The bitches still harass me."

"Who?" asked Viva.

"You know who." Viva could see that in the brief time they'd been apart, something had shifted within her. Her childish demeanor, one of wariness and determination, was fast receding, and in its place was a burgeoning insolence. It was there in the jutting chin and the sidelong squint, a kind of preemptory effrontery, an early negotiation with all that adulthood might bring.

"Did you talk to Maisie or the guidance counselor?"

"Those assholes?" Calla snapped one of the rubber bands around her wrist.

Viva sighed. She had an excruciating headache. Maybe she'd have one shot. But then she remembered there was nothing left to drink. She'd poured the last half bottle of vodka down the sink hours ago.

"Are you coming back to school?"

"I can't," said Viva. "I was fired."

Calla tried to feign surprise, but it was impossible for her to not know what happened. With deep embarrassment, Viva recalled the entire chemistry class peering at her from the third-floor windows. Not to mention the archery club that stood transfixed on the lawn. "What are those rubber bands?" she asked Calla.

"They're for my neural reprogramming. Melody Brankin, your sub, makes us wear them to get rid of bad thoughts."

"What?"

"You have to snap them when you feel critical of yourself. It rewires your brain and makes you a better dancer. Supposedly." The disdain with which she tossed off the explanation didn't completely belie that some small part of her hoped this was true. Calla began to pace, moving her hand in rapid fishlike movements, mentally marking some piece of choreography. She suddenly stopped in front of Viva. Her eyes were the deep blue of the inside of a mussel shell.

"I quit school."

"Why?"

"I just told you why—Sienna and all of them—they hate me. Plus, I missed the auditions for the showcase when I got suspended. Curtains for Calla." She laughed bitterly.

"No, it's not," said Viva.

"You're just saying that." Calla became increasingly agitated and began to move around the living room picking up Viva's things—a small statue of Ganesha that had belonged to Charlotte, a glass paperweight—inspecting them, setting them down. When Calla came to a photo of Viva after her graduation recital, she held it up to the light, inspecting it from every angle. "Too bad you never made it as a dancer," she said.

Viva felt dizzy. She stood up, walked past Calla, and stood before her living room window. Her knee throbbed as it sometimes did at the end of a long day. She had constantly lectured her students about dance injuries—how to prevent them, what to do if they were hurt. But nobody could tell you what to do with the anguish.

"Sorry," said Calla. "I didn't mean that." She snapped a rubber band on her wrist. "I know you had an accident."

The faintest bit of daylight began to leak into the night sky, striating it pale pink. Viva opened the window. "Listen, Calla, you can't quit school."

"What am I going to do?"

"I don't know, but I'll try to help you."

Calla picked up her knapsack and headed for the door. "Check you later."

Viva had no idea where she would go or when she'd see her again. "Calla, wait. Do you want to stay here tonight? I'll make up the sofa."

Calla turned and looked at her. She lifted her chin and considered the offer as if she had plenty of options, but Viva could see the exhaustion and relief in her eyes. She set down her bag.

"But we have to call your sister, okay?" Viva reached for her phone and saw her answering machine flashing. For a crazy moment, and before she could short-circuit the thought, she imagined that Charlotte had called. But it was not Charlotte, it was a man who seemed hesitant when he said her name, a man who said Charlotte had given him Viva's number.

chapter twenty-nine

Wilson was almost twenty minutes late. Viva stood outside the restaurant where they'd agreed to meet, a small steakhouse that catered to the downtown business crowd. She felt her blouse cling to her back, and with regret she stared at her heels, which, though they appeared indigo in her closet, had shifted to a garish bright blue in the light of day. But what was the correct color of shoes to wear to meet a father she'd never known? She thought about a popular TV show where people were reunited, and they always seemed to know exactly what was expected of them, the eruption of joy followed by tears and proclamations. Viva tried to inhale deeply, but the best she could manage was a teaspoon of breath. She'd considered canceling a dozen times since this morning. Nearby, small black birds shrieked and dove into ficus trees surrounding the entrance. Viva tried to remember what they were called. One flew past her head, and she ducked. Where did it go? Not far.

Charlotte had once told Viva her father was shy. No, that wasn't it; she'd said he was prudent. Or was it patient? *Trusting*, that's what she said. Too trusting. Viva had tucked the comment away with other scraps of information—that he was a good swimmer, allergic to shellfish, and played the oboe in college. Not well. Facts she'd gathered over decades. What a long time to know so little.

When they spoke on the phone, her father said he was a sixty-one-year-old photographer who lived in Anaheim. She scanned the sidewalk for passersby, trying to locate one that might fit the bill. There was a man with maybe his mother, a man with maybe his girlfriend, a man in a tux carrying a violin case.

Something was being filmed across the street from the restaurant. A commercial, Viva guessed. Men wearing Civil War costumes were everywhere—hundreds, it seemed, smoking, prattling on phones, lurking near Craft Service, where they jammed fistfuls of M&M'S into their mouths. A young woman in a prairie dress, head covered in rollers, slouched on a folding chair in the back of a covered wagon. She reminded Viva of Calla. She'd managed to convince her to stay in school for the time being. One small victory.

One of the black birds swooped into a nearby ficus. Viva heard it to the side of her head like a power line buzzing. Frantic, agitated. She hadn't drunk in eight days, and the sound seemed to bore into her head.

A grackle. That was the name of the bird.

Across the street, filming resumed, and twenty or thirty soldiers packed tightly together, fake sabers hoisted, gave a battle cry and charged across a patch of grass. She was giving Wilson five more minutes.

"Viva?"

Viva's stomach lurched. She was surprised to see her own nose on the man in front of her—slight bump below the bridge, narrow tip—a nose she considered beakish on a bad day, regal on a good one. Awkwardly, they shook hands, and Viva noted his height. He must have been a foot taller than Charlotte. He had a faint widow's peak, and it looked like he'd put some effort into his hair.

Wilson apologized for being late, and as she followed him into the restaurant, Viva noticed a slight limp. Had he been in a war after all? Something she'd lied about so many times.

The interior walls of the restaurant were red brick, and scythes of various shapes and sizes hung from them. A hostess appeared and led them to their table near a long, gleaming oak bar. Viva considered asking for a different table but didn't. Wilson began to sit down but then seemed to think better of it. He rushed to pull out Viva's chair. She sat down quickly, almost missing her seat, and Wilson pushed her too close to the table.

Sorry.

Sorry.

Silence.

They looked at each other, and it seemed utterly impossible to Viva that they would make it through an entire meal. She had prepared some questions ahead of time, but now she couldn't remember a single one.

A woman wearing a green gardener's apron over a long dress wandered through the restaurant, selling single tulips from a basket. Viva fervently hoped the woman would not stop at their table. She felt her entire body waver and her mouth went dry.

"Special occasion?" The woman bumped into the back of Viva's chair, and Viva could smell and feel her, spicy and damp.

"Special day?" the woman reworded the question, and this time it sounded more like a suggestion.

For a moment, Viva felt a flare of pride. Perhaps this woman saw them as father and daughter. Then just as quickly Viva realized that maybe she thought they were on a date.

Wilson pulled a couple of dollars from his wallet and gave it to the woman. She plucked a gigantic red-and-yellow tulip from her basket and presented it to Viva, who clasped it awkwardly like a scepter. After a few minutes, she carefully placed it crosswise atop their small table, a kind of floral dividing line, beyond which it seemed difficult to imagine either would pass.

"This place was a speakeasy in the twenties," said Wilson.

"Really?" said Viva. "That's something."

Viva felt him study her face, and she wondered if he thought she looked like Charlotte, though she'd always thought her mother was prettier than herself. She recalled how when Charlotte awoke in the morning she looked like a stunned bird, and how every day she did facial exercises to get rid of the lines around her mouth caused by smoking. But she was beautiful. And Viva did share some of her features—the same full lips, but her jaw was more pronounced.

Wilson swiveled in his chair, his eyes (desperately, it seemed to Viva) scanning the restaurant for a waiter.

The happy-hour crowd had arrived, and behind them three businessmen sat at the bar, each slurping an oversized beer from a large goblet, the one advertised on the menu as "the fishbowl." How Viva hated drinkers when she wasn't drinking.

The man in the center playfully punched the man to his right. "Nina, the new receptionist, what about Nina? Her ass is like, like . . ." He fashioned a wild shape in the air with his hands. "It's like, it's like . . ." He struggled, then momentarily brightened. "An outboard motor!" The men roared with laughter.

Viva felt her entire head flush, and Wilson made a production of winding his watch. If nothing else, they shared the trait of being easily embarrassed.

"What's in Anaheim besides Disneyland?" asked Viva. She hadn't meant to sound accusatory.

Wilson said he lived near an orange grove he'd inherited from an uncle, adding that he had a lot of corporate clients in the area.

"Have you seen the billboard with the father and the little boy—the one where they're fishing, and they pull a gigantic cell phone out of the lake?"

"Yes, yes, I have," Viva lied.

"I shot that."

"Outstanding," said Viva. A word she hadn't used since high school. She sat up very straight and tried to resist the urge to pick at her cuticles.

Suddenly their waiter swooped down upon the table, a heavyset man who introduced himself as Mercier.

"What would you like, Viva?" There was something about the way Wilson asked the question that caught her off guard, as if he'd known her a long time.

Mercier, pad in hand, turned to Viva and waited.

"I'd like a glass of—" She paused. Water, sparkling water, orange juice, tomato juice, Coke. She considered them all. Twice.

"I'd like a glass of champagne."

"I'll have a glass of iced tea," said Wilson.

"Cancel the champagne," Viva said. "I'll also have iced tea."

"And a vodka tonic to start," said Wilson.

Viva's heart sank, but she would not change her order again. She would get through this meal without drinking. In the distance, Viva heard a coffee grinder begin its terrible one-note melody. The beginning of a headache poked her at the base of her neck like a cold wire.

Their beverages arrived and Viva watched Wilson take a quick gulp of his vodka tonic. She didn't touch her iced tea, which was served in a bulbous glass, sweat running down its sides, a limp slice of lemon collapsed on its rim.

"What kind of camera do you use?" she asked.

"Camera?"

"You said you were a photographer." Viva couldn't seem to control the edge in her voice.

"Oh, different types over the years. But the first serious camera I used was an old Zenobia-C Daiichi-Rapid." Wilson paused. "Great Japanese camera made in the fifties. Totally manual, of course. Funny little left-handed shutter release."

Viva nodded. She could feel the momentary comfort this topic brought Wilson, the first such moment since they'd laid eyes on each other.

How many times had she wondered what advice her father might give her or what she'd ask him if she ever met him, and now, given the opportunity, it seemed she had nothing to say. A blast of air-conditioning shot from some unseen vent and swirled around her upper body. She began to shake. The restaurant was filling with people and Viva experienced a strange quickening, as if she was watching the entire scene on fast-forward.

"Are you married?" she asked.

Wilson blinked, blinked again, and to Viva, it looked like some kind of ocular Morse code.

"No, not married, but I've been married." Wilson added that he'd just started dating a woman named Phoebe who had three kids aged seven, nine, and fourteen. "But it's okay," he added, "because I love kids." He abruptly stopped and blinked again.

Mercier passed their table and Viva signaled to him. "I'd like a vodka tonic, as well." Mercier took her order with a bemused smile that seemed to her to indicate he knew she'd never make it through this lunch.

"Where do you teach?"

"At a private girls' school—Findley Academy," Viva said. Even though she'd been fired. "It's a good school. An excellent school," she said. And there it was, the need to impress this man, her father, though she barely knew him.

Wilson stretched out his right leg and said he'd sprained it last week when he fell off his bicycle. Apparently, a neighbor backed out of their driveway without looking both ways.

"People need to be more careful!" said Viva, too loud to her ears.

"Yes, yes, they do." Wilson's voice rose to meet her own.

"Some people are completely reckless."

"Yes, they are!" said Wilson.

For a moment, it seemed the spark of their mutual enthusiasm for safety would ignite further discussion, but once again, they fell silent.

Minutes passed. A blast of heat swirled around Viva's head even though her feet were freezing. Finally, she said, "Tell me something you remember about Charlotte."

Wilson paused to think. "The thing about Charlotte was that she always had an ace up her sleeve."

"Like me?" Viva said.

"I guess you could say that."

Viva felt a feckless courage spiral up within her. "Who were you then?"

"What do you mean?

"When you were with my mother. Were you a different person then?"

"I couldn't say. I guess I've always been one to question things."

"Well, here's a question. Why do you think she didn't tell you about me?"

Wilson stared at Viva, and she could see him carefully consider his words.

"I don't know, but she was very possessive. She may have wanted you all to herself."

"If you had known about me, would you have tried to find me?" *Blink, if yes*, Viva thought. *Blink, if yes.*

"I think so. Though I'm not sure Charlotte would have let that happen. Your mother was a complicated person. Easily wounded."

"Charlotte?" asked Viva.

Mercier returned and placed Viva's cocktail before her. "Are you ready to order?" he asked.

"Yes," said Viva.

"No," said Wilson. He put on his glasses and studied the menu.

Viva looked at her drink and peered out the window. It was almost dark, but she could see a lingering row of clouds in the sky, pale, thin clouds that looked like they'd been raked.

When Viva drove down the stairs, there was a moment when her car was airborne. Less than a moment, and with deep regret she savored this instant still. *Stay up until you must come down.*

Swiftly, she slid her drink across the table.

"Don't you want this?" asked Wilson.

"You ever hear of the Huma bird?"

"Sorry?" said Wilson.

"The Huma bird?"

"The one with the head of a lion?"

"Different bird."

"Well, then, no."

Viva saw the quickest flicker of irritation jut above Wilson's left eyebrow.

"The Huma bird can only stay up; it can never come down. Does that seem like a good thing to you or a bad thing?"

Wilson looked at her. "Viva, are you in some kind of trouble?"

"Excuse me, I need to use the restroom," she said. Viva willed herself out of her chair, and as she turned to go, the insole of her high heel became unglued. When she walked, it flapped like a tongue, and there was nothing she could do to hide the fact. She almost collided with the tulip woman.

"Special day? Special day?"

Viva stood before the bathroom sink and studied the circles under her eyes. She was dizzy and thirsty, and in that moment, she felt completely dislocated from her body. She'd once read that under emotional duress a person's body and soul could actually part, that a person could, quite literally, be beside herself.

Viva heard a buzzing in her ears, and she gripped the sink. She recalled a humid summer night long ago, lying on her stomach while Charlotte braided her hair. Viva was almost asleep when Charlotte traced on her back the words *You Are Mine*.

Someone pounded on the restroom door. "Is anyone in there?"

Viva looked in the mirror and splashed water on her face.

"Hello? Hello?"

Viva raked her fingers through her hair. She ripped the insole from her shoe and jammed it into the trash.

Viva left the restroom and walked down the hallway past the emergency exit. It was propped open a few inches, and she caught a glimpse of a waitress smoking in the parking lot. She could slip out of this door and out of Wilson's life.

She turned the corner and scanned the restaurant. Viva stared at him in profile, her own profile, and she took a deep breath. She watched Wilson pour water into her empty glass, then he folded his hands and waited, simply waited, as if he'd do this forever if need be.

chapter thirty

Charlotte's VW van still smelled like her perfume, Fracas, and reminders of her were everywhere—clove cigarettes, smoked, not smoked, partially smoked, stuck in the seat crack and taped to the ceiling. There were twenty-seven dollar bills, four pesos, and a lottery ticket stuck beneath the floor mat. The VW's undercarriage was rusted out from the snowy Glenalbyn winters, and the hole in the floor by the passenger seat, which was once so small Viva could stick her finger through it, had grown to the size of a saucer.

Viva merged onto the freeway and headed south. It would take a couple of hours to drive to San Diego, where she and Wilson planned to meet on the beach to memorialize Charlotte. Just the two of them. Charlotte's van staggered and stalled, and the recalcitrant shift fought Viva, no matter which gear she tried. Reverse wasn't where it should be, and in fourth, the stick hit her leg. She drove slowly as cars and trucks overtook her on the 5 Freeway, and crosswinds pulled the camper about, due to the engine being in the back. It was like steering a boat that was also her mother. Viva looked in the rearview mirror and saw Charlotte's eyes looking back at her—not in shape or color, but in her determination.

Tomorrow was Viva's final day of DUI school. But now the real work began. And how does a person change? How does a total internal rearrangement occur and when can a person say I would no more drink alcohol than drink aquarium water? How does a person pry open that moment, the tricky interstice between the past and present, and say here is change for good? As simple as walking a hundred miles with a stack of plates on one's head. But this is what Viva needed to do. Not drinking would become the new drinking, and it would take a lot of practice, but she knew how to practice.

Early that morning, Viva had made herself a cup of tea, then picked up a notepad and began to sketch a dance. It was the first time in months she'd had a reason to think about new work. Donovan, the choreographer she'd met at Anastasia's performance, had invited her to submit a piece to a local dance festival, and she had the perfect person in mind to perform it, someone who could handle the emphasis on the fifth beat, someone who wouldn't get thrown by the complexity of the transitions.

Viva continued to sketch and beneath the sequence she wrote:

> *Calla,*
> *This is a dance about the challenge of trying to stuff a big soul into a puny human body—or maybe it's about bursting free. Practice these sequences, and we'll work on them next week.*

Viva pulled into the nearly empty beach parking lot. It was a clear winter day and surprisingly cold. Wilson hadn't yet arrived. She parked her mother's van and looked at the churning, choppy surf. Beautiful and fierce, like Charlotte herself. Strong-current warnings were posted everywhere, and the jetty was closed. Viva could imagine Charlotte striding past the signs, defiant to the end. Sun slashed through the clouds and struck Viva in the eyes. She reached for the visor, and when she pulled it down, she saw, written in her mother's hand, faded directions to the campground on the Cape. Charlotte never did have patience for maps.

Viva opened her window. Wind rushed into the van, and she flashed on an afternoon when she was three or four. She and Charlotte were on the roof of an apartment building, playing a game of eating spring air. Viva held her mother's hand as they ran around, gulping it down left and right.

"We're drunk on air," Charlotte shouted.

"Drunk!" Viva repeated.

Charlotte ran with her to the edge of the roof, and Viva thought Charlotte might jump over the side and take her with her. But Charlotte stopped short. She was watching the world below. Simply watching.

Viva wanted to see what Charlotte saw. She wanted to see everything.

Charlotte picked her up and put her on her shoulders. "This is ours!" she said. And in that moment, it seemed entirely possible that her mother possessed not only the entire city but the sky above. "What do you see?" Charlotte asked.

At first, Viva hadn't been able to look. The height. The drop. So far to fall.

"Open your eyes, Viva!" said Charlotte.

And this was what she saw—a house being built across the street. There was only a frame. No doors, no windows, no roof. The spring air blew everywhere and there was nothing it could not touch. A man wearing a yellow hard hat sat on a rafter, eating his lunch. Charlotte waved to him, and the man waved back. Viva clutched Charlotte's head as her mother held her legs. Everything was good. Everything was right, and there was so much to see if she could just keep looking.

Author's Note

While *Burst* is a work of fiction, a few non-fiction sources assisted me in my research and provided great information and inspiration. Joan Acocella's *Twenty-eight Artists and Two Saints* is an exceptional collection of essays that illuminates a broad range of artists, and her writing on dancers helped me consider dance and performing from new angles and with depth.

The Wim Wenders film *Pina*, about Pina Bausch, was deeply moving in its documentation of her electrifying, powerful choreography and expanded my thinking about how to describe dance for both the initiated and the uninitiated.

Oliver Sacks's book *Musicophilia: Tales of Music and the Brain* was very useful to me in terms of learning about musical hallucinations and other aural and neurological conditions. Additionally, Neil Bauman's writing about Musical Ear Syndrome ("MES—A Different Approach") helped me more deeply comprehend a condition that is still not well understood.

Last, during the writing of *Burst*, I discovered the photography of Vivian Maier. Colin Westerbeck's *Vivian Maier: The Color Work* was a book I often returned to for visual nourishment. In particular, Maier's photo "Untitled, 1956" had a profound effect on me. The subject, a woman in a red dress, stands with her back to the camera, hands clasped in a way that on different days seemed to signal different things—anticipation, longing, atonement. The photo prompted me to write an entire chapter of my novel. I'm deeply grateful for this kind of mysterious convergence when it occurs, this cross-inspiration of art forms. Vivian Maier's photography was unknown in her lifetime, and it makes me mindful of the fact that secret brilliant artists walk among us daily.

Acknowledgments

Sarah Bowlin, my extraordinary agent, for your passion for this novel and your remarkable insights and guidance.

Leigh Newman, for your enthusiasm, support, and your editorial expertise.

The visionary Zibby Owens, the wonderful Anne Messitte and Kathleen Harris, and the entire phenomenal team at Zibby Books.

Jamyelese Ryer, for your intensive reads of this novel, your supernatural discernment, and our decades-long friendship.

Clayton Clark, for your deep wisdom, emergency literary assistance, and our walks and talks about writing in the D Garden.

Libby Flores and Mary Yukari Waters, for invaluable early reads.

Laura Cogan and Oscar Villalon at *Zyzzyva* and Olivia Smith, Dinah Lenney, and *Los Angeles Review of Books*, for publishing early excerpts of *Burst*.

Wordtheatre and Cedering Fox, for your enduring support and the amazing performances of excerpts from this novel.

Noepe Center for Literary Arts in Martha's Vineyard, for providing me with a writing retreat and giving me the gift of time and space.

Gunn Espegard, for providing a respite and place for me to work during a particularly hectic season.

Los Feliz Public Library, Brand Library, and Los Angeles Central Library. where I wrote portions of this book.

Eric Goldbrener, for all your support and help.

Mumtaz Mustafa, for a beautiful book cover.

In loving memory of my parents, Dorothea and Raymond, who encouraged and supported my interest in all the arts early on.

Vincent Oresman, always and for everything.

About the Author

Mary Otis is the author of the short story collection *Yes, Yes, Cherries*. Her fiction, essays, and poetry have been published in *Best New American Voices*, *Electric Literature*, *Tin House*, *Zyzzyva*, *McSweeney's*, *Bennington Review*, *Los Angeles Times*, *Los Angeles Review of Books*, and numerous other literary journals and anthologies. She has taught fiction at UCLA and was a founding professor in the UC Riverside Low-Residency MFA in Creative Writing Program. Originally from the Boston area, Otis lives in Los Angeles.

@maryotiswriter